An Ech

For Harry

Hope this gets your
approval!

Best as ever

Milk Atterlu

Also by the same author

The Long Shot

A Shot From The Shadows

An Echo in Time

Michael Atherton

© Mike Atherton, 2018

Published by Michael Atherton

A CIP catalogue record for this book is available from the British Library.

ISBN 978-0-9930645-1-7

Book layout by Clare Brayshaw

Prepared and printed by:

York Publishing Services Ltd
64 Hallfield Road
Layerthorpe
York YO31 7ZQ

Tel: 01904 431213

Website: www.yps-publishing.co.uk

Dedicated to the memory of

8961

Private Charles Atherton

20th Hussars

For those who went before and never came home.
When they said farewell, they didn't think
it would be forever.

Foreword

On the 4th August 1914 at 23:00 hours (Midnight in Europe) Britain declared war on Germany. Sir Edward Grey had made his famous quote the night before: 'The lamps are going out all over Europe, we shall not see them lit again in our lifetime". He was speaking to his friend, the journalist, John Alfred Spender.

For the next four years huge armies would be pitted against one another. The resulting slaughter and carnage is well documented and recorded by the great historians of both their and our time. The world would never be the same and, for millions of men, women and children, it would quite literally be the end of the world. For the brave men and women who gave their all, the lights never came back on.

If you study the history of Continental Europe, the war to end all wars had been brewing for months; years even. Empires were near constant in their plotting and scheming and although 'An Echo In Time' is a book of fiction it is based on fact. The soldiers you will meet did live and, although some of the names of individuals are pure fiction some are not. This is the story of one man's war, from beginning to end. His friends are real as are the horses he rode and the Regiment he served in; the 20th Hussars. 'An Echo In Time' isn't meant as a reference book for the regiment but it does depict the story of a group of men and, in particular, Private Charles Atherton, my great uncle. I have the luxury to be able to write my story but his has already been written.

Special thanks go to Julia and Steve AKA Team Atherton, truly I'm very lucky.

This book is a tribute to those young men of the 20th Hussars who fought and died together in WW1.

CHAPTER 1

They say that in dreams you can't smell, well I could. I could also hear, taste and feel; it was as if I was stood there. As I reached out, I touched the white froth on the horse's neck, he was sweated up and fractious. The warm musky aroma of his hot body was as real as reading this. The horse's bit was green and frothy with freshly chewed grass; the leather, soft with saddle soap, was slippery and shone like melted dark velvety chocolate. The soldier sat astride him gently patting his sweating and steaming neck. "Whoa there, steady lad" was all he said.

All along the line, horses brayed and stamped impatiently as they did whilst out with the hunt except this hunt was far more lethal than the hedges of old England. This was France in 1914.

As I stood there transfixed, I noticed the whites of the eye in the nearest horse, he looked more terrified than I could believe possible. He stamped his hooves and shook his head in defiance. He was wild with excitement and fear but again the rider calmly sat still, his legs clamped gently around the flanks of his mount. His boots looked well-worn and fitted snuggly, the tops hidden by cloth puttees wrapped like a bandage around the rider's shin and calf. His foot fitted into the stirrup. The dark brown saddle was clean and polished; an army blanket was fitted under the saddle to provide comfort for the horse and, to help hold the saddle in place, a long girth strap that reached under the horse's belly. With remarkable ease the soldier reached down, as he pushed his left leg forward, he casually flipped the flap that was there to hide the buckle and tightened the strap; he pulled it one hole tighter.

Along the line there was a palpable anticipation, it didn't seem like fear but I sensed everyone was terrified in their own way. Somewhere I could hear a man vomiting; the nerves and fear had taken over from his military training.

A sergeant called out some soothing words about making sure they kept in line and rode together. He then shouted as, without warning, a roar like a train ripped through the air and rumbled like thunder. It was the German artillery. They were trying to find the range of the lines of cavalry. Somewhere out there beyond the woods, a German observation officer was watching where the shells fell. This volley was way out, at least 300 yards too long, and the shells crashed into the ground sending huge plumes of earth skywards, landing back there they did no harm; there wasn't anyone back there.

Along the ranks, the horses skipped and neighed, anxious to be getting on with their work. The line was 120 men and horses of the 20th Hussars standing ready behind the leeward side of a hill rise just out of sight of the German trenches and supposedly out of harm's way. On the other side of the hill, an infantry attack was ongoing and the signal for the cavalry to charge was to be a star shell fired from a Very pistol. Everyone waited.

The sounds of battle; gunshots, screams of anguish, pain and anger were carried on the wind; there was no escape from the dreadful scene of slaughter hidden over the hillock and then, with a loud cheer, the Germans broke rank and were on the run, routed from their trench and running for their life back to the second line of trenches and the reinforcements they knew to be waiting there. A solid plop from the Very pistol sent the slow rising canister skywards, a trail of smoke snaking behind and with a bang the flare erupted into flame, it was the signal the cavalry had been waiting for.

With a shout of command "Draw Swords" from the troop commanders, there was a loud scraping of steel on steel as 120 sabers were drawn from their hanging scabbards. Now the horses knew the game was afoot, they pranced on the spot some bucking with excitement; their mounted partners, reaching down for the rope neck strap for extra stability, tried to calm them but the adrenaline was coursing round their taut muscles. Most of the horses lifted their clipped tails and emptied their bowels in readiness for the chase, fight or flight in perfect harmony.

The troopers, sat aboard their mounts, knew that this was the real thing, no more training, those days were behind them now.

"The Regiment will advance at the walk, WALK MARCH." The last two words were shouted out louder and echoed along the line by the non commissioned officers and sergeants. It was spectacular to watch and as the horses skipped and walked; the men held their swords in the right hand, tip to the sky as though on a parade back in Colchester, the muscles in their left arms bulged with the effort of holding the horses back, walk soon turned to a trot but the line held straight.

The next minute, the first horses reached the top of the small incline that had been their cover whilst the infantry had fought to get through the barbed wire and over no man's land. These British soldiers were now to the left of the

3

advancing line of cavalry. In the distance the constant "tat, tat, tat" of a distant machine gun played a lonesome tattoo, as would a single drummer.

Then came the command every man and horse had been waiting for, from trot to canter and onto a gallop, the ground heaved to the percussive beat of nearly five hundred hooves. Among the ranks each man hid his fear with bravado, no more nerves, no more being sick, now anticipation was replaced with expectation, every man knew his duty. It was time to ride and each man felt the elation and blood lust.

"CHARGE".

The more experienced riders let the horses go and slipped the fingers of their left hand under the neck rope, it gave them just a bit more security. Amazingly, the line remained relatively straight as the horses near bolted towards the terrified Germans who were literally running for their lives, knowing they would be caught out in the open and overrun within seconds. Where had these horsemen come from? From a distance you could see the swords come from the upright to the outstretched, apparently an outstretched arm and sword were the same length as a lance or a rifle and bayonet, but no one cared for military facts now. The noise was deafening, screams of excitement and rage mingled with the rhythmic pounding of the horses, a cacophony of noise.

The first German fell, a sword protruding from just above his right nipple, as he fell the swordsman followed his target down to the ground with his hand and the sword exited as cleanly as it had entered, blooded but sharp, the next rider reached down with his sword and pierced the stricken German through his throat and with a blooded gurgle he toppled, doomed.

There were others; they were crushed underfoot; bones breaking and lungs exploding with the furious onslaught of the raging galloping horses.

In the German trenches, the men looked on aghast at what they were witnessing, this form of warfare was from another time, no one thought to fire a rifle or machine gun; they were transfixed, it wouldn't last.

The first screaming shell came from the sky like Thor's mighty hammer 'Mjölnir' It impacted the ground with a sickening 'crump' it was a big shell, a 'Jack Johnson', named after the huge negro boxer John Arthur 'Jack' Johnson from Galveston in America, it threw up an enormous mushroom of earth and with it two cavalrymen and their horses, the war had found the 20th Hussars.

The shouts of the commanders could be heard above the din of battle and, almost as though it had been choreographed in the riding school or on Queen's Avenue in Aldershot, the ride came round in a huge semicircle and whilst still at the gallop formed up into small troops, and as quickly as it had started, it was over. Shells peppered into the empty ground where only a minute ago there were horses and carnage; now there was nothing, the fight had finished.

All along the German lines, men were asking each other if they had actually seen a cavalry charge, right there in front of them. The butcher's bill wasn't very large, just a half dozen men, but the ramifications of this attack would ring through the German trenches like a gas bell, it would be talked about for years and men would boast they had been there when the British Cavalry had charged on the Western Front.

The horses were blowing hard, but the troopers were worse. Hands shaking as they tried to unfasten the water bottles from their saddles, each man had a terrible thirst and, as soon as they were safe, they dismounted and with cupped hands offered a drink to their horses. No one spoke. It was very quiet initially, just offered words of comfort and reassurance to their scared mounts. Then as they remounted, a few words and an occasional laugh, it was all very orderly.

As I stood there looking on, one man, the same man I had been stood next to earlier, rode back over to where I was standing and then he did something quite unexpected, he spoke to me.

"Hello Michael" he said using my Sunday name from childhood.

At the sound of his voice I was suddenly awake and he was gone. And so it was that a simple single dream was to be the start of the change in my life.

CHAPTER 2

May 1st 2015

I had been planning this day for at least five years, perhaps longer; but with a certainty that the anniversary would arrive I had, at last, made it to Ypres. As I stood in front of the huge Cloth Hall, it was a spectacular building; magnificent didn't do it justice. It was rebuilt after World War 1 from heaps of rubble, all that remained after the German shelling of the medieval town.

There was a hushed bustle on the cobbled road that is the town square. Cafés and shops form the boundary to the square and yet through it runs a road. It's all very quaint and pleasant. School children walked all around me as they headed to the museum that, in itself, a grand memorial to the hateful days of World War 1.

The town of Ypres, known as 'Wipers' to the hundreds of thousands of British 'Tommies' who either struggled with the pronunciation or couldn't be bothered to try, was ancient. It had been the centre of trade in the cloth industry for millennia and had in itself seen more than its fair share of wars and conflict. Nothing had ever been as totally destructive as the Great War of 1914 to 1918. In that time a million men, and more, had marched along these same cobbled roads up past the old city gate along the Menin Road on their way to the front. The British had held a salient in the shape of a tongue that pushed out into the German lines. There was very little movement in the static lines of trenches that became home and, in turn, graveyard for so many young men. The main industry in Ypres these days is still the War, done with remarkable respect and dignity in the main. Ironic really, that the very thing that destroyed the town is now the main lifeblood of its survival.

There isn't much industry about the area, but the Great war, and the hotels and guesthouses are full of pilgrims and students offering tears and knowledge equally. The shops sell memorabilia and artefacts alongside ice cream and waffles and, every night at eight, there is the ceremony of remembrance at the huge memorial to the dead that have no known grave. The Last Post has been played at the Menin Gate every night since the 11th November 1929, and only halted for the Second World War when the Germans, once again, brought death and warfare to the cobbled streets of Ypres. The fallen even then, were never forgotten and the ritual of remembrance continued back in Blighty until the Allied Army pushed the Germans out in September 1944. On that very night despite fighting in the streets nearby, the local Fire Brigade, dressed in their best uniforms, marched smartly to the gate and played their mournful and proud respects. It has never failed to play the Last Post once since that day.

This wasn't my first visit to Ypres though. I had been a couple of times to visit the battlefields and commonwealth graves from the First World War. There is a fascination, albeit a morbid and sad one, for all things WW1 in Flanders fields not least the amazing museum that they have in the Cloth Hall. This visit was special, tomorrow was the 100-year anniversary of the death of my great uncle. He was mortally wounded and subsequently died along with three of his comrades in 1915 and tonight, along with my closest friend Jim, I would be honouring the man I had never met but whose surname I still carried as mine. The plan was to drink a toast to Charles and the three mates who died that fateful night back in 1915. We had with us a fine bottle of regimental port and two spare glasses; we were determined to continue a military tradition that went back to the days of Wellington. We knew we had to be in the cemetery at 11:50 pm the exact time the shell had exploded, and despite the fact that all the cemeteries would be closed, we didn't see the harm in sharing our bottle with the fallen. It was all very tastefully planned and respectful. Jim had even recorded the Last Post on his mobile phone.

As we talked, we made our way to the Menin Gate ready for the Last Post. As ever it was very busy, it was after all a lovely day; the sun had been warm and the sky blue. To add to the bustle there was a ceremony of remembrance by a Canadian group who would say a short mass and lay a wreath. We held the wreath of poppies we had taken to lay; our respects needed to be paid here at the gate after the main service.

We joined in the group of wreath layers and waited our turn to march to the area dedicated to wreath laying. The Canadian service did drag on, and despite trying hard not to, I was thinking about later on that night and the separate private ceremony at Poelkapelle Military Cemetery we were going to hold. I was miles away when Jim nudged me, "Are you ready?"

The group ahead of us had set off to lay their wreath and we followed them. With military precision we placed our blood red poppy wreath on the stand of remembrance. It was quite moving, and as we remembered the reason we came, I felt a chill of pride shiver down my neck and looked at Jim, more for reassurance than comfort. He caught my eye and nodded, I knew he understood.

We knew that we had a couple of hours to spare so decided to go and eat. It wouldn't be dark for another couple of hours in any case; the last rays of sunshine settled low, throwing long shadows along the main street, back towards the Cloth Hall. There was a chill in the air but it wasn't a cold evening. The crowds of people who had been at the ceremony dispersed and made their way back into the main square for coffee and hot chocolate. For many they would never return and as if a debt had been paid you could see the sadness in their eyes, remembering *your* dead did that. The chatter of excited children lifted the somber mood of the older visitors.

Jim and I found a nice restaurant and ordered beer and food. As we waited for dinner to arrive, we chatted and laughed about the things we had done in our own time in the army. We had been friends for over 30 years sharing our youth as young married soldiers based in Germany. Divorces apart, we had enjoyed life as friends and been each other's best man at the second weddings and, despite our separate lives since leaving the army, we had managed to stay as close as brothers. There was a bond between us that was based on laughter and love and we both felt that we would need that bond tonight when we toasted the fallen. It mattered to us both.

After dinner we checked that we had the things we would need for the nights vigil; torch, port glasses, port, telephone and camera. All was in place, packed neatly in the boot of the car along with Barbour jacket and fleece just in case the night turned cold and wet. We needn't have worried; there was a fresh, but light, wind and it was a fairly clear night. The moon wasn't quite full but it was bright and in the darkness of the lay-by next to the cemetery we were surprised how much we could see. It struck me as funny that we spoke quietly, as if someone might overhear what we planned. At 11:00 pm we entered the cemetery through the iron gates that stood guard inside the arched entrance built out of stone. We knew where we were going, we had done a recce that afternoon and it was a grave I had visited a couple of times before but in the dark of the night it was different and although we could see easily enough we used a torch to ensure we didn't disturb anything on our walk to the graveside.

As we stood looking over the best part of a brigade of men in the cemetery, nearly 7500 men, most with no known name, it struck me the dignity of the setting and, apart from the current 'thieves in the night' style intrusion, all remained quiet and slightly surreal, the moon cast an eerie light over the parade.

As the clock ticked round towards the appointed time we laid out our glasses and uncorked the port. Jim set his mobile to play *'The Last Post'* and I placed a wreath with an explanatory note of what had happened to the men commemorated by this red ring of poppies. I felt I had to explain what had befallen the two men lying beneath the soil. At exactly 23:50 we pressed play on the phone. We stood to attention as all soldiers do and when the music had finished, we raised our glasses and drank a toast to the memory of Corporal William Stanesby and Privates Miles and Clarke

11

and finally Charles Atherton all men of the 20th Hussars killed 100 years before. One shell was all it had taken and four young men gone. When we had finished sipping our glass we refilled it and poured a tot over the two graves in front of us; one belonging to Corporal Stanesby and one to 'A soldier of the great war who belonged to the 20th Hussars'. Both headstones bore the regimental cap badge of the 20th Hussars and the research I had done previously suggested that the headstone marked 'Known unto God, a soldier of the 20th Hussars' belonged to Private Charles Atherton. We two old soldiers didn't need to speak; I don't think we could have at that moment due to the huge lumps in our throats; so we hugged as friends do when they love each other as brothers. We poured more port and dripped a few drops on all the graves in the row, we shared our drink with the dead and in turn we knew they toasted our health whilst we lived.

There were no ghosts, no hoots from an owl, nothing but two men celebrating the lives of a generation lost to madness a century before. We took our photos and tidied up making sure everything was as perfect as before. Jim lit a candle in a little red glass and placed it at the side of the grave and I can remember now how touched I was at this gentle, respectful gesture and as the flame flickered in the night we walked away back to the car parked on the road. We didn't stand and salute, that's Hollywood and not the British way, we just nodded, it was enough.

On the drive back we chatted about what the men we had been toasting would have possibly been like, were they different to us? We laughed at the thought they could have been as laddish as we had been when we served and the scrapes we had got into as young men. Jim said

"I can just imagine them saying, "Oh for Christ's sake Corporal its freezing tonight, how come it's always us that has to do night sentry duty" The lament of every soldier in history when told they are on 'stag duty' at night. Why would they be different?

I laughed and said,

"You can imagine as the artillery shells flew over and crumped into the trenches them going 'God those poor buggers in 'A' Squadron are copping it tonight' Still better them than us." With luck the shells landed in the dark of no man's land and no one was injured, but that certainly wasn't the case for these four. A shell had come from high and smitten them. It exploded as they stood outside 'B' Squadron headquarters dugout killing three of them instantly. Charles Atherton was mortally wounded and died an hour later, drugged and comatose; there was no pain but equally there was no chance of surviving either. At the tender age of 22 years he had died in some far away field that would now be forever his England.

Chapter 3

It was after midnight when we finally went to our rooms; we had taken a nightcap and reflected at the sadness of it all. In that one quiet cemetery all those men, it was a sobering thought but we were determined to celebrate their lives and not concentrate on the tragedy of it all.

We said our goodnights and went to our rooms, there was no indication what so ever that things were going to change and as I slipped between the crisp cotton sheets and pulled the light switch I soon fell into a deep sleep.

One of the things we rarely reflect on when we awaken is how time has no bearing when we're sleeping. Sometimes we wake and feel totally refreshed, only to find we have slept for just a couple of hours and other times we sleep soundly for a whole night and wake still feeling tired, but the point is we don't really know where we are throughout the night clock; we are just 'sleeping' and sometimes, dreaming.

There, in front of me, as though waiting, stood a man. He was small and slight, a young man with just a hint of facial hair trying to be a moustache, it was struggling to be seen. He had soft features and kind warm eyes but he looked sad and down beaten, but not broken, no he was definitely not broken, more resigned. He wore a very smart tunic with golden braid weaving from left to right across his chest. I knew it immediately as the uniform of the 20th Hussars. I had seen it many times in my youth when I had been introduced to the Regiment in the form of old photographs. More recently I had seen the real thing in the regimental museum in Preston. I recognised the face as well, it was like looking in a mirror only 25 years ago, he looked just like a young me.

I can vividly remember feeling very comfortable and safe, it was as if I was wrapped in a blanket of love and a strong feeling of wellbeing washed over me. There was certainly no sign of fear or even alarm, it was all perfectly natural as indeed most dreams are.

Even though I knew I was dreaming it still felt so real. I noticed there was a slight synchronicity issue when he spoke and as soon as the realisation was made it was corrected. Further proof should it have been needed that I was indeed in the middle of a very real dream.

"Hello again Michael, or do you prefer Mike?" he went on to explain he had known me all my life but the whole story would have to wait because we didn't have long before I would wake. Unsurprisingly, within a few moments I was waking up.

When I was fully awake, I looked over at my watch, it was 8am. I felt wide-awake, I remembered it all, his face his voice and most of all, his uniform and how slim and short he was. When I went to the bathroom I looked at my old unshaven face in the mirror, I was smiling.

Clearly the dream had been as a result of the previous day's activities, we had spent the whole week working up to the cemetery visit and it had gone as well as we could possibly have hoped. Add to the emotion of the evening and a few drinks and it wouldn't be a surprise to anyone that I had had a long and very detailed dream about my Great Uncle Charlie.

As I shaved I thought about telling Jim about my eventful dream and decided maybe it would be best if I just kept it to myself, friends and brothers have a nasty habit of taking the mick out of daft dreamers.

CHAPTER 4

Farnworth 1911

Charles Atherton was a good-looking lad. He had great big shoulders and a strong back, all these physical attributes were down to his swimming. He was a serious swimmer, he had started at the local club when he was 11 and had won numerous competitions, when he wasn't in the swimming baths he was at St John the Evangelist Church either as a chorister or at the young men's club. Singing was a family trait, both his brothers sang, Thomas was his elder brother and had a deep baritone voice whilst William, his youngest brother, was not quite so naturally talented. He had a pleasant voice and tried hard not to make a mess of the hymns.

Mr Toms, the Head Chorister liked the Athertons they were triers, but he had a special place in his heart for William because although he was the least talented of the 3 boys he never failed to make everyone smile. But if the boys were good singers then the sister, Elizabeth, was the star of the show. She was a stunning soprano by far the best most naturally talented he had ever heard and it didn't appear that she had to try at all.

At the age of 15, Charles had started work in the local mill as a stripper and grinder. In time he would make a qualified engineer, but his initial task was to help with keeping the equipment in the mill spick and span. Time spent fixing stopped looms cost everyone money; the mill owner, the weaver and the apprentice and the tier in. The knock on effect of a loom not working affected all. It paid as a stripper to be quick and, more importantly, accurate in the repairs or maintenance. Charles had an eye for detail and he was in high demand because he was quick and he didn't make many mistakes, in fact no one could remember him making any. By the time he was 18 he was the master of his craft.

At the end of his shift, the walk home along the canal towpath was filled with nods and hearty hellos. Two things that Farnworth had plenty of were mills and canals, along with a good amount of coal mines in the area no one was out of work. Farnworth in 1911 was a hardworking but happy town. Yet for Charles Atherton something was missing. Yes he was happy at home but he felt, as a lot of young men do, unfulfilled and by the age of 18 he was seduced by the travelling recruitment show of the 20th Hussars. It was on a sunny day in May that he was in Farnworth park, the hustle and bustle of the mill left behind for the day. There was a hotpot waiting for him at home but he was in no rush to be at it. The day was warm on his shoulders and he took off his jacket and stuffed his cap into its pocket. He hooked his finger through the hanging lace and flicked the jacket over his shoulder. His neckerchief was maintaining his decency and he dared himself to pull the stiff starched collar open.

Charles wasn't really a risk taker but today he didn't seem to mind.

The birds were loud, happy to be feeling the warmth and the normally smoke filled air seemed so much clearer today. All in all, he felt very content, he didn't even hear the man walk up to him from behind.

"Hey up" called the man, it made Charles jump.

As he turned around he saw a soldier in uniform, the uniform was dark blue with gold latticework across the chest. Charles noticed that the man had 3 stripes on the right arm of his tunic and, on his head, was a busby with a bright yellow hackle that stood proudly pointing skywards. Charles took in the remarkable man but was amazed at how shiny his long riding boots were, but he had no horse and Charles couldn't see a horse anywhere.

"Hello there, you didn't half make me jump" he said, "Who are you?"

"My boy, my name is Sergeant Aloysius Harris, and I am the recruiting Sergeant for the finest cavalry regiment in the British Army, the 20th Hussars. Now forgive me but you look like a lad who belongs in the army, big shoulders like those could hold any horse to task. If I may be so bold lad, I would say if I hadn't seen you myself I wouldn't have believed you weren't already a soldier out on leave. You're not are you?"

Charles felt himself grow a couple of inches with the compliment, as for horses he had never sat on one apart from the draught horses at the mill, and only then no more than a couple of times.

"No Sir, I'm not in the army, never thought of it to be honest. No, I work up at mill ower yon at Kearsley spinning" he thumbed his hand in the direction of the many chimneys in the near distance.

The Sergeant asked him if he fancied a cup of tea. There was a tent set up by the bandstand with tables and if he was lucky there might be some jam sandwiches left. Charles very much liked this sergeant chap, he seemed like a 'reet grond mon' as his brothers would say. Despite all Elizabeth's efforts to improve their speech, these lads were as broad as they were honest but to an outsider it was as near a foreign language as Russian.

They walked chatting as if they had known each other for years. Familiarity was easy for Charles he was a very easy-going lad and Sgt Aloysius Harris seemed like an older brother rather than a stern sergeant from the army.

Over by the bandstand was a small camp, as promised by Sgt Harris, comprising only three bell tents and a couple of bay horses tied up pulling furiously at a hay net. The tack was over a temporary saddle rack.

The two horses gleamed, each had a stump for a tail but it was an immaculate stump and their hooves shone like night, as clean as Charles had ever seen his shoes, even for church. As the two men walked over, a large lurcher type dog came trotting over towards them. Charles liked dogs but slowed as the dog approached them.

"Oh don't worry about him lad, that's just Dylan Gregory, my dog. He's friendly enough unless you're a ne'er-do-well" As he said the last bit he winked to Charles to let him know he was just joking. Come and have a cup of tea and a sit down, let's have a chat."

Charles was very taken with the uniform, two of the men had the same dark blue tunics and yellow braiding and the third just a khaki jacket and trousers with boots and what looked like bandages wrapped around the top of the ankle boot and up the calf.

"You ever heard of the 20th? We're called 'Nobody's Own' 'cause we aren't one of those posh mobs and nobody can claim us to be theirs". Harris laughed, "we are based in Ireland presently, that's where old Dylan came from, took him of a didicoy who beat him I did, gave him a right shiner for good measure. What kind of man beats a dog, I ask you? You got any animals lad and whilst I'm at it what's your name? I can't keep calling you lad can I?"

Charles felt the dog push his hand onto his head with his nose and instinctively he scratched behind Dylan's ears.

"Charles, is my name Sir, Charles Atherton, I live ower top yon, and no I don't have any pets Sir, my mam's got a bad chest and they make her wheezy"

Harris leant over and patted him on the shoulder, "He likes you Charles, not many he sits with, you ever ridden a horse? And please just call me Sergeant I'm no sir, I don't have a commission and we save all that sir stuff for the officers. As I said the Regiment is in Ireland but we are on the move, we've been there 3 years and it's time for us to come back to good old blighty. We are moving into some barracks in Colchester. My job is to find us some new men to join us there and as soon as I clapped my old eyes on you I thought 'Aloysius, there's a likely looking lad' Have you ever thought about serving the colours Charles?"

He hadn't, well not until now. Now he was thinking.

"Who's at home Charles and how old are you if you don't mind me asking?"

As Charles took a cup of tea from one of the lads Dylan lay down at his feet.

"Oh there's my mam, my sister and a brother William at home, my older brother is living with his wife and baby daughter just up the street. I'm the middle lad and I'm 18, as of last month" Charles felt so at ease with these men, he felt like he had known them for an age.

"Well Charles, we could do a lot with you, what are your hobbies and how do you spend your time? We will teach you how to ride, shoot, march and all things soldiering, but there are no pressed men anymore. You have to volunteer to join but the pay's good and there's 3 meals a day and a good roof over your head. We travel about a bit but we ride, not like the bloody infantry who march everywhere. We move over to Bury tomorrow for the rest of the week, if you feel like you want to join up come and see us there. We are at the militia barracks where the Lancashire Fusiliers are. We break camp here first thing but we are there for a few days."

And as he drank his tea, Charles pondered a life in the army; he found he was nodding as he worked things through in his mind. He would talk to his mother tonight and with William and Thomas. His brothers had always been close to him and he felt if he talked it over with them that they would see him right.

That night at home he spoke to his family, each of them said he should follow his heart. Tom said "There's not much here for you Charlie, you'll be in that mill forever, hell love you don't even had a lass to leave behind." Charles felt himself blush, and so his mind was made up. Tomorrow he would get the tram to Bury and if things turned out right he would take the King's Shilling and join the army.

CHAPTER 5

It was a week after I got back from Belgium that the first headache started. In modern parlance we would call it 'a cracker' but, for me, it was really unusual – I wasn't the headache type. I said my goodnights and retired injured to bed. Sleep came very easily as it most often did, and by the time my wife came to bed an hour later, I was sound asleep.

The dream started with laughter, real belly laughs, from a group of men who were just messing around in a large riding school. One lad was on a horse and was galloping round the school like a circus act. In the centre of the riding school stood a Sergeant next to a Corporal shouting "Sit up, sit up." The Corporal was shouting as well but he was clearly having fun, "Don't you dare fall off in my riding school Miles, if you fall off I'll have your guts for garters." Over in the far end of the riding school, which was about 60 yards away, sat five other men on horses, all looking slightly anxious but in fits of laughter. The Sergeant saw them and yelled, "Gentlemen, I hope you're not laughing at poor Private Miles and his slight predicament." As he said the last word, Miles lost his grip and, on a corner at the gallop, he slid off onto the sandy floor of the school with a very undignified thud as he hit the ground.

The Corporal corralled the bucking horse with soothing words and cooing noises. "Whoa there, whoa good lad, shhhh." The horse nodded his reluctance to stop but steadily came to a stand near the other horses. One of the riders from the other horses slowly slid of his mount and reached over to the braying escapee. Its nostrils were wide and eyes excited and slightly wild. He took hold of the reins and slowly patted the horse's neck, the horse threw his head back but calmed quickly as he realised the man wasn't going to admonish him, just pat his neck. As the black horse snorted in victory, Private Charles Atherton gently blew up his nose, it was a very natural thing to do and the horse, instead of being angered, nuzzled his neck and snorted gently. The rest of the men watched on in fascination, it was like witchcraft the way Atherton had an affect with horses. On more than one occasion he had been asked if he had gypsy blood in him. He didn't of course, he was just good with animals and especially, as it turned out, with horses.

Private Miles came over to collect 'Arthur' his horse. "Thanks Charlie" he said, "How do you do that? The blowing up the nose thing, where did you learn that?"

Charles just shrugged; he really didn't know where he learned it but had a vague idea it was Eric Johnson the drayman back at Kersley Mill who had shown him in what seemed a lifetime ago.

"Atherton, you're next. Get back on your horse and let's see you take on this fence, get this right, for the love of God and don't fall off." It was Sergeant Allison calling the shots. "Gentlemen this is all basic riding, by this stage in your training you should be able to do this with your eyes shut, Private Atherton here is going to show you how to do it, aren't you lad?"

Charles climbed aboard his horse, this one was called Apollo, who was a handful in the wrong hands and a monster in the right ones. Only the more able riders got to sit on Apollo, Atherton turned to face the Sergeant.

"Yes Sarn't I'll do my best Sarn't." He could feel the power of Apollo underneath him. He gently placed his leg down the flank of his mount and like a shock of electricity he felt Apollo stiffen and come alive under him. He didn't need to kick him on there was an understanding, almost a synergy between them. Some of the more senior riding staff spoke of it in the Sergeants' Mess at the various breaks, the ability that Private Atherton had on a horse. Apollo walked with a powerful forward drive, as Charles held him with his fingers the horse bent his strong neck like a bow; a gentle squeeze and he went straight from a walk to a perfect collected canter. The others just watched in amazement as the horse did a cursory buck and Atherton slipped his hand down the horse's neck and steadied him with a click from his tongue.

"Stop that clicking! You're not a bleedin' clock" shouted the Sergeant "Now bring him round and count the last three strides in before you take off."

"Yes Sarn't, sorry." As he came round the corner the horse saw the fence, he knew it was there because everyone else had had a go and every one of them had fallen off. Charles felt the horse bite down on the bit in his mouth and as quick as a flash he flicked his fingers each side of the reins and Apollo instantly released his bite on the metal bit.

"Good, see what he did there you lot, look how the horse is under him, Atherton, push those heels down a bit and sit up, don't you yank that horse in the mouth when he gives." There was no chance of that. Charles Atherton had the hands of a soap seller, they were very soft and forgiving. Charles could feel the rhythm under him, there was no rushing, no panic like the others just a gentle squeeze with his lower leg and Apollo was on final approach to the fence.

"Call out the time, those last three strides, shout them out nice and loud"

As the fence got closer he could just see the 'strides', the imaginary distance that equated to the length of a cantering horse's stride. As the horse got to the exact point, Atherton called out "1, 2, 3" and on 3, as if on a magic carpet, he took off. He leaned slightly forwards towards the horse's neck and his bottom hardly left the saddle, just enough to take the weight off Apollo's now arching back. It was only a small fence, no more than 3 feet, but it was an enormous jump and the pair cleared the fence by another 2 feet, easy.

"Good man, now get hold of him, don't forget the jump isn't over yet. Land and sit up and drive away to the next obstacle. For the purpose of this exercise come round the school and take the jump again, only this time at the far end of the school, close your eyes and trust your instincts."

Once more Apollo tossed his head in anticipation and as he rounded the bend, Atherton could feel the horse gather himself. He had cheated a little on the previous jump and he already knew how many strides there were from the corner to the fence. In his mind's eye he could see how many strides he had to make and with a relatively confident one-two-three he let the horse have its head and exactly on three Apollo's mighty neck came up to meet him and once more Sergeant Allison and Corporal Magee looked at each other and shook their heads.

"Atherton, tomorrow morning at 07:00 hours you are to be at the front of 'B' Squadron Forge with Apollo. Tack him up in hunter's and report to me for a day's hunting. I think you're ready. You others ride to the middle and prepare to dismount." The six riders came together in the centre of the riding school and awaited the next command.

"Ride, ride dismount" and the six men slid their right legs over the back of their mounts and after the regimental pause of 2-3 stepped down onto the floor.

To me it all seemed so familiar, even Corporal Magee was known to me, in fact he had taught me to ride all those years ago. It sparked a memory that was still there when I awoke in the morning.

CHAPTER 6

Old soldiers never die

Ernie Scattergood was at least 85 years old when I first met him. He was an old man with a lot of knowledge about horses and riding in the military fashion. One day at Aldershot riding school, a lad younger than I by a fair way was taking a riding lesson in the huge riding school that had been the home of the cavalry for a hundred years. I was at the other end of the riding school trying to come to terms with my new-found hobby. History was right here in this building; Winston Churchill had learned to ride there in 1895 when he became a commissioned officer in the 4th Hussars.

At the far end of the school there was a balcony set into the wall. In years gone by instructors would have sat on this balcony watching their students as they did exactly the same as I was doing right now, trying not to fall off. Today there sat an old man called Ernie Scattergood and he was casting his aged eyes over me.

I had only sat on a horse a couple of times but I seemed to have stopped falling off quite so often and although I clearly lacked any style I did have what is colloquially known as 'stickability'. It was after this particular lesson after I had dismounted and was walking my horse back to the stables that Ernie pulled me to one side,

"Where did you learn to ride Mike?" he asked

"Here" I said "It's the first time I've ever ridden, it's my wife's hobby really"

Ernie shook his head in disagreement "Come with me, I want to show you something in my tack room." To call it a tack room was being very generous; it was a spare stable in which Ernie had years of knowledge and a million old photographs stored. He had been a riding instructor for the Mounted Section for his entire career finishing with the mounted Military Police back in the day, the day being in the 1930s.

"You might not realise this but I used to be quite a teacher as a horseman and I started as a Lancer before I went to the Hussars. Why am I telling you this? Because you ride exactly the way we used to teach, and no-one teaches that way anymore and haven't for 60 years. It isn't a natural way to sit on a horse, it's a taught one." He showed me a polaroid photo he had taken of me being very ungainly sat on a big horse, he then showed me an old photo taken in the 1920s The position of the rider in the picture was exactly the same as I was sat in the polaroid.

But that was a long time ago and now was just a memory; I hadn't sat on a horse for over 20 years, it made it all the more fascinating that I could remember it so clearly. It was all just a bit strange.

It was morning and my head felt fuggy. My wife asked if I was ok which I clearly was but I felt slightly tired, what we might today call 'that Monday morning feeling.' I was aware of the dreams but they didn't seem connected or indeed relevant. I just put it down to the week away and getting back into the swing of things. It had been a fantastic trip but too many late nights and more beer than I would normally drink had left me with a desire to have another holiday, this time for a rest.

CHAPTER 7

Colchester 1914

Life in the 20th Hussars in early 1914 was full of fun and activity. Charlie's social life was so much more involved than back in Farnworth. He had new friends, it seemed like a whole world of friends to him, hundreds of new men to introduce himself to and as for activities, he hardly knew where to start. He was now a very competitive swimmer for the Battalion, he competed at regular galas in Colchester and indeed Aldershot. Each time he represented the 20th he could feel himself burst with pride.

His circle of friends was always very supportive of everything he did and as a lad, Charles Atherton was extremely content with his lot. One of his closest friends, Tom Kelly, had been in the Squadron for only a short time when he first met Charles, but the two of them had hit it off straight away. They were amongst the best riders in the 20th and went hunting and tent pegging together on most occasions unless Charles was swimming. Tom had joined as a married man but his wife, Alice, had stayed back home in a village called Langwith up in Derbyshire and on the odd weekend, when the two men were stood down from duties, they would eagerly travel back home to Tom and Alice's home.

It was a huge change for Charles who had only a very limited experience of the countryside and what it had to offer. He had seen a lot more of it since he joined up and out riding with various groups either hunting or tent-pegging or just hacking out on exercise of horse's rides. He was a keen student of all things rural but the thing he loved about Langwith was the church. He wasn't a pious man particularly, but he did find an inner peace in church. He would always attend church parade on Sundays, even if he were granted a weekend pass. He would go to church and sing, when he went home to Farnworth he would wear his Hussars uniform and invariably he would be gifted refreshments on the train and once home he would be treated like royalty especially by his little niece Mae, the daughter of his brother Tom and his wife Emily; although only a toddler, Mae adored him and he would take her on his back and give her rides around the house whilst she shouted excitedly "gee gee" and giggled as only a child can.

There were dalliances with the fairer sex but nothing serious, in truth Charles had never even kissed a girl, he always felt his time would come and one day he would meet the right girl for him. He envied Tom Kelly with his lovely young wife Alice. It was obvious they were very much in love and once Tom had finished with the army he would return to the estate with tales of exciting do or dare and his enthralled audience would gasp at the tales he told. The spring of 1914 was full of promise for the future. Two young men with a life of ambition and dreams to fulfil, both with families back home and both very loved by those kin. Little did they know what was to befall them in the next year, the friends they would lose and the sights they would see, then the laughter might have stopped but as is the call of youth they were invincible and no harm could ever become them.

In Europe across the Channel, there were dark deeds afoot and, on the 28th June 1914, Serbian-backed terrorist, Gavrilo Princip, shot dead Archduke Franz Ferdinand, heir to the Austro-Hungarian throne. No one knew exactly what the consequence of this dastardly deed would be but most understood the gravity of the situation. If diplomacy failed there would once more be a war in Europe and with the various accords and coalitions, and also written treaties and agreements, it was hard to see how Great Britain and her Commonwealth would be able to avoid its own involvement. The escalation of events gathered pace. On the 28th July 1914, Austro-Hungary declared war against Serbia, this declaration of war drew in allies and supporters on both sides. Germany supported Austria-Hungary but Russia, another mighty power, stood by the Serbs.

In London The British government, led by the Prime Minister Herbert Asquith, agonised and toiled over whether to support France and Russia or to remain neutral, but Great Britain couldn't allow a German domination of Europe. If France and Russia were beaten, a victorious and hostile Germany would threaten not only Britain's home security. It could very well threaten its position of power in the world.

It was with a very heavy heart that on the 3rd August 1914, Foreign Secretary Sir Edward Grey addressed the House of Commons on Britain's position in the European crisis. Eventually the decision was taken out of his hands; Germany's invasion of Belgium, to get to France, put Great Britain on a war footing as Britain had, since 1839, guaranteed both Belgium's neutrality and her independence. This brazen disregard by Germany to respect the alliance between Britain and Belgium had literally crossed a line. An ultimatum was given to Germany and should they choose to ignore it and not give the appropriate reply to London by midnight, then Britain would place all her military assets at Belgium's disposal and would be at war with Germany. The response never arrived.

CHAPTER 8

August 4ᵗʰ 2014

It was a lovely evening in England. The house martins were swooping through the warm clear air, whilst below the smoke from the barbecue spiraled skywards carrying with it the most amazing smell. I had enjoyed a lovely few days and wasn't even aware that I hadn't had a headache for maybe a couple of weeks. But tonight I could feel the pain behind my right eye. This sharp pain was a precursor to a throbbing headache that would come to me within the next couple of hours.

Having enjoyed a couple of glasses of a half-decent Australian red, I was certain a paracetamol would sort it out. However, over the next short while it was obvious to me that I needed to catch some kip, it had been a long day and what, with cutting the lawn and various other gardening related activities, I was knackered. Our guests had left and after bringing everything back in I kissed my wife and said I was going up; she would 'follow shortly' she said and as I closed my eyes, I was reassured to know she would be there if I woke in the night.

I clearly remember feeling very calm and comfortable, there was no angst or stress just a slight headache as I drifted off.

I could almost feel the chill of the evening air and I remember looking to make sure I was dressed appropriately for the time of day. I was surprised to see I was wearing a pair of khaki trousers, heavy boots and a thick itchy woollen shirt. It almost looked like a uniform but I knew it wasn't. It certainly wasn't the same uniform the men in front of me were wearing.

There was an excitement in the air, the whole area was bustling. All around there were people shouting orders and as I looked around the stables even the horses were 'hunting jumpy' – a term I had heard whilst watching these men setting off in the early morning hunts.

They had all been out on the challenging hunts now. Each man was rushing but there was no sign of panic or anything other than urgency. One of the soldiers stopped opposite where I was and as he flitted past me he shook his head he shouted "It's war!" looking at no one in particular. He then rushed off to the tack room to continue his packing.

War; I had no idea. It was only then that I realised this dream was different; my heart was racing and I could feel the passion in my blood. I wanted to be there, wanted to be involved but even as these thoughts were flooding through me, I realised I was just in a dream, it just felt so real. The difference being 100 years; this was 2014 and the war that had just been declared had started on this day but a hundred years ago.

CHAPTER 9

To war we go

New men were pouring into the camp. On August the 5th 1914, Colchester was buzzing and every few minutes a cheer would ring out as another 'old and bold' member of the Regiment would turn up to honour his reserve commitments. The Yeomanry had been mobilised and along with the 20th Hussars the Royal Scots Greys had travelled from their camp in York and the 12th Lancers had mobilised from Norwich. Together they would form part of the 5th Cavalry Brigade of the British Expeditionary Force.

There were so many horses turning up that at one stage they had to double them up in the stables. A new riding camp was set up nearby to train the new arrivals in the basics of military horsemanship. I had never heard the word 'remount' but that was the term used for these civilian horses, offered freely by the local hunts, farms and even private houses had offered their horses.

It took a few days for the organised chaos to take shape. The Quartermaster's Department was issuing uniforms and saddles; and saddlers were working overtime day and night in shifts. The Armourers were checking weapons and swords and scabbards handed out. The Farrier Major ensured that all the horses had new shoes fitted and all the smithies in Colchester came to lend a hand under the Farrier Major's experienced eye. Within a week all was in place. The Regiment was due to leave barracks on the morning of 16th August.

The whole Regiment were paraded at 06:00hrs and the band struck up at 06:30. The road to the railway station was lined with cheering men, women and children and when we arrived at St Botolph's station, bunting and cheering crowds greeted us. It was very exciting.

They had no idea where they were headed but all were loaded onto train carriages and the horses were loaded onto livestock carriages with hay nets for each one. Sergeant Aloysius Harris cheered his men away; he was too old to go back to war. Clearly everyone wouldn't fit onto one train and the other three trains were stacked one behind the other just outside the station, the best part of eight thousand men and all equipped ready for war. Excited and scared the atmosphere was electric. The quiet ones just smiled and nodded knowingly to one another, these were the men who had been there before and they knew what was to come. The others, more naïve than ignorant, had no idea. Within six days all would know the meaning of war and the horror and fear for both horses and men. "La Grande Guerre" was just around the corner.

When they arrived at Southampton, it was unbelievable just how busy the town was; after all, war had only been declared a week before. There in the port town stood the British Expeditionary Force in its full glory. The men and horses were settled overnight and with the sound of crashing and banging from the docks and stevedores shouting and yelling, the equipment of war was loaded aboard the S.S. Indore ready for departure to Havre and in the middle of the night the ship silently cast off and left.

Arriving in France was a wonderful feeling for both men and horses. Many of the men had been sick on the crossing over and as soon as the 'Indore' tied up, the heavy work of unloading began. Suddenly there was a shout as a horse being winched over to land fell out of his harness. Fortunately, the poor animal was only a couple of feet from the floor and no doubt felt rightly manhandled so kicked and squirmed until finally he broke loose. No sooner had his feet touched the ground than he was off at the gallop straight back towards the sea and with a huge buck he jumped as high as he could over the barrier and without knowing his fate he plummeted down to the murky water below, a good way below. With a mighty splash he disappeared under but within a couple of seconds he bobbed back to the surface.

There was a frantic shout from the Sergeant Major "Bloody hell, that's mine!"

The horse didn't fancy the swim back to good old Blighty and after a couple of minutes he swam back towards the ship where-upon a brave officer dived in and got a rope around the poor frightened animals neck. With a bit of cajoling and a push and a shove they managed to get the Sgt Maj's horse back on *terra firma*.

Back on dry land he was rubbed down with some straw and an army blanket thrown over his back to help warm him up. The Sergeant Major called the horse 'Lucky' after that. The men all laughed when the Officer Commanding said he would shoot anyone else trying to desert his post. The rest of the unload went relatively quietly after that.

CHAPTER 10

France, beautiful France

The first night was spent in a shed near the railway station. The horses needed feeding, as indeed did the men but horses first. Then the men, and finally the officers. This was a long-standing tradition going back to the days of Waterloo, interestingly the battlefield of Waterloo was not much more than a two days' ride from where they were setting up camp for the night.

France was beautiful, the evening was warm and bright, the late summer heat had died from the midday sun and men and horses soon settled down to night time routine. There were no sounds of war, no explosions or shells falling. To many the war seemed a jest, merely a yarn and a million years away; yet within 4 days these same men would be galloping for their very lives.

The next day they mounted another train to Amiens, another magnificent city. All along the road to the embarkation point we were soundly cheered and to a man kissed. Many a lad was seen to be blushing including Charles who was, by any standards, handsome, and also it should be noted without his cap badge, given freely for a kiss to some brazen harlot for a mere moment of joy, oh the ebullience of youth. The collection of the spoils of war had already begun.

When finally they arrived, hot and tired, there a bustle of activity but, before long, the horses had been washed down and a water fight between A and B Squadrons had begun. The men were soaked, and to all this I was a spectator, no bodily contact or communication to me other than a chance nod by Charles as he rode past. I knew it was a dream but such was the detailed picture I saw I knew it was no ordinary dream, well not like I had ever had before.

In the evening, some of the men were allowed to take a walk out to the town of Amiens. Soon they discovered that the beer was cheap but the wine was cheaper and, like England, the streets were quiet and populated mainly by women and children. The menfolk we met were older, the young men had left to join the French Army and they had already marched north.

* * *

When I awakened the bed was a mess, the quilt thrown onto the floor and the radio was on. The fug of sleep gradually cleared from my eyes and as I sat up my headache had once again been consigned to last night. Over breakfast I told my wife of the dreams I was having, enjoying. She was flippant but I knew she had been concerned about the headaches, enough to leave me to sleep in. Apparently, I had been quite vocal in the night. She left the kitchen saying

"I didn't realise you spoke so much French".

The day's schedule was full; we had plans to take friends away to France to see the battlefields in a few weeks. I needed to book a couple of hotels and travel tickets and, as ever, have a quick look at the details of their particular family members who had made the long march to war all those years ago. I always liked to try to find some details of where their fallen were laid, after all it was so easy these days with the Internet and all the different social media pages. I don't remember much of the rest of that day because that was the day I had my first seizure.

CHAPTER 11

A Head full of marbles

We sat in the doctor's surgery along with the sick lame and dying, I hated doctor's surgeries they always seemed to be so miserable with kids running away from stressed mothers or worse, mothers who couldn't care less. The receptionist was as ever very inquisitive and as ever I was as belligerent as a bull elephant

"What is the matter with you?" she demanded

"Are you a doctor?" I enquired

"I need to know so I can tell the doctor, now stop being silly and tell me what's wrong with you" That was a big mistake; I could almost hear my wife roll her eyes skywards. She would be thinking 'here we go'.

In my most authoritative voice, which was getting louder I said, apparently "What is the matter with me is between me and my doctor, thank you." Then I fell over, it was just a serious bout of dizziness but I felt a real fool. I could see that my wife was concerned as she helped me sit on a chair.

"I'm sorry, I just felt rather dizzy, like my head is full of marbles. I'm ok now thanks love"

She sat holding my hand; I could feel her reassuring grip, her hand felt so small yet so important. Eventually we were called into see the doctor. A large man from Africa, his mouth smiled but in his eyes he seemed hostile, I couldn't really care less, it was obvious that the receptionist had told him how awkward I was being.

"What is the matter with you sir?" he asked in an overly loud voice as if I was deaf.

I explained I had been having headaches for a few weeks and that they seemed to be mainly in the evenings, but worse, I had had some kind of seizure that morning and just again in the waiting room I had fallen over whilst feeling incredibly dizzy. He hardly looked up from his computer screen.

"Mmm, you seem to be quite overweight"

What? How the hell was this relevant?

He looked in my eyes and then in my ears, took my temperature and proclaimed, "you have an ear infection, I will prescribe you some antibiotics, try to lose some weight"

And that was the end of my examination and indeed appointment; We were dismissed.

Back in the car I said "I don't have an ear infection" I grumbled, "there's nothing wrong with my damn ears" but we had collected the antibiotics and went for a coffee together in the town. It was here that I had another fainting attack. I burned my leg with the hot coffee.

CHAPTER 12

First Contact

It was August 21st 1914, and today was really the first day of the war for the 20th Hussars. As I looked on from my ethereal position, Charles Atherton walked over towards me and as he sat down on a hay bale he said "I know you're here, with me, somewhere. I've told the lads we have a guardian angel."

As he spoke I could feel the early morning warmth of the late summer sun, the breeze wafted softly across my face and ruffled my short hair. I felt very real and absolutely 'in the moment' but all along knowing no matter how real it felt, it wasn't my world, it was theirs.

"'B' Sqn are going on patrol in a few minutes stay close to me, I'll feel safer if you are." He got up and went over to his mount, 'Apollo'. After his exploits back in Colchester he had been issued '501 Apollo', the number was an army identification so the horse qualified for rations and veterinary treatment should he need them, and after all Charlie seemed to get on with the horse so he was issued it, not that that bothered him, he really liked the horse.

The men were buzzing like a hornet's nest, the horses, excited and jumpy were as keen as mustard to be getting on, all in a day's work to an army horse but this time it just felt a little different, a little more serious than a day's hunting. The 30 men and horses all gathered round a young Captain, to me he looked too young to be an Officer but the men jostled and bumped into each other to get a better position to hear what he had to say. "Today we have been tasked to watch over a bridge to ensure the enemy don't get across it. Make sure you have all the ammunition and bring water; each man will carry water in his bottles. It might get quite hot and both you and your horses will need a drink."

I couldn't help thinking what a rubbish briefing that was; but very quickly the men had mounted up and formed into a section ready to ride out to meet the enemy. On the other side of the road the same thing was happening with another Troop, the competition was palpable as to who would snag a German first. One of life's huge lists of games played out by soldiers throughout history.

'Jocular' would best describe the mood as the men chattered away about what the day might bring. The horses were calming down now, well rested and fed which was more than could be said about the men sat on top. Looking on at the scene, Charles was clearly one of the lads, he was chatting to the others whilst gently patting his horse's neck. Each man had his kit with him, including the long sword and a Lee-Enfield 303 in its holster; plenty of ammunition was stored in the leather bandoleers around their neck and chest. Their tunics were buttoned right to the neck and I remember thinking they would soon be boiling hot inside the heavy cotton jackets. The horses all had docked tails and hogged manes; they looked fit and strong as they snorted in the morning air.

The bridge they were riding for was about 3 miles away and with a wave of his hand Charles and the rest set of at a steady walk, best to walk for the first part otherwise the horses would get giddy and start farting around, within a few minutes they would break into a gentle trot towards the war. By the end of today they would all know what war was and having had a taste of engagement some would want no more of it.

It was a surreal ride, side-by-side the men had stopped talking as there, up ahead, stood a bridge.

Charles was riding with his mates, Ernie Miles, Tom Kelly, Bill Stanesby and Bert Clarke who came from the same neck of the woods as Charles in Blackburn. Bert had a particular twang in his accent and people struggled to understand him when he got excited, it used to make Charlie laugh because they would just gawp at him as if he was talking a foreign language.

The Captain shouted and held up his arm "Halt."

The ride came to a standstill. In the distance there was gunfire, it was the first time anyone had heard it in anger, they knew it was the sound of battle because it was so frantic. The gunshots were coming from over the bridge towards the railway station.

As they waited they heard the sound of horses galloping on the cobbled roads coming towards them. They recognised the first runners, they were the second part of the Squadron led by a Lieutenant. In hot pursuit of the Troop were some grey looking horses with lancers sat atop. Initial thoughts were these would be the Scots Greys but they didn't carry lances and with a feeling of real dread we realised they were in fact the Hun.

"Make ready" came the command and all the men drew their 303s and cocked the bolt. One trooper fired a round off as he tried to lift his rifle with shaking hands but the bullet headed skywards and avoided hitting anyone, it earned him an instant bollocking from Corporal Stanesby "Be careful you bloody fool."

"Sorry Bill, I must have pulled the trigger"

Stanesby's face went bright red "Its Corporal lad not Bill, the war's started and you need to forget all that 'Bill' nonsense from now on it's about discipline and rules."

By now the lead horses were on the bridge, it looked like a point to point race, there was certainly no order just 30 or so galloping horses with some terrified riders on board.

"Take aim" cried the Captain

The large German Ulans were very close with their lances in the charge position one lance scraped along the rump of the rear horse and it accelerated harder to avoid a second stab.

"Fire"

There was a volley of rifle fire, none of which hit anyone but it did have the effect of stopping the Germans very quickly. They slowed down and wheeled around to gallop for the cover of the nearby houses. There wasn't time for a second volley and the Captain shouted, "Cease fire." With that the men lowered their rifles and as the leading riders from the other troop got to our front there was a cheer. It was soon stopped by the NCOs. The scene resembled a circus; despite all the training the men and horses had both back in England and, latterly, in France, when it came to the 'hey lads hey' it was carnage. Bucking horses had thrown riders off and men and animals were all over the place and men were busy running around almost in panic trying to catch their own horse and keep a wary eye open for any Germans who were literally less than 200 yards away. They needn't have worried too much about the Germans who were almost hysterical with laughter at the show the British Cavalry were putting on. The German commander was pointing out that this was indeed the "contemptible little army" that the Kaiser had demanded be exterminated.

Back in the British lines the humour wasn't as obvious and the senior officers who had witnessed the chaos had learned a valuable lesson; they weren't yet prepared for war but they had precious little time to get ready because the Germans had the edge and that just wouldn't do. The ride back to the camp was subdued and quiet, at least for the first ten or fifteen minutes then someone started to laugh, it was as infectious as measles and within a few minutes nearly everyone was howling laughing; nearly everyone. The three officers at the front had no desire to laugh, their mission had been an abject failure and when they got back there would be hell to pay.

On their return there was absolute madness going on with people shouting and horses being tied up and watered; the Sgt Maj was in full flow, he was busy tearing into a young Corporal who had been laughing along with the rest of the other troop who had returned just prior to 'B' Squadron's two Troops. Things had been as bad with this Troop as with 'B' Squadron's but the results were that one of the Lieutenants had been wounded and worse, left behind in the chaos that was the engagement. Men were missing and horses had run away or been killed. The pain on the faces of men was haunting and yet all who saw them knew that this was only the start. The realisation was that they would have to liven up their own games pretty damn quickly or they would be the laughing stock of the British Expeditionary Force and its Commander, General French, didn't tolerate fools gladly.

Once the horses and men had had time to sort themselves out, the Regiment was moved forward to a new location, a sugar factory along the way. But the day had more events to offer before lights out.

The first shell exploded a long way short. The next landed within a few seconds and was much closer. Shrapnel whizzed past the heads of the men and horses. This was the first time either men or horses had seen the German artillery, their first taste of what was to become a very regular meal of death and pain. It was at this time Charles and his mates decided that this wasn't going to be the jolly they had anticipated and, as they rode on, the mood became more somber and serious with each step. The loss of the Lieutenant had hit the men hard, he was a cheerful soul and well-liked by the men, but there was also men from the ranks missing and that really didn't sit well. No one who was in the '20th Hussars' liked the idea they had lost men to the Germans and to make matters worse, it had started to rain, and there is no one more miserable than a wet, cold cavalryman with wet tack and a cold wet horse., and because the horses were tired the men had dismounted and walked at the side of them.

By the time they had made the sugar factory there was a fire lit and some hot food but following the age-old tradition of the British Army, horses were fed before the men and the men were fed before the officers. It had been a shit day and tomorrow didn't promise much better. The men changed their wet clothes for whatever they had that was dry, one horse had shrapnel in his neck and the Veterinary had removed it and stitched the wound. The Farrier had plenty of work to do and as they listened to the tap tap clank of the farrier's hammer each man was lost in his own thoughts of home. Charles Atherton looked totally fed up and as he pulled a rug over Apollo's strong neck and back he gave the horse a hug round his long head. He settled down next to his horse who slowly drifted off to sleep, as he did he looked over at his mates, Charles just nodded to himself and closed his eyes.

CHAPTER 13

First love gone West

In Farnworth, Rebecca Long had been walking out with Charles, well walked out, to be precise. She had taken a walk with him only once and they had talked and been suited. He looked magnificent in his army uniform and she had worn her Sunday dress with a parasol. She was quite taken with him. He was kind and gentle and had a lovely complexion with ruddy cheeks and laughter lines around his stunning blue grey eyes. Yes, she could imagine walking out more with Charles Atherton. That was until Alf Green turned up later in the week, he was a different kettle of fish altogether.

Alf was a rough house, a street fighter and a brawler. He was well acquainted with trouble and, more often than not, the police. He had a soft spot for Rebecca and they had walked out earlier in the year, before Alf had to go into hiding down near Birmingham for getting a little over enthusiastic in one of his many pub brawls; only this time he had left a chap with a broken jaw and a fractured skull when he had smashed a bar chair over his head. It hadn't gone down well with the local gypsy family with whom this poor fellow was living, and word was that Alf was wanted by the gypsies who wanted revenge for the assault. A bare-knuckle fight was demanded.

Many people said Alf had it coming and the sooner the police collared him the better but Rebecca was strangely attracted to this rough man despite the fact she was quite a gentle soul and came from a very nice Jewish family. Youth doesn't often listen to the blatherings of older (some might say wiser) members of society and Rebecca was no exception. She had spent the night with Alf not two days after her walk to the park with Charles. She had lost her virtue in an unkind manner; there was no affection, no kindness or love, just brutal sex that left her bruised and sore. Worse, she had been seen out and about by friends of Charles who, like good friends do, had warned him off. She just wasn't his type. He was broken hearted, because he thought she might actually be the one. There had been no one else to compare her to so how could he know, but he did like to think she might have been a future suitor. He left Farnworth with no illusions; he had been dumped. Well if that was how it was meant to be, so be it. Alf Green was welcome to her.

As Charles boarded a train, the steam and soot wafted around the station, he climbed aboard 3rd class and sat on a bench seat, he felt quite fed up.

It matched his mood before he fell asleep. In France a year later, he still thought about her, Rebecca, there hadn't been anyone since.

As it turned out she had been to see William, Charles' brother at their house on Peel Street. She had begged for an address where she could contact Charles and after a little consideration and head shaking both William and Elizabeth had agreed. That was the easy bit as far as letter writing went, once she had penned her letter it could take weeks to find Charles out in France. Although the Army Postal Service did its best, by definition the cavalry were a mobile unit and didn't stay in the same place for very long.

Charles had written his details for William, his brother Tom and sister Elizabeth and they had already sent him a couple of letters, none of which he had yet received. Conversely he had written letters and they had arrived very quickly back to his home. In them he told everyone he was doing fine and that, despite certain restrictions on information he could tell them, once the letters had cleared the censors the main information was just chitchat.

"The men are doing splendidly" he had said and he seemed to be having a grand time of it.

Tom and William had both been away to the recruiting office to join up but the news that Tom had a heart murmur had meant he couldn't join the Royal Army Medical Corps. His eyesight wasn't the best either, even with his spectacles, so the best the Army could, and would offer him was a home posting. He accepted of course, how could he not? He had to deal with the disappointment and do the best he could.

William's attestation had been a slightly different story; he had been accepted but delayed, there had been over 100,000 men all trying to answer Kitchener's call, it just was too many all at once. The logistics of clothing, training, arming and transporting all these men was just too large, so he had to wait, a little while at least. Thomas and William would be sent to do their basic training in due course but for now both men were stuck at home. Elizabeth the sister and Tom's wife Emily were delighted, but nodded their frustration when the men were around.

At Kearsley Mill the men were thinning out, some of the lads remembered Charles Atherton joining up and more recently seeing him at the temperance bar when he was on leave. "He had made the right choice, we should have joined years ago as well" they said. Now there was a queue at the town hall, all joining up to serve their country.

In the long lines of terrace houses all over Bolton, and indeed the country, arguments and harsh words such as 'selfish' 'and why you?' were being exchanged between worried wives, mothers and their husbands and sons. The answer was always the same. "Hush now woman, it's my duty and I have to go, besides it'll all be over by Christmas and we'll all be back."

History would show different, war has a voracious appetite for men and the first 100,000 would be followed in quick succession by 200,000 more as the menfolk of Britain and the rest of the world marched, regardless of the cost, it seemed, into the battles ahead.

CHAPTER 14

Fortune favours the brave

The next few days were a blur, boredom interspersed with sporadic action but the bond between the men seemed to grow and get stronger every day. Letters came and went but Charles held one in his pocket above all others, the one from Rebecca sat in his tunic and was read every day. In his mind there was hope of a new beginning but the word was the war wasn't going as well as first believed, no longer were the men expecting a quick skirmish and then back home to Blighty. Charles and his mates had forgone the home 'in time for tea and medals' routine for a much longer event.

August 1914 on the French – Belgium border was hot when it wasn't raining.

The next day was very autumnal, there had been a wind blowing overnight that had dried most of the woollen ware. First light meant first parade and as would become the norm a 'stand to' in readiness for a surprise attack from the enemy. Out past the sugar factory all was quiet; it was like any other day in any other country, when there wasn't a war on. Unfortunately, that wasn't the case here, today there was a war on and the plan was to put patrols out to see if they could make contact with the advancing Germans.

Breakfast was some bread and jam for the men, and fodder for the horses. The piquet guard had fed the horses early and, as the men washed and shaved, there was an air of civility and normality in camp. Chat soon turned to banter and banter to laughter. This was the way in the army. Grooming was a good time for the lads; quiet time with one's horse was always a good time.

In the distance there was a short rumble, almost like thunder and as the men came outside the factory to see what the noise was, the first salvo of shells screamed overhead and landed in fields behind with a deafening 'crump, crump.' Huge mushrooms of earth sprouted towards the sky. On a hill behind the factory stood an impressive windmill and in that windmill there stood an Army Officer with some field binoculars. He was the Observation Officer for the Horse Artillery unit who were stationed close by. In the distance there was a second rumble of guns and a second volley of shells were in the air.

"Untie those horses and get them in some cover; quick man move yourself!" came the irate shout.

The Sergeant Major looked magnificent as he stood to his full height and defied the Germans to try to hit him. They needn't have worried, the shells weren't after the 20th and as the second volley roared overhead they peppered the windmill. Its mighty sails buckled and the huge wooden slats that made up the sails turned to splintered firewood as huge, ugly pieces of iron from the exploded shells ripped them apart. A mixed volley of shells made up of high explosives and shrapnel smashed into the ground around the windmill one shell had a direct hit on the doorway. It was perhaps twenty feet too low and just carved a massive hole into the wall where the doorway used to be up until a few seconds before.

Down in the courtyard of the sugar factory, we could hear the Officer whistling a tune as he lit his pipe. There was a retort of gunfire, this time it was our guns letting loose their deadly load. There wasn't a need for a second go as the shells totally destroyed the German Battery away in the distance.

The horses had barely tossed a head and carried on munching at the hay at their feet. As the Observation Officer, we now called 'Whistling Willy,' walked out from the big hole in the wall he smiled and laughed. He was puffing madly on his pipe and out from behind him staggered the Signalman; he looked like a ghost as he was covered in grey dust from head to foot. He had been on the floor below the Observation Officer relaying the information back to the British gunners' battery by telephone and when the shell smashed into the building he had literally been blown up into the air like a rag doll, but he had already sent the coordinates given him from above. Fortunately for him the shell that caused his discomfort had been a shrapnel shell and not a high explosive, else they would have been his last coordinates.

Yesterday they had seen an airplane for the first time. One or two of the men had taken a shot at it and, to everyone's surprise, it had turned off and flown away in a different direction so maybe it had gotten too hot for the pilot and his observer. The rumour was that local folk had been colluding with the Germans, passing information as to where the British units were. Later this would be disproved and the real truth was that the Germans also had their own version of 'Whistling Willie' and aeroplane spotters but as yet the British had to depend on the man in the windmill and his signaller; it seemed to be working though.

Following the excitement, the men were called to a briefing for the day's activities. At the briefing the situation on and around the area was made clear, to the left of the sugar factory was the town of *Mons*, to the right some 20 miles way stood *Charleroi,* where the French were holding ground, but it looked decidedly dicey with the French. It seemed the Germans didn't really know the British had arrived in France; they were waiting for the troop ships to land in *Calais* much further north. Much to the amusement of the lads the Officer said it would be a very unpleasant surprise when they did. Moral was good, it wouldn't stay like that though, things were about to get so much worse. As it transpired the Grey's had been in contact with the Germans the day before so our being there wasn't as much a secret as we thought. It was Sunday and, in the distance, they could hear the church bells ringing, calling the faithful to prayer. It wasn't hard to imagine there was no war at all but Sunday the 23rd August changed everything for the officers and men of the British Army and, more tragically, for the local civilians who had no idea of the misery that was about to be unleashed.

CHAPTER 15

They're Coming

'They're coming. They're coming!' yelled the first man back at the near gallop on the cobbles, sparks flying as he tried to slow his horse without falling over or skidding into a hay cart. He was closely followed by the rest of the patrol. 'A' Troop had been out on reconnaissance when they had spied the first columns of German soldiers over the other side of the canal. There was much to do, the Royal Engineers had bridges to demolish and all along the whole canal bank for 10 miles or more, troops were running to take their 'stand to' positions in readiness for the forthcoming attack. This was it then, this is what war is about, chaos. Then the artillery barrage started from the German side, some wildly inaccurate but, more worrying, some was deadly accurate fuelling the belief along the line that either there were spies amongst the civilian population, or that the people themselves were giving the Germans information.

All along the canal there was a mist just above the water, soon this would be replaced by smoke from the rifle fire and cordite from the few machine guns the British had. Out along the flank towards the left stood the French Army but here near the city of *Mons,* it was the British who would be playing the game of war today.

Within a few minutes the rest of the patrols were coming back, each with similar reports of enemy activity all along the front. The Germans were indeed coming and cometh the hour they would find to their cost, would indeed cometh the man.

"Everyone get your kit and mount up in Squadrons. This is it boys, time to put the Germans back in their box of tin soldiers. All Squadron Commanders immediately report to the CO for a briefing. Sgt Maj, get the men mounted and ready to ride out in 15 minutes." It was the first time the 2i/c had raised his voice and it was clear there was a certain excitement in the air.

'B' Squadron were dispatched out on a patrol to some nearby woods and 'A' Squadron set up locally, in the distance they could hear the barrage growing in intensity. All wondered where the shells were landing but had to confess they were pleased it wasn't near them.

It seemed just as the men were about to go and do something, they were stood down again. This, as I had already learnt, was the pattern of war, very much the forbearer of 'everyone on the bus off the bus' a phrase I was to learn a great many years later.

As day turned to evening, news came to us of the dreadful fighting that had been going on throughout the day along the canal. Hundreds of our infantry dead but thousands of Germans killed, we hadn't escaped losses either. It transpired that the 20th had lost a very good man, a Lieutenant, with a huge future, and with him two of the lads. It hit the 20th hard. As the news of Mr Soames filtered through the rest of 'B' Squadron it was hard to see the men so upset. These men were very close and knew each other as brothers; it was obvious to even me and, despite the stiff upper lips, men wept quietly into their horses' necks as they brushed some

61

imaginary hay from their hogged manes. One of the men had been wounded and even as the medics in the aid post were treating him, he was able to cast some light on to what had happened to the three. There had been a scrap with the Germans and he had seen the Lieutenant right there, firing his revolver and then he fell. It was so quick; the others had to run, but as they mounted their horses there came such a volley of rifle shots the horses fell as did the men. It was with this volley he was hit. The rest of the lads managed to gather themselves together and ride back but he had suffered a shot just above his buttock. The bullet had hit the saddle and deflected into his right arse cheek, an inch higher and it would have caused real problems with his kidney, but, as it was, the saddle took most of the shock and although he was hit, it didn't look too bad. Still he was going back to the Field Hospital and from there it was thought, back home. The thing that stood out was he was so damn angry that he would be "missing the show". He might not have felt that way if he knew what the next four years would bring.

As day crept into night there was the constant sound of the guns bellowing their foul loads. It was away in the distance and the men couldn't see where the shells were landing, but the reports were the Germans had broken through and crossed the canal. The 20th Hussars were to provide cover and resistance whilst the rest of the Army withdrew to a better fighting place. The French, as it turned out, had already set off without telling anyone and this left our right flank very exposed. It was time for the 20th to earn their corn; they had to protect the right side of the line whilst the rest of the Army retreated with something that resembled order.

CHAPTER 16

First Kill

The ride was fast, there was urgency to the gallop and getting to our destination, the horses were blowing hard, and the men were blowing harder.

Word was that the Germans were about to cut off a number of the infantry who were slow in catching up with the men in front. They had been fighting a brave retreat and had, through no fault of their own, been left behind and exposed. The Germans were in close pursuit and there was a danger of them getting around the side of the column, then they would be able to set an ambush for the tired and confused British. The 20th were sent to make sure that didn't happen.

As they crested a hill over the farmland it was obvious they wouldn't be able to get into position on horseback. The skyline they had just come over was the perfect firing position to provide cover. The ridge ran in a large semicircle almost like a natural amphitheatre. They could see the Germans running to the left and there in front of them, at the bottom of the dip, were the British Infantry. Between the two was the crest of the hill where the now dismounted cavalry stood. They wheeled around to give themselves the cover of the crest and went to ground.

Sgt William Blackie called to the men and organised the Squadron into a firing line along the ridge. There were

36 men after the horse holders were dispatched to hold the horses and lead them down the hill about 150 yards. It looked like the whole German Army were coming.

"Steady lads, get comfortable and take off your cloth hats and put them under your chests." It was a trick he had learned from someone to help keep the men's chests down and stop them lifting their heads too high.

As I watched, Charlie, Stanesby along with Sam Atherton, who was no relation, and Dick Sutton formed a little Section and then there was a small gap and another four men formed another and another, all along the ridge there were nine such groups of men and a young Lieutenant in the middle area looking through his field glasses at the advancing Germans, who were now very much closer and easily within rifle range.

"Pick your target and then the next one." Instructed the calming voice of an old head, confident in his abilities and more so in the Lee-Enfield 303 in his mens' hands, Sgt Blackie spoke with an authoritative voice but his quiet manner just seemed right.

"Take aim, steady, steady…. FIRE"

There was a ripple of thunder from the ridge and a line of Germans fell face down without ever knowing where the shot had come from. All along the line there was a click click, click clack as the men smoothly worked the bolt on their rifles then another 'crack' as the next volley left towards the doomed target.

Charlie noticed the man he aimed at fell like a stone. He felt nothing and moved another round into his empty chamber and fired again; the same result, down went a man but Charlie didn't see him hit the floor he had already lined up number three.

All along the ridge death was being delivered at an impressive rate and to add to the carnage the men at the bottom of the ridge, the supposed German targets, had joined in the fight and now there was a wall of lead pouring into the panicked Germans who had turned round to retire away but were still falling in their droves. Charles and Stanesby were firing so fast their magazines were quickly empty and changed for full ones with the hand of professional soldiers, so swift hardly a heartbeat was missed and then the murder started all over until the Germans had retreated beyond the skyline.

"Cease fire!" a long, loud shout came from Sgt Blackie and to a man the firing stopped, not one late one away; "Good lads, that'll show the buggers not to mess with the Nobody's Own" he said.

In the distance there was a rumble of artillery, almost lost in the cacophony of noise that was playing all around, that was until the first shells landed.

There was a 'Crump Crump' as the first two shells landed at the bottom of the ridge but within a second or two, a further ten explosions and all on target at the foot of the hill. Men, horses, carts and equipment were hurled in to the maelstrom of splinters and shrapnel. As Charles looked on from his elevated and, as yet, safe viewing point, he saw three men stood looking at each other oddly, two had lost limbs, and arm and a leg, but the third was fine just shocked and amazed at what he was seeing. There was a flash and the three were gone, obliterated. Charles felt his heart and his jaw drop, he had never seen death and as the reaper walked collecting his harvest for the day, Charles knew he had seen evil; the kind of evil only war could produce, one where wounded and sound were killed in a flash. Stanesby touched Charles's sleeve and gave a gentle tug, it snatched Charles back and he closed his mouth. He was aware he was pointing and as he looked into his friends eyes he noticed the look of shock on Stanesby's face as well.

"Did you see?, Did you? Hell, they just disappeared in a cloud of smoke, all three of them". Charles was simply astonished that such a thing could happen. There on the fields of battle he had lost his innocence, he had killed a man and watched as others were killed in front of him. He didn't think it made him a man, it belittled his Christian beliefs, it had made him less of a man, an animal and he felt less worthy than his trusted mount 'Apollo'. The misery of war had been with him for a few weeks but the reality of war had struck him like a slap to the face and that had happened less than two minutes ago. All along the ridge men were feeling the same but no one was talking, all was quiet and the birds had taken flight back into the sky but they were sharing the airspace with a deadly load as the second volley of artillery was going to arrive imminently.

There is a peculiar sound when an artillery shell is heading towards you almost like a wobble in the air more than a shriek, the men all looked skywards as if they would see the shells heading towards them, only for a second then Sgt Blackie roared "Get down" and as each man dropped to the floor the hillside erupted, on the other side of the peak on which the 20th were standing a tirade of fury punched and exploded into the ground. If any man had remained upright he would have died instantly as large horrible shards of red hot metal lanced across the top of the ridge. As it was, most men were battered by the noise and concussion of the shells and then covered in dirt and sods of earth. They could feel the earth move beneath them, a portal to hell about to open and swallow them. There were perhaps twenty explosions before it stopped.

"Everyone ok? Anyone wounded?" shouted the Lieutenant.

There were two wounded, small insignificant wounds, one a piece of shrapnel in the scalp of Dick Sutton and the other a bad bruise as a man had landed on the sight of his rifle when he dropped to the floor. He had a nasty gash above his eyebrow and it would need wound powder and stitches when they got back but, other than that, they had been fortunate.

Charles noticed he was soaking, the weather was fine but certainly not raining. His tunic was drenched and he was so thirsty. Everyone was soaked in sweat their hearts racing, pumping blood, and adrenaline coursing round their excited bodies. There was no sign of the Germans, they had retreated into some woodland about a mile from the hillside. Their dead lay all along the top of the ridge and when the count was finished, all the bodies were collected together and from the bottom of the hill a Padre appeared. It all seems so surreal, less than half an hour ago these men lain out in front of them were alive, intent on killing the very men who had helped collect the dead and wounded and were, even now, treating those very wounds as they would if they had indeed been their own men. The Padre said some words from the book and the dead were left covered with various blankets and raincoats from their backpacks. Souvenirs had been collected and nearly all the *Pickelhauben* German helmets had been nicked. Charles couldn't bear to have one, to him it just felt wrong to steal from the dead, even uniform.

It was time to collect the horses and return to camp, there was a general feeling of '*Bonhomie*' amongst the lads and there was a significant amount of back slapping, this turned to hilarity when Sgt Blackie made the men pick up the brass and place it into a sandbag. It had been the rules since bullets had replaced muskets, on the range everyone collected their brass cases from the spent rounds so they could be refilled somewhere.

Old habits like old soldiers die hard. It was a myth, and in the forthcoming weeks, months and years it would prove to be so as old habits and soldiers died. The race to Paris was on.

CHAPTER 17

Run boys run

Everyone felt tired. The ride back to camp was at the trot and men suddenly felt all the fatigue of a day both in the saddle and in their first contact with the enemy. Charles felt a great unease, it lay heavy on his shoulders and as Apollo trotted along, Charlie felt sad. He hadn't ever thought about killing another man, he deplored violence and today he had been exposed to a lifetimes violence in about twenty minutes. Hundreds of Germans had crested the hilltop and dozens had died, some he thought as a direct result of himself. Bill Stanesby noticed Charles' somber mood and caught up with him. Dick Sutton was riding next to Charles in the column and Bill nodded the wink to Dick and Dick moved so Bill could take his place next to Charlie.

"Are you alright Charlie" Bill, like most of the men in the Regiment liked Charles, he was a good man and fair to everyone and Bill shared his beliefs in life, they got on well. Charles looked up, he hadn't even realised his riding companion had changed, "Oh, hello Bill, didn't see you come in there, sorry I must have been day dreaming, did you say something?" Bill repeated the question.

Charles nodded, "To be honest, I was just thinking back over, that was a very strange experience wasn't it? I was so excited before and whilst it was all going on but after and now, I find I'm feeling very sad and a little bit angry for killing someone. He was someone's son, father, husband, I don't really have anyone but my brothers and sister, my mam died last year and my father years ago, there isn't a wife waiting for me and today I stole someone's life and caused someone so much upset. Its just made me think a bit Bill, I'll be fine, we are fighting a war after all, I just didn't expect to feel like this."

Cpl Stanesby didn't speak he just nodded, he knew what Charlie was feeling, he was feeling the exact same way.

"You know" he said after a couple of minutes, "I was quite scared, when we were waiting that was, I didn't expect that Charlie, but once it started I didn't see them as men, they were just targets, just for a few minutes, targets not men. Then when it had all finished I was busy looking out for those that aren't as quick witted as you, that daft bugger Sutton was shouting and whooping like he had gone mad so I was busy quietening them down before the Sgt set about them. It was only after I felt like you do. I don't like it Charlie, not anymore than you, but we have a job to do and I noticed how well you did yours today, I'm not the only one who noticed either. How many do you think you dropped?"

Charles had only thought about the man he remembered, he didn't think about how many others he might have shot, it was a difficult thing to think about and he felt sick to his stomach knowing he had taken more lives.

By the time they got back everyone was packing ready to move again, the retreat was in full flow and the Regiment had to drop back further just to keep up with the rear of the Army who had already set off earlier. The Germans were in hot pursuit and the French had taken flight, it was to be a fighting retreat to a stronger position but, as dusk approached, there was little time to feed the horses let alone the men. Food had to be taken 'on the hoof' and Charlie, despite feeling knackered knew he had to plough on. The black dog of depression would be pushed back into the box in his mind as indeed it would for many, there was a job to do and the 20th Hussars were going to do it to the best of their ability, or be dammed trying.

CHAPTER 18

Whose side are they on?

At some stage, the troops were tasked with different jobs. Charlie, Ernie Miles, Tom Kelly and Bert Clarke were placed in the care of Cpl Bill Stanesby who in turn was under the charge of Sgt Bill Blackie and, at the top of the tree, was Lieutenant Andrew Johns, a young subaltern who had been at the forefront of as much action as he dared.

The seven men were tasked with catching up with the lead army elements who were miles ahead and really needed to slow down. Easier said than done said someone from the ranks as the Squadron met for orders.

"Men, you have been given this mission because you ride as well as any in the Regiment and we need to make haste" The Officer Commanding stood on a hay bale to give him some height. The 'Greys' are ahead and they have sent a rider back to here but, damn the man, he's gone and got himself wounded and needs to go back to the hospital, so you are to catch up with the Greys and give them the coordinates we will be at by 23:00 tonight. Ride hard lads and don't get caught out in the open. From there you are to change horses, if needed, and ride to the Army Headquarters and report to the General Staff about what's happening here. We are holding the enemy at bay but all the while we are fighting a retreat back to the main army group, its slowing the blighters up and many of the infantry have managed to escape because of the excellent work you have already done."

Bert Clarke was a dour man, he rarely had any humour and when he did, it was at the expense of some unfortunate soul having a bad time. He grumbled a lot but tonight more than ever, he didn't like being tired or hungry and they were gifts abound tonight. No one had slept for at least 24 hours and the men had to grab what they could from open ration packs to make sure they ate anything, this was the last thing anyone would want but the seven knew the importance of the mission so, apart from Bert, there was no gripes.

"Why'd they go and pick us?" he said "haven't we done our bit for the day?"

It was Tom Kelly who rounded on him first, "Bert, why don't you stop moaning? We're at war, don't you realise everyone is tired? Look at Mister Johns, he looks dead on his feet and he isn't complaining, is he? We're all in this together whether we like it or not so shut it a bit will you."

It was a sentiment they all shared, no one likes a moaner.

The horses had rested for a couple of hours and been fed with a mash of oats and water. There was little or no time for the men to grab much more than a hot brew of some weak, insipid tea but sugar was in good supply so the tea was hot, weak and sweet, almost perfect. Some hard biscuits for dunking and, for some of the men, a quick wash and shave. It was time to get going.

They rode out of camp in single file, there was always a chance that there might be someone watching and if they were, an artillery barrage would soon be heading their way, so one at a time and at a bit of a canter for the first couple of hundred yards. There was a copse of trees along the road and it had been agreed they would stop there and collect themselves together.

Charles was riding next to Tom Kelly. They were good mates and the banter soon picked their tired spirits up. Home was a popular subject and for Tom he talked incessantly about Alice and how she was the best wife a man could wish for. Charlie always agreed, she was very special and he was fond of her, she had always made him most welcome and it helped that her dad was the butcher so meat was always on the table and in plentiful supply.

The troop had been riding for about two hours when they happened across a chateau. Lieutenant Johns had said they would stop for a short while more to give the horses a rest. They had covered a lot of ground considering it was night time and dark.

As they rode towards the gate it became obvious there were other people there. Lieutenant Johns stopped the ride, to listen, there on the night-time breeze he could hear voices but he wasn't sure if it was German or French.

"Préparez le cheval sur ses pieds, dépêche-toi, nous n'avons pas le temps."

He recognised the word cheval, horse; it was French.

"Walk slowly lads, nice and steady we don't want any jumpy Frenchies with itchy trigger fingers." It was the Sergeant and he was right, as ever. Lieutenant James dropped back a couple of positions in the rank, it was good practice to leave unsure situations to the more experienced men and James knew when to listen, it's what made him both popular and welcome with the men he commanded. This was his first real sortie away from the Troop Commanders and he was keen not to cock it up.

"Bonjour, hello in there" called Sgt Blackie " We are 'cavalerie anglaise' can you hear me? We are coming in, don't shoot." The column walked slowly to the gates and inside the courtyard they were met with a truly dreadful sight.

On the cobbles lay a horse, it was barely alive, its eyes wide and fearful but its heart was weak and old. Its shoeless hooves were ragged, worn to the sole. Worse still was the fact it still wore the full tack of a warhorse but clearly its fight was done.

Stood above it was its rider, he was holding a whip and as he beat the poor animal to get it to stand Sgt Blackie shouted to him. "Hold the whip Frenchie, hold it man, don't you dare strike that animal once more or I'll take your hide." His Scottish accent was as strong as anyone had ever heard, it was clear and obvious he was furious.

Once more there was a crack as the whip came down and struck the prostrate creature, it whinnied pitifully; Sergeant Blackie was an animal lover, he liked them much more than people and in a flash he was off his horse and he punched the French trooper with so much venom the Frenchie fell on his arse. It wasn't enough for Bill Blackie though and he followed the stunning right hook with a lethal vicious kick to the man's ribs, who groaned as all the air in his body emptied.

"You cowardly French bastard, I'll kill you." It was Bill Stanesby who grabbed the Sergeant to haul him off, " Hold on Sarge", he said as he struggled to hold onto the furious Scotsman. Lieutenant Johns shouted "Sergeant, control yourself" and Big Bill Blackie shook Stanesby off like a ragdoll. There was the loud crack of a rifle and the sickening thud and gasp of someone falling, it was Tom Kelly. He had been shot.

From the darkened doorway stepped a French Cuirassier, his plumed helmet blew in the wind, his rifle was still smoking a sure sign he had just cleaned it and applied too much gun oil to the barrel, it was the last thing he ever did. With a swoosh a blade from a English steel blade sliced him across the neck, it almost decapitated him but as he fell to the floor Lieutenant James jumped from his horse and kicked the rifle away from the Frenchman.

The man who had been beating the horse was up on his feet, he was big and even without his cuirass, he was a barrel of a man. He went to grab his rifle but a second shot of the night felled him on the spot. Bill Blackie had taken the shot from the hip, he didn't even aim it but the bullet smashed into the Frenchman's chest and he was down, dead before he hit the floor.

Two more French soldiers ran out from the building and before they had time to shout, they raised their hands to the sky "Abandon, abandon" they shouted. They were lucky they weren't shot on the spot but Johns said they were surrendering and everyone blew out a large breath.

One of the Frenchmen went to the body with the sword wound, he was gurgling as blood filled his lungs and he was clearly going to die imminently, he had no fear in his eyes, just resignation of his fate. The man knelt next to him and took his Officer's body to his chest and, with a final gush and cough, he died.

"Anglaise?" He said and Lieutenant Johns went over to him. As he did he showed the Frenchman he wasn't going to hurt him, he slid his blooded sword back into his scabbard and Bill Blackie shook his head, he knew it was going to be a bitch of a job to get the dried blood from the inside of the scabbard.

"I'm sorry about your Officer, he said, but he has shot one of my men" and as if a magic spell had been broken all eyes turned to Tom Kelly; Charles was with him holding him as if sat up; Tom was dead.

The Frenchman spoke very broken English, but enough to say he was sorry that his comrades had caused this skirmish.

Bill Blackie had Stanesby hold the collapsed horse by the bridle and with his service revolver he dispatched it, there were tears in his eyes as he pulled the trigger. The poor animal would suffer no more.

All this action had taken less than ten minutes, it felt a lot longer, but in that time 3 men had died and ultimately the horse that had caused such a passionate response was now finally at peace as well.

Lieutenant James collected Tom Kelly's identification and Miles, Clarke and Charles buried his body in a shallow grave with a wooden cross. There would be trouble, everyone expected it but the Frenchman said neither of the two Frenchies would be missed, neither was popular one a bully the other an aristocratic pig. They would tell their Commanders that the two had been killed by Germans. They would lie and say they had a heroes death fighting the Bosch.

It remained to be seen what the British would say, but it was agreed that Tom was killed by the enemy, this way Alice would be granted a pension after the war. Everyone agreed apart from Bert Clarke who said it wasn't the truth. Bill Blackie took Clarke to one side and had a little one to one chat and when they came back Clarke was more than happy to go along with the tale, for Alice's sake.

CHAPTER 19

Aug 1914

Rain, there isn't much that's worse for a cold, tired and particularly miserable group of soldiers, but today it would excel and as the 20th were being sent in small groups to all sorts of different locations the grumbling grew worse and worse. Moral wasn't very high, this war was meant to be much easier than this; over by Christmas they had all said, no chance. The British Expeditionary Force had been severely tested, it hadn't quite broken but it was all bent out of shape and breaking was a near thing.

'B' Squadron had two Troops of men patrolling some nearby woods. There had been reports of German cavalry and despite everyone's caution, the lads were keen to get some action. They felt they had been running away far too much; they understood the reasoning, but still it irked them, and they were as keen as mustard to get stuck in to the Germans.

Here in the woods it was dim, almost dark, but at least the rain wasn't landing on them. On the road that ran along the side of the woods, there were some men on bicycles, part of the civilian population whose life was disturbed but not yet destroyed, and the daily work went on regardless.

In the distance, through the murk and mist, there stood a group of mounted cavalry. As often happens in war assumptions are made and the assumption was that the men were Belgian soldiers or at least French. If the 20th could make contact with them, maybe they would be able to point then in the direction of the enemy. As they carefully picked their way towards the mysterious riders the undergrowth was getting thicker, it slowed 'B' down, it saved many men from falling that day. As they lead riders broke into the clearing they realised, too late that they men were in fact a German Unit, who like themselves, were lost, but like a disturbed hornets' nest, aggravated and very dangerous.

The first few shots were high and wide, both sides had rushed headlong into a battle that neither could foresee and as much as the Germans shooting was bad, the British was its equal, and although brief the encounter was soon over, the Germans held the upper hand and the Troop scattered in all directions. Charles dug his heels into Apollo's side and was relieved by the urgency Apollo showed in his response. As he turned on his heels to run, Charles felt the wind knocked out of him by a low hanging branch of an ancient oak. Funny that the very tree with which we associate with our brave soldiers had now knocked one over. Charles felt himself lifted from the saddle and, as Apollo dug his mighty hooves into the woodland, he left behind his rider. Charlie had committed the ultimate sin in horsemanship, he had fallen off.

Charles rolled into the undergrowth and not a second too soon as two mounted Germans came past him at the gallop. The tree which had caused him to come off had, in turn, saved him as he hid in its embrace of low branches and scrub. He wasn't injured and he soon got his breath back, but Apollo and his comrades had gone. For the first time in a long time he felt dreadfully alone, where, just a few moments before there was war and chaos, now there was silence and peace. There wasn't any sign of anybody else around and now, in the quiet in the trees he could hear the beautiful song of the birds. Charles knew nothing of birdsong, back home there were the common birds found in a smoke-filled mill town, dirty starlings, sparrows and the ever present pigeons with their soot stained feathers. He had no idea what kind of bird was making the lovely noise he could now hear but it sounded beautiful. He thought it best to stay hidden for a while to ensure the Germans didn't find him on their return, he needn't have worried, they weren't coming back this way ever because they had caught two of the men they had been chasing, and one was the Lieutenant, he had been captured along with some of the squadron but Charles had somehow managed to avoid capture for now. It was getting darker in the woods and as he lay there he wondered as to the time, he had no watch, he'd had no need for a watch, he was told where to be and when, his watch was left behind in his personal stuff in his back pack. Although he was concerned, he felt a great tiredness come over him, the adrenaline had all gone and he was safe in his little hidey-hole and even though it was raining outside the wood, it didn't seem to be getting down to ground level so he was warm and dry. He thought hard about what he should do. Should he move and risk the Germans still being around? He couldn't hear anyone nearby; or should he stay put for an hour to make sure the path was clear? He tried to remember the route they had taken to get to the edge of the woods. If he could remember the way in, he would easily remember the way back. The best course of action would be stay put for an hour, he felt sure this would give him the best chance, he nodded an affirmation to no-one but himself. He hoped Apollo had followed the rest back and, if he was being honest, he hoped the lads would return to try to find him. That would be the best, he should stay here for an hour or so or at least until the daylight subsided. He was still thinking this through as he fell asleep, safe.

The tip of the long German lance rested ever so gently on his chest. He barely felt it as he slowly opened his eyes. He hadn't heard them coming but he had moved, that's when they saw him. Not sure if he was dead or wounded, the two German horse mounted Ulans approached cautiously. One let his lance gently rest on the British soldier's chest. The lance was huge, over 10 foot long, and the square steel point was sharp and deadly. All he needed to do was push it home into the Englander's chest, but he noted the spurs on the prone soldier and recognised he was a cavalryman, like himself. There was honour, there always had been, and as the big German allowed his prisoner to come from his hiding place, he smiled to reassure his prisoner he meant him no harm, his war was over.

Charles looked first at the point of the lance then along its shaft to the man holding it. He was smiling, almost a familiar friendly face but he knew no Germans. Charles crawled out from the undergrowth and put his hands in the air, he was unarmed and certainly not in a dangerous mood. The realisation was, he was a prisoner of war. Neither spoke the other's language, so all communication was in the form of mime. But Charles was under no allusion what the consequences of any rash move might be.

CHAPTER 20

Captured

Charles felt embarrassed, he didn't really know what to feel – so embarrassed was better than shame – and he certainly didn't feel any joy at being a prisoner, so embarrassed fitted.

The Germans were a good sort it seemed, they hadn't roughed him up and in fact had walked alongside rather than behind him, but they were on huge horses. Charles had nodded his surrender to the mounted Germans and even though he was captive he still had time to fuss the horse his captor was riding. He stroked the horse along its nose and gently played with the horse's lips. The large horse was magnificent and it nodded its head furiously when Charles stopped, almost demanding he carry on, all three men laughed, horses did that to you. They were a common denominator and if you understood horses you understood horsemen. Charles noticed the uniform of the cavalryman wasn't a million miles different to his own he pointed to his shoulder tab that said 20th Hussars and said "Hussars" he pointed a finger at the German. The Germans face lit up into a huge smile he pointed to himself and said "Ich bin ein hussar, bist du ein hussar?" He slid his cape from his shoulder to reveal the number 3 on his collar. Charles didn't know what it meant but he could hazard a guess that this fellow was a hussar as well and that he belonged to the 3rd something or other so he nodded and patted the horse on the neck. The German offered him a flask and smiled, they didn't seem too bad these Germans, he thought, as he sipped the strong brandy that made him cough. Charles wasn't used to strong liquor, he was much more comfortable with a Dandelion and Burdock from the temperance bar. He did drink beer but not often, truth was he wasn't struck on the taste and following a very inexperienced evening with the lads back in Colchester, he had been drunk and was very ill for the next few rides. He didn't care for alcohol much after that. So he took a sip and wiped his lips dry as he handed the flask back.

As the three men rounded the lane he could see the rest of this German's Squadron in the village square ahead. Sat around in a circle were some other chaps, only these didn't have any caps on and thought he recognised one or two of them, but the rest he didn't know. No wonder they didn't come back for him, they had either been captured as well or scattered. As Charles and his escort walked towards the gathered huddle, it was Stan Greenbank who saw Charles first, he called out "Hey Charlie, over here." Charles felt his heart rise, sat there in a huddle were 3 more 20th Hussars, one was the Lieutenant. He was talking to a German Officer who appeared to speak extremely good English. Next to him stood their Commander who didn't speak any English but was clear in French. Fortunately, Lieutenant Michelle spoke French and, between the 3 of them, they seemed to be communicating very well.

It was Charles' escort who announced to everyone that the men they had captured were in fact, Hussars, like themselves and in an instant the mood changed not that it was bad in the first place. Each man had had some rations and a drink but now the drink became much more palatable and was served with a back slap or handshake.

As Charles looked around he could see one or two horses that belonged to the 20th and there, stood as bold as brass, was Apollo. Charles said to his guard, "Can I see to my horse please?" and pointed to the horses. The guard wasn't sure what he meant but asked someone who said "Yes, absolutely." Lt Michelle said "Atherton, you can go and see your mount, don't try anything stupid though." Charles was both relieved and offended all at the same time. He really wanted to say to the Lieutenant that it was his fault they were captives, it was HIM who did 'something stupid' by trotting over to the Germans who, he said, were in fact French. What did he know? "Thank you, Sir," he replied biting his tongue. Charles wasn't given to profanity so he just thought 'arsehole' but didn't say it.

He walked over to Apollo who snorted in excitement to see his master, not that Charles ever thought the relationship was like that, he saw Apollo as an equal and as he got hold of Apollo's huge head he played with the horse's ears. He noticed the girth was still tight so drew attention to the guard who knew immediately what Charles wanted and nodded his approval. Charles loosened the strap, he looked to see all the other 20th Hussars' horses were the same and set about loosening their girth straps as well. He also let the bits down a hole on the bridle's. Apollo nodded and head butted him as if to say thanks.

The large German who had been on horseback but a few seconds before came up besides Charles, he had two mugs of coffee and he offered Charles a brew. "Is he your horse" he asked; Charles was surprised, he had assumed no one spoke English, especially this chap who, it turned out, spoke very good English.

"Yes, this is my horse; Apollo" Charles replied; he put the hot cup of steaming coffee on the step so it didn't get knocked over.

The German said "My name is Gerhardt what is your name?" it was slow but very clear English and Charles wanted to ask why he hadn't spoken to him before? Maybe it was the confidence of being with his mates?

"Charles Atherton" he said, "20th Hussars"

Charles was just moving the metal stirrup up the leather stirrup straps and passing the leather through so the metal was secure and not bouncing on the horse's flank. He turned around to look at Gerhardt as he picked up his brew, "Thanks for this" he said.

"Oh it is nothing", said the friendly German, "you would do the same for me, we don't want to be here either but this war isn't our plan, like you we are professional soldiers but Hussars on two different sides. Your officer, he is arrogant yes? Young and arrogant, we have the same problem in our army, we call them 'Arschloch'"

Charles laughed and said "He is, but he's only a boy, not been with us long before we came out here, this will make a man of him though. Being a prisoner will hurt his pride."

"He will stay a prisoner Charles Atherton, but you will be released tonight once it is safe for you to go."

Charles was astonished at what he had just heard, "What? free to go, tonight? why would you let me go?"

"Ah we are Hussars together, and you are my prisoner, and I already like you, you are like me. It is clear you care very much about your horses. We won't be able to send you back with an escort and you would just try to escape if we tried to make you go yourselves. I would feel bad if you got killed for trying to escape and we are many in the area. You will be better if you ride alone back to your own side. We will keep the Officer and the others, but I have decided to send you back to your Regiment with honour." Gerhardt patted him on the shoulder, "I am on guard tonight and after the men go to sleep I will wake you. We might meet again Charles Atherton, in happier times,"

Charles offered his hand in friendship, honour was a hugely important quality to him and when he gave his word he meant it, and when he offered his hand it was his guarantee of sincerity.

"Thank you, do the others know?" he was still slightly stunned that he was being allowed to return to his own lines but he had been taught a valuable lesson about his supposed enemy, they were much more honourable than the French he had met, it made him wonder if they were fighting the wrong people.

"You will be leaving after dark, our Officer wants you to slip away and be safe, there are no other cavalry out tonight so you should get back safely. Your young Officer is glad to be staying, maybe he wont be a loss to you."

As daylight faded and the long shadows of dusk began to stretch along the wooded lined road, the four prisoners sat and ate their small ration of food. Charles sat on a fallen log looking at his comrades, he was a slightly apprehensive and worried the others might feel there had been a betrayal in that he was going to be freed; he felt had to say something. The other Hussars weren't from his regular Troop, one wasn't from the Hussars at all, he was an infantryman who had been left behind. The thing that really disappointed him, almost disgusted him, was the way these other men were happy to be prisoners of war. They knew that barring some travesty they would be safe from here to Christmas when the war was surely bound to finish. Why get yourself killed fighting in a scrap that'll be over in no time? "We will be returned home in one piece, every bit the hero" he'd heard one say. They were glad to have been caught, and obviously they were in no rush to escape. Charles thought he should say something but safe in the knowledge he was going back, he didn't want to risk failure, if they wanted to stay then let them, as the German had already said they weren't any loss if that was their attitude.

CHAPTER 21

Escape

As darkness fell, the make shift camp were turned in to sleep. Charles wasn't tired his very soul was burning to be getting on with it. He had moved his blanket further away from the others so he wouldn't disturb them when he left. He didn't have to wait long.

Within the hour he could hear the quiet footsteps of someone coming towards him and with a gentle touch on his shoulder he got up quietly, he needn't have worried, no one cared if he stayed or went, they had made their minds up they were staying. Apollo was tacked up, his saddle had been placed on his strong back and his bridle had been put in place. He let out a welcoming neigh as he smelt his friend and jockey stroke his thick neck. Charles whispered into Apollos ear, "Steady old love, we'll be home soon" Gerhardt offered his hand to Charles who took it and held it firm, "Thank you Gerhardt, I hope we both survive this daft war and who knows we might well meet again, I'll keep an eye out for you if we come into contact again and maybe I will be able to return the favour". Gerhardt offered Charles a leg up and quietly Charles mounted his horse.

"I have heard your men are heading towards Le Cateau" he pointed in the right direction for Charles to set a bearing. "There are no mounted patrols planned tonight but I cannot say about infantry, be careful and trust no one until you get back to your men. I have fed your horse and there is water in your drinks canteen along with some bread. Good luck Charles Atherton, 20th Hussars." He handed Charles the reins and with a final nod of respect to each other Charles rode out of the courtyard and onto the lane that ran parallel to the wood. Within 50 yards he had disappeared into the dark shadows. His escape had been made good but he could have no idea he was jumping from the frying pan into a very hot fire.

CHAPTER 22

The cat is out of the bag

Charles rode steadily for the next 3 hours, every now and again he would hear some troops moving in or near his vicinity and each time he would dip down or hide in the shadows. He knew he must be nearing the retreating British lines but he hadn't seen anyone on foot, let alone on horseback.

"Halt! Who goes there?" Charles about messed himself

"Friend" he called back

"Advance friend and be recognised"

Charles rode very quietly so as not to spook anyone or indeed his highly alert Apollo who could smell the soldier hiding in the tree line.

"Who are you, and where are your regiment?" asked the sentry

"Private Charles Atherton 20th Hussars, who are you?"

"Stand there, don't move a muscle or I'll shoot" A man wearing a kilt stepped out of the dark and pointing a very ugly bayonet towards Charles he said,

"Why are you alone?"

"I have escaped from the Germans, I was trapped by them last night but I have managed to give them the slip but my Unit is not to be found. I'm not even sure where I am but if you might stop pointing that ruddy great rifle at me I'd feel a lot better."

The Scottish soldier lowered his rifle a little but kept it pointing in the general direction of horse and rider.

"I'm Tam Ryan Gordon Highlanders wait there and I'll get the Guard Commander"

Charles stood and looked up to the night sky it was perfectly clear but no light from the moon. It was a cold night and now he had stopped riding he was feeling the cool nip in the air. Presently a young subaltern came to where Charles was waiting.

"Hello Private, er; Atherton? my lad here tells me you have escaped from the Boche, is that right?"

"It is sir, I left them about four hours ago and I have been trying to find my lot since, they have moved I am guessing, but I have no idea where to. Do you know or have any idea where they are Sir?" Charles was aware that it might look a little odd him being separated from the rest of his Troop but the truth was, he was hopelessly lost, he was extremely lucky that the man was British and not German.

"Where were the Germans the Officer asked, how long have you been riding? Get down off your horse lad, come and get a hot brew you look knackered." The Officer had hit the nail on the head. Charles suddenly felt weary as he slid down from the saddle. He loosened the girth for Apollo and fetched a bucket of water for him to drink. He patted the horse's huge neck, he had been a superstar of a horse and Charlie knew the Apollo must be hungry. The guard asked "does your horse eat oats?, We have tons of the damn stuff in the canteen for porridge. I'm sure we could get some if he needs them." Charlie could have hugged him. "Please if you could spare some they would be perfect." Within a few minutes, a bucket with some wet oats had been delivered and devoured, and a drink of water from a bucket taken. The kindness of some people who would share what small amount they had was touching. A warm cup of tea with a tot of rum was Charles' blessing as well as some hard tack biscuits and plum jam.

Charles knew the 'Gordon's' they had been in Colchester Garrison at the same time as the 20th Hussars, in fact they had been deployed together and it wasn't long before he met one or two he knew from the Garrison Swimming Club. They all looked old and haggard, and he knew that they had been retreating for the past few days with little or no time for sleep or rest.

The Orderly Officer came to Charles with a map. He was smoking a pipe and the smell of the tobacco was heady and sweet. It was a familiar smell to Charles, as quite a few of the lads in his Troop smoked a pipe.

"You're a way from your lot Atherton, they're down to the South of us here by about 15 miles. If you ride at a trot you should be there in a couple of hours. I have a man who is going South so he is happy to ride along with you, two of you stand a better chance than one on his own. I suggest you rest up a while and let your mount have a breather. There doesn't seem to be much point in you trying to navigate there in the dark, it would be easy to get lost. There are British troops all along the line ready for another crack at the Germans tomorrow. We are staying here to hold them as long as we can which is why I'm very interested in the fact you have given them the slip, where were you? Can you show me on this map?"

Charles followed the map with his finger, first North to the Southern edge of the woods then around to the West and North up the tree line towards the old Roman road and pointed to a small chateau,

"It was around here Sir, I was the only one to get away and I rode South for a good while before I came across you and your men here"

"Did you gallop or trot?, if it took you a couple of hours of good trotting or a gallop then they might not be that far behind you, eh"

"They were all asleep when I slipped away, no one was showing any signs of moving till daybreak Sir"

"O.k, it's now 03:00hrs so go and get some shut eye till 05:00 then you can get going. Don't worry about your horse, one of the men will throw a rug over it and let's get you away to your Regiment. I'll give you a letter to prove you're not a deserter, it'll be ready for when you go."

Charles lay in the hollow of the shade of a huge tree, he pulled the blanket over his head and within a few seconds was sound asleep, a dreamless deep sleep.

He was woken at 05:00 with a warm insipid sweet brew of tea but he did have a sausage butty, something he hadn't had for months, and it was delicious. His companion for the ride was Tam Reeks and he had a message to deliver to HQ somewhere south of where Charlie was hoping to find his mates. Apollo was 'tacked up' ready to go, Charlie checked his horse's feet and to make sure they were clean and wriggled the shoes to make sure none had come loose. They were all fine and with a spring up onto Apollo's back he was seated and ready. He gave the horse a pat along his thick neck and slid his hands up to the big ears and gave them a scratch. Apollo shook his mighty head in a playful way.

"Good luck lads" it was the Duty Officer come to see them away,

"Aye Sir, and you, I'll see you when I get back later today" Tam was a useful horseman but he hadn't ridden anything as spirited as the Adjutant's horse before and he looked anything but confident. Charles reached over and patted his comrade's shoulder 'It'll be reet Jock, sit up and just follow me." And with a wave they were on their way.

It couldn't have been a mile later when they heard the first artillery shells in the air. Charles had heard the distant 'booms' but not sure what side had started the shelling, he just trotted off down the road. The 'Swoosh' of the first big shell whistled over his head and with a huge crash ploughed into the far side of the woods from where they had come. The battle of Le Cateau had begun.

CHAPTER 23

Homefront

Rebecca had been lucky, she didn't fall pregnant to a man with no heart or love for her. She had learned a valuable lesson and regretted her indiscretion with Alf Green.

Charles Atherton had her heart, she hadn't seen or heard anything from him since he had left for the war, but wrote to him every couple of days. Her handwriting wasn't partially good but even she noticed how much better and neater it had become over the last few weeks, despite the fact she hadn't yet received a letter back. She understood that the Army was on the move and, secondly she knew she had hurt Charles badly with her stupidity. She needed to tell him how she felt and now the fear of an unwanted pregnancy had passed she felt brave enough and, indeed relieved enough, to show her true feelings. A tear ran down her soft cheek, she hoped she might see him soon, the war would be over by Christmas, everyone said so, then life would return to normal and maybe her soldier boy might come home to see her again. She held that dream close to her heart as she licked the flap on the envelope and stuck it down with a kiss, she let the tear fall onto the paper, it left a faint stain, a sign of her love that no one else would ever share. It would be her secret gift.

She walked to the shops and posted her letter, she picked up some shopping to make a hotpot and walked home to her mother's house on Peel Street. At number 19 she saw Elizabeth at the step washing the stone in her old, and somewhat tatty, pinny. She smiled and waved and Elizabeth stood and stretched her aching back.

"Hello love, you been shopping?" Elizabeth Atherton was a kind lady, old before her time. Now that her mother had gone, she had passed in 1913; leaving her as the lady in a house she shared with her brother William and, latterly, Charles. Thomas had married and moved with Emily and his young family but, as was the way, he hadn't moved far, two streets away to be precise.

"Hello Beth" (never Liz that was far too common and never Elizabeth that was the family only) "Have you heard anything from Charles?" She had asked this question every time she saw Beth and the answer was always the same.

"He is moving all the time I suppose. I saw in the Bolton Evening news that it's been quite awful at a place called Mons, but there was an angel! it saved a lot of our lads, did you read it? He'll write love, once he knows how you feel. Have you sent him another letter? They might have to get a mule just to deliver your letters. Dear Lord you don't half send some." She laughed and they hugged.

"Your mam was out on the step earlier, tell her I've got some new salts for the stone, it seems to make them shine a proper job. If she wants some I'll pick some up next time"

"Any news about William going off yet?" asked Rebecca

"He has to report to Bury next week, Tom is staying on home duty. I'm glad. I have two brothers doing their bit and another one here. Apparently, Tom is going to be guarding the prisoners up at Leigh, it's his eyes that are bad so they don't want him. He should stay at home with Emily and

Mae, she's a little bugger let me tell you. Had her head stuck in the rails again last night, luckily we managed to soap her ears but one of these days she'll get proper stuck." again they both laughed.

CHAPTER 24

Hell and Shrapnel

The noise was deafening. Shell after shell roared over the top as the two horsemen picked their way along the final few miles to safety and their own lines. Tam had managed to sort out the ride he was on and the horse had begrudgingly given in a bit to his strong hand. Charles had tried to show him how to relax his hand but the best he had managed was to stop him jerking the bit in the frightened animals mouth. "You've got hands like a farrier Tam, go soft on his mouth, look, like this." Once more he showed him how to give a little with the reins so the horse's mouth didn't get yanked.

"Hell's teeth Charlie, those shells don't seem to be getting any less, some poor bugger is getting it hot today."

Today; Charles hadn't thought about the time of day but it was light and still raining, he guessed it must be after 08:00 but wasn't sure.

Presently they came to the road, it was here they would part company; Charles to the right and East, Tam straight on to his HQ. They could see the headquarters in a hollow valley up ahead about ½ a mile. They shook hands and bade each other good luck. Charles knew he had about 5 miles to go before he would be in the area of his own Regiment, he checked to make sure he still had the letter in his pocket that said he wasn't a deserter. With a wave the two men went their own way. He nudged Apollo and they stepped off into a trot. About 200 yards up the road, Charles heard the hiss and whizz of a shell just overhead. He ducked instinctively as it passed him, he looked over his shoulder just in time to see it land, right besides Tam and his horse. They both died instantly and Charles felt his shoulders heave as he tried to suppress a scream and closed his eyes as if to not see it but too late.

Tam's demise was the start of a deadly hour, for in that sixty minute period there wasn't more than a breath between the scream of a shell and its destructive impact. It was as if Charles was riding along the front of the line that separated the two warring armies. He tried to count the impacts as he calmed Apollo, it was with Gods blessing that neither had been hit. Charles could hear the solid lead balls of shrapnel whistling past his head, each one a death penalty, unserved but willing. He wiped his face with the arm of his tunic, his nose was dripping but he was alarmed that when he looked it was blood that had smeared along the sleeve. He thought he must surely have been hit or wounded but there was neither pain or indeed sign of the wound. He then noticed he was bleeding from his right ear, Apollo had a nick in his ear, a shrapnel ball had skimmed past and cut the large pointed extremity but the horse's dander was up and he pumped a spray mist of blood across Charles' face. To the onlooker it would have seemed as if both the rider and horse were mortally wounded but there was no more than a fleshwound on Apollo's ear, and the concussion of the explosions that had made Charlie's nose and ears bleed, he wasn't injured at all.

All along the road he could hear the dying creaks as trees and branches fell to the destructive powers of man's imagination. It wasn't that long ago that cannon balls were the worst it got, now shells exploded in the sky and belched death from a thousand lead balls from within.

It took Charles a lot longer than he thought it would to reach a crossroads. There were still road signs not all removed by the French yet, he followed the one directing him to *Tergnier*. It wasn't far, about another few hours by his reckoning if he walked on foot for a bit and rode.

In the distance there was the omnipresent rumble of artillery, he had no idea who it belonged to but it was just there, constant. He saw some civilians walking along the road. He was glad to see some other people, for the last hour or so he had felt terribly alone as if he was the last one left. These poor wretches had their worldly possessions on carts and what few bits they had managed to pack showed signs of the country folk and the way they lived, a catalogue of life dating back a hundred years all jumbled up on the back of traps and trailers pulled along by tired horses and driven by even more tired people.

"Bonjour." Charles hadn't mastered French at all and said in a Bolton accent. It sounded most peculiar more like "Bon Jewair." The French were a very forgiving audience who stopped and looked at him with sympathetic eyes, he looked dreadful, covered in blood and his eyes had dark deep shadows that made him look a lot older than his 20 years. He realised he must look shocking when a farmer's wife crossed herself, he hadn't thought about how he looked. Someone offered him a drink, he had expected nothing but was very surprised when what he thought might be water from a flask turned out to be wine. It made him cough, he wasn't used to wine or any other form of alcohol but he was grateful all the same. "Thank you. Mercy bou coups" he said and someone smiled and then laughed, it started as a titter but grew into a deep and relieving laughter, there was no embarrassment at his dreadful French, it had been the catalyst for a huge stress reliever and the laughter of these poor displaced people was music to everyone's ears. Charles was given a wet cloth. He wiped Apollo's head and neck to help cool him and clean him up a bit, then, after it had been rung out and wet again, he wiped his face. He was surprised how much blood was in the cloth and then understood why the shock of seeing him had caused such concern. When he was finished wiping himself down even the stubble of his unshaved chin felt softer, it was not much more than 'bum fluff' his mates told him but he felt more of a man if he shaved. That would have to wait until he either found his Unit. He had no shaving kit with him, he had left it all behind what seemed like weeks ago but in fact was only a few days. Water appeared in a bucket and a nose bag of hay for Apollo, he got stuck in and Charles was given some bread and cheese, it tasted delicious, he was truly humbled by this rag tag refugee who had little to give but gave it anyway. He took off Apollo's saddle and rested it on the roadside, he even slipped the bit from Apollo's mouth and then he kissed him on the nose and the French laughed, so different from the French Army he had encountered just a few days before. It made him think of Tom and that made him sad. They rested on the roadside for an hour, Charles felt weary; he badly needed some sleep but he knew he had to keep going. It couldn't be far now, just a few miles at the most.

It was time to walk, he had ridden Apollo for far longer than he would normally have and, given that food was scarce for both him and his horse, he wanted to spend as little time burdening his mount. He left the tack as loose as he could but tight enough to make sure it was safe and not going to fall off. He was loaded with equipment to help lighten the load on the horse's back. It felt uncomfortable at first, but he soon got used to it and, after a few minor adjustments to balance it better and some firm handshakes to the local French who had been so kind to him, he was on his way.

He walked through the village and out onto the country road that seemed a million miles from a war, crops were mainly in but here and there a field lay un-gathered and the crop was withering slowly in the autumn weather. Rain had been heavy for the past couple of weeks but when the sun came out it was as hot as hell, much hotter than England in autumn. The plus side was there was plenty of grass and Apollo made sure he took advantage of every stop to have a good munch. Charles didn't mind, everything he possessed needed cleaning it was covered in 'clarts' and he knew he would be in for a rollocking if Sergeant Blackie saw it.

After he had walked for about an hour he came to the outskirts of a small town. It was here a rider suddenly appeared without any warning and he heard his name being called

"Charlie? Charlie Atherton is that you? We heard you were dead."

Charles looked at the man, he knew him! "Arthur, oh thank the Lord, are the Regiment here?" Arthur Davies was from "A" Troop but he had been in "B" Troop before the mobilisation. He knew Charles well enough from days hunting in Colchester. He had been a Lance Corporal until he lost his 'stripe' for being worse for wear with drink. He had been involved in a brawl in a pub along with quite a few others from the barracks, civilians were always good for a fight after a few beers, but on this occasion, Arthur had walloped some ne'er-do-well a little harder than intended and been arrested by the Garrison Police. The subsequent charge cost him his rank.

"Come along Charlie, there's a few people want to meet you I'm sure." He led the way. Charles followed leading Apollo, it wasn't far. Just up the road they came across the rest of "A" Troop. There was a lot of back slapping and hand shaking when Charles told them what had happened. The young Officer in charge said it was important to get him back to his Squadron so he could answer some questions. With that the reconnaissance trip was deemed done. Charles tacked up Apollo properly and with a swift leg up was ready to follow his mates back to the Regiment. He felt sure there would be a huge telling off waiting for him and, suddenly, he was nervous. The Sergeant Major was a fearsome man and, if he thought Charles had in any way been slacking, he would have him on a charge 'toot sweet'. So it was with some trepidation that he approached the outpost where the 20th Hussars were resting for the night.

He needn't have worried though, Captain Sanford came to meet the ride and his exact words were 'Oh thank Christ, you're alive Atherton, we thought you had been killed. Come and tell me what happened and where you have been lad. There's some food waiting. I'm sure there'll be enough for you, go and sort your horse out and bed him down for the night, he looks knackered lad and I have to say you don't look too grand yourself"

Charles gave him the letter he had from the Gordons' Officer to show he hadn't been trying to desert, it probably hadn't saved his life, but at the very least it gave the Sergeant Major something to read, which was handy because he came striding over to Charles whilst he was bedding down Apollo.

"Atherton" he said, "where he hell have you been?"

"Sir, I was knocked off my horse and captured by the Germans, they had some of our lads in a camp but I managed to give them the slip and get away." He didn't know if his little lie would be seen through, he wasn't a good liar, it was against his better nature, but he wasn't sure if he wanted to tell the truth either. If he did he was sure to drop the men who had decided not to escape in the mire.

The Sgt Maj said "The Adjt has just given me the letter you gave him, I know the Officer that wrote it, we were drinking pals together back in England, is he ok?"

"He was Sir, last time I saw them, but his area took a right pasting with artillery after we left." It was the first time he had thought about Tam, he needed to inform people as to what had happened to him, he would tell the Adjt when he saw him.

"Dont worry about your kit, I'll get someone to sort it out for you lad, go and get some food and then get over and see Captain Sanford; once you've seen him he will tell your Troop Commander that you're back, but I want you to go and get some sleep. You look like you could do with a rest, so get that lot sorted and then get some kip here. Dont talk to anyone about what happened until you have seen the Captain,"

"Yes Sir" he replied. It felt good to be back with the lads, safe and sound. His little adventure had come to an end and he felt relieved it had. He filled a sack with some straw, it would make a bed of sorts and he would kip here with his mate, he had a thick blanket and he was dog tired so he didn't have any doubts he would soon be in a deep sleep. He cleaned himself up before setting off to see the Captain. He nodded to a couple of his mates as he walked over the cobbles, he knocked on the door and waited.

"They did what?" Charles had never heard Captain Sanford shout but he was furious that any man from the 20th Hussars would rather be kept as a prisoner of war than fight with his mates here in the Regiment

"I hope we survive this war Atherton, then when they get back I will see them Courts Martialled for cowardice. An Officer as well, it makes it all the more galling. And you did well to get away, well done"

Charles had spilled the beans, told the truth as to what had happened. He didn't want to be seen as someone who had escaped from the enemy when, in truth, he had been released by a compassionate enemy. He felt bad for telling about the others, but truth was truth, and it sat like a ball of unease in his gut that people would abandon their mates and take the easy way out rather than fight on. He felt better in himself for having told the truth and to hell with the consequences. He was dismissed with a warning that the Commanding Officer might want to see him in the morning to tell him what was barely believable. In fact, had it been anyone else who was doing the telling, Captain Sanford might not have believed him, but this lad Atherton was a good lad, honest and a good soldier, well liked by his mates and seniors. As the Captain spoke, he had an idea.

"Atherton, how would you like to go back to Blighty for a few days or so? We have some reinforcements due out to join us in the next few weeks and I am aware that you were good friends with Private Kelly. You might like to go and see his wife and family on your way to seeing your family in the North. It wouldn't be for long but you might be able to kill a few birds with one stone. Word is the race for Paris is about done, the Germans are losing too many men and have started to slow their advance. We are going to be heading North. There's a new race afoot, the one to the ports up North so we could do with you giving the new men a few words of encouragement. Let me talk to the Commanding Officer and your Troop Commander, after all we thought we had lost you. I have just written a letter to your sister, it looks like I can tear that one up, that's always good news. Let me clear it with the Colonel and I think we might be getting you away for an errand back to England. I will write to the Officer Commanding back in Colchester, there are new men arriving daily and they might be grateful for your help, just for a few days.

Charles's head was in a spin, he understood what had happened but didn't understand how quickly it had, this morning, only 12 hours ago, he was a million miles away and very much in harm's way and now he was off to England for a few days, maybe even a few weeks.

"Go and get some rest Atherton, you look done in lad. Well done and thanks for bringing me the news of the Gordons' runner. I'll make sure the news gets back to them. I'm sure we will talk tomorrow. Dismiss."

Charles felt himself stiffen and he saluted smartly, then he turned on his heel and almost marched out. As he left the room he walked straight into Sergeant Bill Blackie,

"Oh hello Sarge, sorry, I didn't see you there."

"Hello Charlie, are you ok lad? I heard about what happened. Long day eh? I have one of the lads sorting your kit out, you go back to the stables and make sure your horse is ok and then get your head down. Are you sure you're OK? it must have been a bugger getting split away like that, well done you for getting away and finding us again, we have covered quite a bit of ground since you left for the patrol."

Charles nodded and Bill put his hand on his young shoulders, Blackie was older than most of the men, a career soldier he felt a real empathy, a simple connection, with his men and this one, Charles Atherton was one of the good ones.

"Go on lad get some sleep."

Charles went back to the stable and grabbed his blanket, he was asleep in seconds, the last thing he felt was the warm air from Apollo's nose as he smelled his human friend. It was as wonderful as it was soporific and in a heartbeat, Charles was asleep.

CHAPTER 25

The Long Way Round

It felt very strange being back in Blighty. The war had hardly started but a month ago and it was a huge surprise that he had been sent back to the barracks in Colchester. The train stopped and he stepped onto a very busy platform with soldiers as far as the eye could see. It was all very orderly, some were with sweethearts, a last kiss goodbye before the off to a great adventure. One man from the "Norfolks" bumped into Charles.

"Hello mate, you coming or going?" it seemed a strange question as he was clearly just getting off the train. When he looked down the platform he noticed another train already parked up. This train wasn't so joyous, it was an ambulance train. It had been loaded at the docks with the wounded and now some had died from wounds on their way back to base hospitals in England. It was the first time Charles had seen one, he had heard about them but now, stood looking at one, he became more aware of the letter he had in his tunic pocket. This letter was for Alice Kelly up in Langwith. Tom and indeed the rest, had all taken time to write these 'last letters'. Each man hoped they would never be read and all of them had given their letter to a mate. Tom had given Albert Miles his letter and in turn Albert had given his to Ernie Clarke and Clarke had given his to Charlie. Charlie had given his letter addressed to Elizabeth, Thomas, William, his sister and brothers, to Walter Stanesby. Each man had promised that should one of the Troop be killed in action, then one of them must try, at all costs, to get the last letter to the people back home. For many this didn't happen until after the war had finished but today, Charles had Tom's letter in his pocket. All things being equal, he would be able to get there for the weekend and then up to Farnworth to his kin. First though, he had orders for the camp. He hailed a taxi cab, and noticed the horse was looking a bit knackered. It wasn't hot but he was sweating under his rigid collar. His blue uniform was looser now. He had been away from camp for over a month and some hard riding and rubbish rations had seen him drop a few pounds but gain a few years. At 20 he was looking more grown up than most, still without his whiskers or indeed any bum fluff on his chin, but it was a blessing he didn't have to shave all the time, there wasn't much clean hot water back on the front.

"Where to soldier boy? If it's local, it's free." The cabbie was older than the hills with a rugged and gnarly face. The camp was about a 20 minute ride away and soon the two were chatting as if they were old mates.

"Have you seen much out there? is Fritzy running away like it says in the papers? Our lads are rampaging over them according to the Colchester Times."

Charles knew different, there had been running but it wasn't the Germans who had run. Mons and Le Cataeu had seen hundreds, if not thousands, of our lads fall in the cause but Charles knew the Germans had paid a heavy price for the land they had gained and now it was their turn to retreat.

"The Frenchies are getting their game together and have turned around, we thought they were going all the way to Paris but some strong words from their leaders have won the day and now, along with the British they are charging after the Germans towards the coast in Flanders. I read the Belgies had flooded a lot of the land and its proper slowed the Germans down thank God. With luck we will get them stuck in the boggy land and then deal them the sort of punishment they dealt us in France".

"Have you seen much?" It was a fair question, and Charles didn't mind telling a bit of his adventure. It was hard even for him to believe that, in the space of just a month, he had killed a man, seen others killed, met a German and watched as brave men lost their fight to live. He had also seen cowardly men capitulate and give in and, what made it worse, was they were on his side and from his own Regiment.

As they arrived at the camp, Charles shook the cabbies hand, "If you can stay out of this mess you should, war isn't the adventure they tell you." Charles meant it as well. He picked up his back pack and turned to walk into the camp, there was a familiar shout almost a roar from the Guard Room.

"ATHERTON!! Bless my soul, if it isn't my boy Atherton returned from the front."

As he turned there was a wet nose nudging his hand. It was Dylan Gregory the lurcher and there, under the porch of the Guard Room, stood Sgt Aloysius Harris. He looked resplendent in his dress uniform and striking moustache – waxed at the edges, but not turned up as the Germans thought stylish to do, but out straight so as to bedazzle anyone watching Sgt Harris talk- he had a hypnotic tash.

Charles was pleased to see him, and walked over to greet him.

"Hello Sarge, it good to see you, and Dylan. How goes the war here in Colchester?" There were new recruits and old sweats mixed in squads and marching around the parade square to the roar of the drill staff and a beating bass drum. Charles felt sorry for them he had been there and done that, he knew how hard these lads were being pressed, and he understood how they needed it before they went out to France.

The two men shook hands, "Why you back lad, you're not injured are you?" There was a fleeting glimpse of panic on his face

"No I'm fine and in fighting order. I've just been sent back to give a message to the C.O. from the Colonel out at the front and then I have to go and see Tom Kelly's wife and give her a letter from Tom. You did hear about Tom?" As he spoke, he realised that he hadn't, he could see a familiar dread creep over the Sergeant's face.

"No lad , we haven't heard much here, is he wounded?" Charles slowly shook his head, what a daft bugger he was, he hadn't realised at all how slow news got back. "Have we got time for a brew Sarge? I'll bring you up to date with what's happened this last month."

"Let's go to my office. Oh Lord this is the worst of news." He was clearly upset, the men he had recruited were important to him, that much had always been obvious.

As the kettle whistled its melodic tune so familiar to every household up and down the country, Aloysius warmed a pot on the hearth before measuring out three spoonfuls of tea, "One for you, one for ma and one for the pot. Now tell me

Charlie, what happened out there, is it as we hear a cushy business? Will it really be over by Christmas?"

Charles took a minute to compose the right wording before he said " It's a rough beggar in truth. We have lost quite a few of the Regiment including Tom. I was there when he copped it but we have never seen anything like these Germans and the artillery. Don't think ill of me Sarge, I'm no coward but it's a hell of a game when they send those 'Jack Johnsons' over, bloody great big shells the size of a man and a big black cloud when they go off. It's not just them though, we have been running like the clappers to withdraw back to Paris and there are thousands of Germans, thousands. We shoot them and two more pop up so they must have a plenty of men. I was taken prisoner by one lot, as were some of the others but for some reason they let me go, the others; (he looked around to make sure no one else was earwigging) the others didn't want to be let loose they would rather stay as prisoners than get stuck in, Officers an' all. Makes me sick to the pit of my stomach. Our lads are magnificent they hardly ever say a cross word, apart from Bert Clarke, he moaned whenever he had the chance and, to be fair, there was always a chance when Bert was around." It made Aloysius laugh, "Aye Bert can rattle on, you were there when Kelly died? How did it happen Charlie? I remember going to his village and meeting him, not that long ago, he was married to a young lass, pretty young thing. It's a crying shame. Do you want a bit of sugar in this tea and a splash of milk, its fresh this morning?" Charles hadn't had fresh milk for months and he smiled as a steaming cup was handed to him. Like every soldier in history, a brew sorted most things out. He finished his tea and had a good chat, they covered all things military, then the world and, as is tradition, once they had put the world to rights they nodded to each other. It was a knowing nod, the world wasn't right, it was a damn mess and sitting here drinking tea wouldn't make much difference. Charles had a job to do and a message to deliver, an orderly was sent to collect Charles when the C.O. was free to see him. Charles tidied himself up in front of the Guard Room mirror and rubbed his boots with a rag. They looked a lot cleaner than they had an hour ago, before Sgt Harris had given him some boot polish to clean them with. He was fit to pass muster and so, with cap placed squarely, he marched into the Commanding Officer's office.

Once Charles had been dismissed, he had a travel warrant for the train to get him to Langwith and onwards to Farnworth, with a return to the port at Portsmouth in a week. The C.O. had been very pleasant and, despite all the formality of the Army, had shaken Charles by the hand, he even patted his shoulder. Charles thought it was a very 'human' touch and as he left the office, the C.O. wished him luck and God's speed. He genuinely was grateful for Charles going to see the widow Kelly, he had written a letter as well from the Regiment but would delay sending it until the following week. That way, it would give her time to come to terms with her loss.

Within the hour Charles was at the station, his train due within the next 20 minutes. He had a lot of men come and shake his hand and twenty minutes went in a flash. Once on the train, he was confronted by the guard who was an 'old sweat'- Boer War apparently. He marshalled Charles to First Class and sat him in a carriage telling him refreshments would be served in the dining car, his account had already been settled and his ticket upgraded for the whole trip. It was the least he could do for him. Charles felt slightly embarrassed, he hadn't ever travelled First Class before, but he had a sound upbringing and manners were manners no matter who you were.

CHAPTER 26

Goodbye to all that

As the train pulled into the station, Charles grabbed his small bag of belongings, he knew today was going to be a painful and sad day.

The door was opened for him from the outside, it caught him by surprise as a porter with white gloves stood in the doorway to collect his luggage, of which, of course, he had none. The two men smiled politely at each other, one thinking 'How are you travelling first class?' the other thinking 'I'm sorry, I know I shouldn't really be sat here.' It was slightly awkward but Charles showed the porter his new ticket and the smile broadened and a knowing nod accompanied it. Charles felt like an imposter but, conversely, felt deserved of the privilege, it was less than two days ago that he was in the fighting in France, he did deserve it.

The station was very quiet, as he looked up and down the platform there were only officials stood by the steaming train. As he let his eyes follow the other three carriages no one else had alighted. He could smell the heady, oily, musty aroma of the engine. It reminded him of England and all she stood for it was, he thought, traditional and safe, familiar to just about anyone old enough to go to school or work. Leather, smoke, oil and muck. All these things were part of his world and, as he pondered, a voice from over his shoulder made him jump.

"Hello soldier, what brings you to Langwith?" It was a man who was about the same age as Charles with broad shoulders and a pleasant face.

"Oh, Hello" said Charles, "I'm sorry I didn't see you there I was miles away." Charles offered his hand and when he took hold of the stranger's hand it was rough and strong but not domineering or aggressive just an honest working hand belonging to an honest country man.

He had been here before of course but not for a few months and as he gathered his bearings as to which exit to take he said to the chap, "I'm going to the village, I have a message to deliver to a lady, well the wife of a friend of mine actually." The man looked at Charles and his smart uniform "Isn't that the same uniform that Tom Kelly wears? 20th Hussars if I remember." Charles nodded.

"It's a letter for Alice, Tom's wife, that I have, I just need to remember how to get to their house, do you know them?"

"Yes, everybody knows Tom and Alice. I heard Tom had been killed though, that's right isn't it? Alice has moved back in to her parents' house at the shop, I'll take you there if you want. It's on the way back. My name is Jack, by the way, Jack Adams. I work at the big house as a game keeper. Come on I'll show you the way."

Jack had a bike, but he walked and pushed the bike alongside. It was only a ten minute walk into the village and, along the way, the two men chatted and nodded their salutations to people along the walk.

"Charlie, I won't pry, but it was quick for Tom wasn't it? I mean he didn't suffer did he? I've known Tom a good while and I'd hate to think he died slowly or in great pain." Charles shook his head, "It was very quick Jack, he wouldn't have known anything about it. I was with him which is why I'm bringing this letter for Alice and, also, I want to tell her how much the lads liked him, none more than I. He was a thoroughly decent chap, a 'reet good mon' as we say. He is missed by his pals I'll tell you."

They came across the main road and there in front of them stood the Barber's Butcher's shop. It didn't look like there were any customers, so Charles licked his hands and smoothed down his hair a bit, he shook hands with Jack Adams and said he hoped their paths would cross again and then he went into the shop. A bell rang as he opened the door. It made him jump, the second time he had been shaken since he got off the train, and whilst he tried to compose himself, a huge barrel chested man came to the counter.

"Hello lad, can I help you?"

Charles felt his mouth dry and his stomach churn, he had been dreading this moment since he found out he was to deliver the letter.

"Hello Sir, my name is Charles Atherton I was a friend of Tom's." He didn't need to say another word, Harry Barber took his arm in his podgy thick fingers and, for a moment, Charles thought he was angry, he wasn't, he was delighted and the tear that came into his eye was a tear of recognition not anger. " I know you Charles. We met when you came home with Tom. It's good to see you lad, you look done in, when was the last time you had anything hot to eat or drink? Come in to the back I'll close the shop for an hour or so, Alice will be thrilled to see you."

Charles felt his resolve dissolve, he could feel a thickening in his throat and a burning in his eyes as he tried to compose himself. Just a simple act of kindness and recognition had undone his stiff upper lip. He just managed to get a hold on himself when Alice came to the door.

"Ma', put the kettle on, we have a visitor come to see our Alice." He made himself look away, he couldn't bear to see his daughter so heartbroken, and he realised it was a difficult job Charles was doing. He moved past her into the parlour.

Charles touched his peak with his hand, as a salute to a lady. She stepped forward and hugged him, then as if someone had pulled a plug she dissolved into a million tears for her lost man.

"Oh Charlie, it's good to see you. Thank you for coming to see me I thought perhaps Tom's friends might forget me now he's gone." Her young face was red and her eyes were wet but she showed a fierce determination to stay composed. It was a struggle, but she would manage.

"Mrs Kelly, Alice, I'm not sure what I should say. I wanted to come and pay my respects but it's been difficult what with us being out in France an all. I've just had some errands to run back in Blighty and I have a bit of time to come and see you. Tom wrote you a letter before.." He stuttered, he didn't know what to say or how to continue, "Before he was hit." He reached into his pocket and gave her the letter, he had been so careful not to crease it or the envelope, and, when he gave it to her he felt a shiver go down his back. He was letting go of his friend and handing him back to his young widow.

Alice took the letter and put it on the table, she would read it later there had been enough sadness already today already and her delicate eyes were swollen from the painful tears.

"Can you tell me what happened Charlie? Were you near?"

Charles thought for a second or two before deciding that he would slightly change the story, but not so much as to lie.

"We were in a French Chateau with a couple of the other lads on a patrol. We rode into the courtyard to rest and water the horses when we came across this French mob with horses that were clearly exhausted. They were beyond cruel what they had done to those horses, and, as we were arguing with the Frenchies, a sniper shot poor Tom. He didn't know anything about it and he was in my arms when he passed. I carried him with one of the lads and we buried him properly in the chateau garden. I'm so sorry he's gone Alice he was a good friend to me."

Alice reached out and took Charles' hand. He realised his were shaking there was a tear running down his cheek and Alice stopped him from wiping it with his sleeve as she caught it with a finger. Charles had never seen such tenderness and, as if he had been given permission, he put his head in his hands and sobbed quietly. It wasn't a manly thing to do, but it had been waiting and he soon caught hold of himself and apologised.

"I'm sorry, I didn't expect that to happen. We have lost quite a few of the lads out there and I think I am as tired as can be. It's just caught up with me, I'm sorry. Tom was my best friend and now he has gone we all miss his sense of humour and his friendship. I have a little parcel for you it's not much but these things were Toms and he had them with him. Inside his backpack Charlie had carefully wrapped Tom's watch and crucifix, he wore that every day and didn't take it off even for a bath, Charles knew how important it was to him so he brought it back for his wife. Next there was a dead flower, it was blue and white and preserved by pressing it between his prayer book pages so it maintained some, if not all, of its colour. These flowers were all around the area where they had buried Tom, and Charles had picked a few to take as mementoes. He was glad he had thought to do so, and even more touched that they clearly meant a lot to Alice, when he explained why he had them. Finally, he gave her Tom's warm scarf, it was round his neck most of the time. It was a gift from the hunt on the day he left to join the Army and it seemed right that it should go back to his family. It was a delicate and sensitive thing for a lad from Farnworth to think about and, as he handed them over, he said "I hope you don't mind, but they were with him when we laid him to rest." Alice was touched and her mother, Elizabeth, wept quietly in the corner. The loss had been hard to bear, but seeing one of her son in law's friends, who clearly felt strongly about it all and was so obviously upset, had touched her maternal soul. She stood up to make sure the tea was mashed properly.

Again, Alice put them on the table, tenderly and carefully, as if these were her Tom laid there before her. She picked up the scarf and held it to her nose. With a long breath, she inhaled the last of his scent deep into her soul. A tear ran down her cheek and she wiped it with the corner of his scarf.

"Now then Charlie lad, you must be famished." It was Harry, he broke a spell and he placed on the table a tray of sausages they sizzled and spat. Next to it he placed a big brown loaf with some homemade chutney and a pat of butter. Charles suddenly felt hungry, more than he remembered and, being polite, he said "Ladies first, please." But Harry was ahead of him, "Alice you go and wash your face lass, and read that letter Charlie has brung all the way from your

Tom. When you've done, there's some more bangers on the stove and I'll bring them in. Go on love, go and have a quiet minute with your mam." The ladies looked at each other and retired into the back room. Harry couldn't bear to see the pain on his girl's face any longer, but he knew it to be the right thing, a necessary thing, to do. It was for the best.

My darling Alice,

Well my love, this is the saddest of times for I have left you behind and given myself to the cause. I know there can be no boundary to the heartbreak I have caused to you my darling and to your dear parents.

Please be brave and forgive me for my loss. I would give my life gladly should it make yours easier but a sacrifice for King and Country comes a close second.

Now my sweet, you must get over this sadness and remarry. In time this war will end and lives will return to normal. You are a precious rose and not to share your life with anyone again would be a dreadful shame, you deserve to be happy and have the children we wanted.

I will always watch over you and the Heaven I imagine is a place full of peace. It will be filling daily with the brave lads I see here and whose company and fight I have shared these past few months. I have missed you so much these past weeks and months, and I know we will meet again in the afterlife, but first you must live a full and productive life else we have failed twofold.

*I don't fear death but I don't welcome it either, and
hope I played my part in a successful job done out here.
I miss the hounds and the life I had, the hunting here
is a much harder game. Please give my best regards to
the hunt and Master.*

*Please don't grieve. I have given myself willingly and
died an honest death doing my duty. No man can ask
for more other than beg you bear the burden with the
pride and love I feel for you dear, lovely, Alice.*

*Darling wife, I have to go, I had hoped you might never
have to read this letter but alas it wasn't to be. I am
called to my maker a proud and duty filled soldier.*

I shall love you for all time and beyond eternity

Your loving husband.

Tom

Alice felt the life drain out of her, she felt faint and weak,
her arms flopped onto her lap the letter held as if never to
be let go. Elizabeth reached over and took her daughter in
her arms as Alice mewed a cry so pained it cut through to
Elizabeth's very soul.

In her arms rested not only a lady of 20 years, but a
girl of 5, widowed by a war she couldn't understand with
a loss so hard to take. The repercussions of this war would
stretch and wind its long limbs around the world and with
it carry grief to millions. It would grip mankind in a way
never before felt by so many and so far away. This was the
first war that involved a world, after this the world would

never be the same, and Elizabeth was reminded of the words she had read in the newspapers 'The lamps are going out all over Europe, we shall not see them lit again in our lifetime'. For her, Alice, the lights had indeed gone out and as she lay there in her mother's arms, it seemed as if the darkness of grief had embraced her in its suffocating grip as death had embraced her late husband.

Charles finished his meal, he was very grateful for the nourishment and doubted he had ever tasted better sausages. He felt a load had been lifted from his broad strong shoulders, his duty to a friend fulfilled and, as much as he was distraught as any good soul would be, he knew that now the wounding of poor Alice's heart had finished, now the healing could start. The waters of renewed happiness would trickle and one day if she was lucky, it would build into a stream but it would take a slow meandering course before her broken heart was mended.

He knew it was time to leave. He had to get home to see his kin before he would return to the front and, if he was blessed, he would see this war over sooner rather than later. Only then could his heart heal and his Christian soul be soothed. There were firm handshakes and a polite hug, he thanked Harry for the meal and said he would pray for Alice. As he turned out of the doorway, Harry followed him with his bowler hat. "I have a delivery to do, jump on the trap I'll drop you off at the station." Charles would have preferred the walk, but felt he shouldn't refuse kindness. In fact, it was Harry who wanted to thank Charles but had felt uncomfortable with the emotional whirlwind that was his home.

"Charlie lad, I can never thank you enough for what you have just done. I can only hazard a guess at how difficult that was for you. Tom would have been delighted to have you as a friend, and he was damn lucky to have a mate like you. If you're all like that over there in France then Fritz doesn't stand a chance, you'll whip him like a beaten dog and if you ever get a chance to pay those blighters back for Tom, you stick the boot in for old Harry Barber."

In no time at all they were back at the station, and Charles climbed down from the trap. He said his goodbyes to Harry, and then went to the front and gently blew up the horse's nose. As he scratched his long head, the horse nodded playfully and Harry watched as this stranger made a friend for life of an old nag.

CHAPTER 27

Homeward Bound

The trip home was as pleasant as he could have wished, although he felt uneasy sat in First Class, he was made very welcome by everyone he met. All wanted to know about the front and how was it out there? He found it hard to believe he had only been gone from Blighty for a few weeks but so much had happened. One chap asked him about an event he had hardly heard about, but knew 'The angel of Mons' had been a topic mentioned in France. Not that he knew much about it, or, in fact, believed it existed. It seemed as if the good people of England and the Shires knew more about what was happening than he did. Still, it helped pass the time.

When he finally arrived at Bolton, he had a quick stop to change trains. It was either the train or the tram, and it so happened there was a train due right away, so he crossed one platform and got aboard the train for home.

He was aware for the first time that he missed home, the mills, the people, the noise and the clatter from clogs on flagstones. He smiled as he thought about how his feet had suffered when he joined up and had to change his beloved clogs for army boots. Then he laughed out loud much to the alarm of a lady sat opposite. What had caused this outburst was the memory of the faces of his fellow recruits when he started his basic training a million years ago the memory of him pouring water into his brand new boots then putting them into a bucket full of water overnight. Once they had soaked through he packed them tight as he could with paper and slathered a full tin of 'English Army Blacking' on them. He left them to dry slowly and he smiled when he remembered Tom Kelly saying he was mad as a March hare for wasting so much blacking. It had cost him a penny and Charles, who wasn't a betting man, said if Tom could make his boots more comfortable, he would pay for the blacking for him. It was almost a bet, and one he would have won because, within a few days, sales of boot blacking had gone mad at the local shop. Tom used a mixture of saddle soap and polish but never got the same deep luscious shine. The main point, however, was all the lads had clean comfy boots. He felt a slight pride in teaching the lads in his group the joy of comfortable boots. Charles felt he owed a lot to his clogs.

It didn't take long before the train arrived at *Farnworth and Halshaw Moor*. The train gave a huge bellow of steam as if to announce his arrival and a hiss of air from the brakes made him close his eyes and soak it in, he was home.

90 Park Street is less than a five-minute walk from the station so, with his pack and a certain swagger that military men have, he set off to surprise his sister and, with luck, tonight both his brothers Thomas and William. There was a certain urgency to get home all of a sudden.

He knocked at the door, it was the rent man's knock so he knew it would be heard even in the back yard, he stood as smart as punch and nearly burst with pride when his big brother Thomas opened the door.

"Good God in his heaven, its Charles." He grabbed his sibling and although it wasn't quite the done thing, hugged him as only a brother dare.

"Hey Up Tom, how you doing old love?" There was a scream from the back room as Elizabeth heard his voice. She wiped her hands on her pinny and almost pushed Thomas out of the way. As she hugged the poor man in the doorway there were tears running freely down her face, " Oh joy", she said, "oh joy, oh joy". Charles and Thomas started to laugh and within a second he was allowed in.

"Tea" it was all he said, Thomas knew he wouldn't get a word in. He was visiting his sister today, Emily being at work, and young Mae, their daughter, was in the yard playing in some sand. Thomas walked into the kitchen and put the kettle on the stove, he closed the bottom half of the back door so Mae couldn't come to any harm and went back in to the front room.

"Ner then, what's tha doing yom? Tha's narn tinjured ist thie?" Charles smiled, he hadn't heard the proper Bolton accent for a long time. "Bill Horrich is back, wounded, it's a greet big un anall. Look at thee, reet posh int uniform, thas looking grond I'll tell thee that fer nowt."

Charles felt as if the weight of the world had been lifted from his young shoulders.

"Wheres Will?" Charles hadn't seen anything off his older brother but was surprised when Thomas said,

"He's away with th'army, started his training lad has. 'Beth isn't happy about it but he gone and joined up, and I'll tell you another thing, so have I, but I've been rejected to home guard due to my eyes being so bad."

Charles felt sick, he had seen the Infantry getting a right pasting all the way back from Mons, he didn't want to imagine his brother doing that. "Who's he joined? And you yer daft begger, you've a wife and child, what are you thinking

Thomas?" He knew he sounded angry, he was angry; but he also understood what men are like and the thought of his brothers not doing their bit was worse than them going to war and taking their chances at the front.

Thomas tried to calm him, "Charlie, lad, this war isn't going to be finished anytime soon and your lot are soon going to be needing a rest. We all know you're going to need replacements and so that's what the lads are doing. There's been a big push for men to join from Lord Kitchener, and there's women handing out white feathers to all and sundry who don't join. I'll tell thee, you're damned lucky to be there already cause there's no bugger left here to do the damn work. Mills are near empty of men and yon lasses are weaving, can you believe it, women weaving. The quicker we get shot of this Kaisers lot, the sooner things will get back to normal. William has joined the Loyal North Lancashires and I did try to see if I could get along in the Medical Corps but now It turns out I might have a dicky heart murmur and my eyes are rubbish without my glasses. I have ended up in the 3rd Manchesters. They have a Prisoner of War camp being set aside in Leigh and I've been told to report there in a month to do my training. I'll be home every night so Emily is happy and Mae, well she's the apple of everyone's eye and too young to really understand where people have gone. Why don't you go and get some old clothes on? Mine'll fit you, I have some slacks that'll do grand and a shirt although yon shoulders will fill the bugger."

"Thomas, mind your tongue, this isn't the tap room." It was Elizabeth back with a pot of steaming hot tea and a Victoria sponge with a thick cream and jam filling. Her little brother was home, she needed to tell Rebecca.

"How long before you have to go back love?" She asked.

"I have 3 days here, my boat leaves on Friday afternoon so I need to leave Thursday and get a sleeper. Here look what the guard gave me when I boarded the train". He showed them his First Class tickets and meal coupons.

"Oh Lord you won't be talking to us next, this sponge won't be up to much compared to the hoypoloi and posh nobs" Elizabeth teased. Charles had to concede, this was the best afternoon tea he had ever taken.

It didn't take long for word to get out that Charles was home. Rebecca knew before he had finished his tea and cake. Her mother had seen Charles walking down Peel Street right past her house from the train station; her having her hair done only yesterday as well, it all boded well, maybe it was a sign? She hurried to finish her sewing, she wasn't much of a darner but needs must especially with this war on. She washed her face, no one would doubt her pretty, almost boyish, looks, she knew she would have to go and see the Athertons and, although she was nervous, her heart was pounding with excitement as well. Her mother looked at her with a smile.

"Your soldier boy's back I hear, best you get a shuffle on and go see him, he won't have long at home" They all knew of her mistakes, but no one bore the blame more than Rebecca, she really felt like she might have made a huge, catastrophic error and she had to try to rectify it right now. She put a scarf over her head and tied it under her chin, her dress was light and airy and her good Sunday shoes clean, all the signs of a simple girl with simple needs, with a glance to her mum, for approval, she headed to the front door.

"Wait 'Becca, hang on a second" Said her mother as she went into the kitchen. She appeared a short while later with a cake tin and inside the tin were four large Eccles cakes, they had been intended for tea tonight but a gift to Charles might help break the ice.

"Oh Mum, that's very kind, are you sure?"

"Go on, get a hurry on, I'll make some more whilst you're out, I've plenty of fruit. Don't you be too forward young lady, if you want him as a sweetheart then don't rush him, he knows his mind does that Charlie Atherton, let him decide. Remember, I love you."

Rebecca stepped out and walked to Darley Street then onto Park Street and her destination, number 90, was little more than a hop, skip and a jump. She knocked on the door, pinched her cheeks to redden them a touch and smiled when Beth answered the door.

"Oh good news travels fast then", she said, "Come in there's a handsome sort of a chap sat in the front room and I'm sure you'll be a sight for sore eyes. What've you get there?"

"Oh, some Eccles cakes my mum made, she thought you might like them with some tea."

"Oh, did she now", Beth laughed, "Come in love, the kettle's boiled."

As she walked through into the living room, Charles was sat facing the door, their eyes met as he stood to greet her and instantly she knew she loved him.

"Hello Becca, don't you look a pretty picture? I'm sorry I didn't let you all know before I got back, but it all happened a bit sharp. Still, I have a couple of days before I have to go back. Come and sit down, please." He offered her his chair as he stood. Thomas noticed Elizabeth stood in the kitchen doorway, he thought she had a tick as she gestured to him with her head to come away and leave the two alone for a minute. As he stood, he nodded, "I'll just go and get a fresh pot of tea, yon mon drinks it like water" he smiled to the couple who looked as awkward as they both felt.

It was Rebecca who broke the silence.

"Listen Charles, my mother said I shouldn't be too forward and that you know your own mind, but I just have to say something. I'm dreadfully sorry about what I did to you, it was a silly girlish mistake and I fully understand if you don't want to talk to me. I have tried to explain it all in my letters to you and the fact you haven't ever written back would suggest you want nowt to do with a silly girl, but I am sorry, that's all in the past and I can't change it." She could feel herself blushing as she became more upset, why wasn't he saying anything to her?

"Lass, there's been no mail. I have only been in the same place for a couple of days at a time and we haven't really had any letters from home, so you see I have no idea what you're on about. Why would it pain you so about what's done? As far as I know you didn't have any interest in me, and Alf Green was taking you out, are you saying that Alf is all done?"

"No letters?" she enquired "What. None? I've written to you most days to say how sorry I was. I did walk out with Alf, but he's a brute and he left me high and dry. We went out twice and, by the second time, you had already gone back. I never even had a chance to say goodbye to you. Charlie Atherton I'm not backwards in coming forwards, never have been but I am more than fond of you, and there it is." He reached out his hand to stop her talking, he really wanted to kiss her lips to stop her, but was too afraid.

"Fond of me? Why that's the best news I've had in many a month. Me? I thought you and that Green fella were courting so I've left it be. Bugger me, all this while you've been writing to me and I've been thinking of you. I'm soft on you 'Becca, I have been for yonks. Oh, this is grand, can we walk out tonight? I don't want you to think I'm brash but I don't have long on leave."

There was a polite cough from the door, it was Thomas, Elizabeth was right behind him and bumped him into the room, Mae was holding her hand as the three bundled into the 'moment' although, to be fair, the moment had finished.

CHAPTER 28

Love knows no Bounds

Charles didn't care much about 'Becca's past, he didn't dwell on the fact. It helped that she didn't tell him everything that the vile Alf Green had done to her. For Charles it had simply been an error in judgement on her side, and he was grateful she had changed her mind. She was a bonny lass he thought, blessed with brains and knowhow and, maybe a little lacking in the worldly wise attitude of some girls her age. What, with most of the menfolk in Farnworth, Kersley and Bolton falling over themselves to join up, he likely could have had a pick of the bunch. Young and desperate love filled the air, men in new uniforms, ill-fitting and stiff, walked around like strutting cock hens with any lass who might care to be seen with them. Charles looked far more dapper, he even wore his braided jacket and pill box hat for a walk out on his way for a photo at Thompson's the photographers, a portrait that would be passed down from family members to generations in the future. 'Becca was as proud as punch and sat there in the very park Sgt Aloysius Harris had recruited Charlie from, but a couple of years ago. The last of the Autumn sunshine was over the park and 'Becca had packed a small picnic for them to share on the lawns. There was rabbit pie, cooled and cut into thick wedges, and egg sandwiches as well as tongue and ham. There was some fruit cake and, to wash it all away, Sarsaparilla in a glass bottle and a cork top. For the good folk of Farnworth it would have been a feast, and Charles understood the effort it would have taken to produce the basket of food. It wasn't that food was scarce, it wasn't but just going to the bother of collecting the stuff would have been a bind, whatever, it had been sorted and he was ravenous. As he finished she asked him what it was like, she had waited deliberately until they were alone because she didn't want him to feel he should make it fanciful in any way.

"It's pretty dull most of the time, we still have jobs to do and the horses need fetching so that side of life isn't much different to manoeuvres we have done in the past. But, when the shells start, by hell it's a different game then alright. I don't mind telling you 'Becca, it can put the fear of God into a man and I'm no exception. Sometimes, if you're close enough you can hear the shrapnel whistle past you in the air, it makes a 'whizzing' noise as it flies past. I've seen men badly wounded by the stuff and me, myself, have been lucky so far. It's not for the faint hearted when the blood's up and the men are magnificent. It makes a man proud to be a part of it. I don't believe all this nonsense about it being over by Christmas though, the Germans have a lot of men and the 'Frenchies' are a murderous lot when they aren't complaining. Those Germans are far superior to the French and even we have our hands full when they attack on our front."

"Have you killed anyone Charles?" She said it before she thought about it, it just came out. He sat there and looked out over the park, he didn't say anything at first, he was struggling with the concept that he had killed more than one man, he had been responsible for killing many more. She quickly said, "Oh Charlie, I'm sorry, I didn't mean to ask that." She reached over and hugged him, it was a reaction more than familiarity, but it broke the spell of a nightmare and then they kissed. For the first time Charles Atherton kissed a woman, it was clumsy, almost comical, but there was a tenderness and desire he certainly hadn't realised he had before. He had knocked her bonnet off with his hand, it lay on her shoulder held only by a hair clip. She casually reached around with her free hand and shook it off her head and, with that, her long hair tumbled onto her shoulders. He pulled away and looked at her, she looked magnificent. He went to apologise, but she kissed him again and held him tight to her body as if to never let him go. She hadn't ever loved anyone but her family, but today she understood the meaning of true, unadulterated, love. This raw emotion was meant to be for behind closed doors, not in the public park and slowly they released each other, then they laughed, not at each other but at the world because at that moment they were indestructible and could overcome anything the world had to throw at them.

Tomorrow he had to set off back to his other family but for today he would enjoy this one. No one knew what the future held and as Charles looked round the park at the crowds all enjoying a day with their families, he couldn't help but think of the family he had left at Langwith. This war was already cruel, and he thought it was only going to get worse but he didn't have to tell 'Becca or the people in his home. Ignorance is bliss and there was no point in scaremongering.

The two young lovebirds spent the rest of the afternoon just falling in love. Charles was 21 years old and knew nothing of the fairer sex, 'Becca was no older, but she had wisdom beyond her years, it was a woman's lot to have to know things that men could only ever dream about. She knew nothing about war though, and, for Charles, he wanted it to stay that way.

CHAPTER 29

Return to war

The next morning, everyone was sombre. Charles didn't want any fuss, it was important to him to just get on his way, but 'Beth, Tom and 'Becca wanted to make sure he was sent off properly. The smell of bacon cooking permeated throughout the house and Charles was aware his mouth was watering. He had his backpack and was dressed in his khaki trousers ready for his journey, he had placed the borrowed civilian clothes folded on the bed. As he walked down the steep staircase he could hear the three of them talking, Thomas had to go to work, he had only spoken to his Foreman last night to see if it would be possible to start an hour or so late due to his brother being back for the short time he was allowed. Of course the Foreman agreed there would be no clocking on for Thomas, it had already been sorted and, although he didn't agree with time cheats, he had covered the Foreman on many an occasion in the past, heavy drink and early mornings didn't always mix and the Foreman liked a drink. As Charles came into the kitchen, Tom nodded his arrival and simply said "Ey up Charlie lad, did you sleep?" There was a twinkle of mischief in his eyes, he knew full well that Charles had come home well past midnight but daren't ask what he had been up to with the young lady stood in the kitchen avoiding the bacon. As Charles passed through the back door to the toilet, 'Beth said she would warm some fresh water for his wash and shave before he dressed back in his uniform ready to go on the train. 'Becca couldn't join in the bacon butty feast because of her Jewish upbringing, but she loved tea so there was a pot steaming on the hotplate. She was torn, she really didn't want Charlie to go back, but she was also proud beyond belief that her suitor was doing his bit. With luck, the war would end soon and then, maybe, they might start to court properly, just at weekends she understood. But that would be a wonderful step up from the lonely heart she knew she would have to nurse once Charles had departed for France. She looked at his strong back and blushed. Elizabeth just shook her head and smiled.

After breakfast, the group all felt awkward. There was a necessity for Charles to go, and everyone knew it, but if they could all hold time in their hands the seconds would be hours and the hours days. Even Thomas was reluctant to leave the happy table but he had to make a move and when he slid his chair back on the Lino, it broke a magic spell and everyone suddenly moved quickly. The pots were put back in the washing bowl, 'Beth said she would clean them later, 'Becca went to the back door where Charles' tunic was hanging to let any creases fall out, and Charles fastened his boots and putties all smart and tidy. He put his tunic on, and his hat, he was ready to leave. He hugged his brother with a very heavy heart, he hadn't even seen Emily, Thomas' wife, and he bade her his love. She would understand that time had been short, but next time he was on leave, or had a pass, he would make sure he saw her and spend more time with Mae. They shook hands and with no words spoke a book full. It's what brothers did.

They all left together, 'Becca and Beth wearing their headscarves, Thomas in his flat cap and Charles sporting his military peaked hat.

At the station the mood turned to sadness and, at Charles' insistence, the ladies hugged him, kissed him and left without turning back. He said he might not get on the train if he saw their tears, so he was quite forceful in his instruction for them to leave 'toot sweet' and as the train pulled into the station, it tooted its whistle as if in recognition of the sadness before it. The steam billowed around Charles like a cloud and he was lost to his family and loved ones. France awaited and he knew not where the Regiment would be. All he knew was that he had to report to the Marshalling Clerk at the port and he would be put on the appropriate transport to the right area. It was going to be a great adventure. As the train pulled out of the station he noticed he wasn't the only soldier bidding farewell to his home. Out of the windows, hats were being waved and young men, with little knowledge of the future, put on brave faces for the sake of loved ones.

CHAPTER 30

The race to the sea

Charles had made good time. He had hit the London stations and caught a troop train to the coast. It had been an ambulance train on the journey to the city, and would revert back to that role tomorrow, to bring the casualties of war back to Blighty hospitals on the South coast and inland. The heartbreak for anyone who saw them, was how full they were and, because of this, they ran mainly at night to avoid the main hustle and bustle of London.

Once at the dock at Southampton, he boarded a steamer bound for France and, although the hustle and bustle of an army on the move was unnerving, it offered reassurance that the sheer numbers of British soldiers going to France must tip the balance in their favour. If this war was going to be over quickly, then these men would be needed at the front, and the sooner the better.

All the talk on the boat was of how to kill Germans, keen young men with no idea of war thought Charles, he knew the reality of war, he had already seen and experienced it first hand and, if he was asked, he might say he didn't want to see it anymore. On the deck there stood an Army Chaplain. He was delivering a sermon and, as was common with military units, there was an avid crowd. As Charles listened to his words of godliness and right, for the first time in his young life Charles doubted the words of the church, this war wasn't godly and they weren't fighting the 'good fight'. The men he had killed were no more evil or demonic than he was and, although he had heard of the dreadful things the advancing Germans had done in Belgium, he found it hard to believe that the same man who gave him his freedom had committed those supposed war crimes. The Padre banged his fist into the hard cover of the Bible and shouted that this was a good war and in the Lord's name that justice be served of the evil Germans. Charles shook his head, he wasn't conscious that he was doing it, but it had been noticed by a Sergeant Major stood on the periphery of the ad-hoc church service.

"You don't believe him then Private?"

Charles looked round and found the smiling face of the Sgt Maj looking straight at him. "I believe in the Book Sir, but that nonsense he's spouting just isn't what I've seen so far Sir."

When he looked, the Sgt Maj was from the York and Lancaster Regiment, as were most of the lads sat or stood in front of the Padre.

"Sorry Sir, but it's just my view and belief."

"You already been out there lad?,"

"Yes Sir, I'm just coming back from a week's leave. I need to report to the Load Master at the dockside to catch up with my unit Sir."

"These religious types are all blood and thunder lad, bluster and bull shit, but those lads sat listening are barely away from their mother's tit. They need this kind of stuff to fill them with the desire to kill the enemy. Sounds like you don't lad, you seen much action then?"

"I've seen a lot more than I wanted to. I was at Mons when the Germans pushed us all the way back, and then I fought in the retreat to get away from them, and yes it's not a nice thing for these young men to experience Sir."

"You killed anyone then lad, with a sword or a lance, you are mounted aren't you? What's that, 20th Hussars? Are they with swords or spears then"?

Charles smiled, 'spears' he hadn't heard them called that before.

"No Sir, we have swords, not lances, the Lancers have them not the Hussars. I have killed some of the enemy but with the rifle not the sword, well not yet anyways."

"How long you been in the Army then lad? You one of the 'Old Contemptibles? How long you been in France?"

"Is that what we are Sir, Old Contemptibles, is that what they call us? Well yes, in that case I am, and I came over towards the end of August. I am very lucky to have been dispatched to take some orders back to England and from there I had a few days to do some admin for one of the lads who fell. I visited his family, you know Sir, to give them his things and what have you. I'm looking forward to getting back to my Unit now though, I feel like I've been away long enough."

It wasn't long before the climax of the sermon demanded they men fought a good fight, a brave and noble fight in the name of the Lord against the heathen, and Charles felt his head shaking again at the pomposity of the Padre, as if he knew anything. There was a rousing cheer from the men in front of him and the Sergeant Major shook his hand, as he did he winked at Charles "Stay safe lad and good luck."

In the distance, on the horizon, Charles could see the smoke from the fires inland from the coast. They were away to the South of where he was and he wasn't sure where they were supposed to land, he asked one of the sailors,

"Boulogne, mate, don't know where you go from there though."

As the ship got closer to the shore, the sea became a bit choppy, and it wasn't long before Charles heard the familiar sound of the poor chaps suffering from sea sickness. It had never bothered him, but he had seen it when he came over in the first place and on the way back to Blighty last week, was it really only last week he thought? Christ, he had covered some miles since then. He wasn't sure how long it would take to find the rest of his mates but quite where they were he had no idea.

Slowly, the big ship came closer to the shore. He could see the docks and the tall cranes on the quay sides. He was travelling light, so didn't have to worry about unloading equipment or kit, everything he had was in the backpack, the rest of his gear had been left behind with the Regiment. As the ship came into dock, there was a tap on his shoulder. When he turned round it was a fresh faced lad no older than 19, if that. On his shoulder was the regimental tab of the 20th Hussars, he was a replacement sent out with ten others.

"Are you with us mate?"

"With you?" enquired Charles

'Well I haven't seen you before, so wondered if you were a replacement like us."

Charles felt a tang of anger rise in his chest, he wasn't a 'newby' he didn't even look like a newby.

"No I'm not a replacement, I'm from "B" Squadron, who are you?"

"Oh sorry Sir, I'm David Lang I didn't mean no offence Sir"

"Hang on Lang, I'm not a Sir, I'm a private just like you.

There's no need to call me Sir. Charlie Atherton, that's me, I'm just coming back from Blighty."

"Have you been out here before then Charlie? We have just come from the Depot. There's 10 of us. Do you know what we are supposed to do when we get off the ship?"

Charles realised he was considered an 'old sweat' and, much as he didn't know what he was going to do when he got off, he did realise he had more of a clue that these new lads.

"There'll be someone who knows Lang, once we get off stick with me and we will find the Dock Master, he'll be able to direct us." There was a bump as the huge vessel nudged the side of the dock, he thought Lang was going to faint, "It's alright, it's just the ship docking. Where you from David?"

"Colchester, we have just finished riding school and basic so here we are, all volunteers mind, all ten of us." As Charles looked over Lang's shoulder, there was a gaggle of men trying to get to him. That'll be the other nine, he thought, shit.

"Alright, alright pipe down you lot. Christ you're like a bunch of washer women all chattering away. Come over to the side out of the way before one of you gets knocked over." he managed to corral them into a small space out of the way.

"Right, listen in, my name is Charles Atherton, Charlie to my friends and I have been in the Regiment for a couple of years, and out here since the start of it, so it might be useful for you to listen to what I say. I'm not being bossy but you don't have a clue yet, and I not much more neither, so I'm going to ask you to stay put whilst I find the Dock Master and see if there's any orders for us. Sit down out of the way and have a drink of water, some of you look a bit ill still from the sailing so get your land legs and wait here for me."

He quite liked being in charge and he smirked to himself when they all said "Yes Sir." He shook his head and left. Eventually he found the Dock Master's office. There was a long line of men waiting outside, as well as a corresponding line of omnibuses on the other side of the road.

Eventually, he was seen by the Captain who took all the information off Charles; the other men cleaned the saltwater from their rifles and checked that their kit was made secure. In no time, they were off to the station to catch a train, this time it was very much cattle class travel, Charles's days of luxury were done. Although the sounds of battle were a long way off, the business of war was all around. Men marched and sang on their way to the front, horses were led to farriers and made secure and fed for the night. It was a bustling arena of worry and angst but, tonight, when all was quiet and there were not so many eyes to see, the casualties would come on the trains, then back to Blighty on the very same steamer the marching men had disembarked. It was hard to believe the war had only been ongoing for a couple of months and yet, here were thousands of new men. Some were replacements for casualties, but the vast majority were new soldiers built on a promise by the men in charge.

The thing that alarmed Charles most was that these weren't kids, young men yes, but there were men of all ages all trying to do their bit. King and Country meant the world to all the men of Britain. Across the divide of oceans, men of the Commonwealth were answering the call to arms, the long arm of loyalty reaching across the globe and pulling the young men into a turgid mire of death and heartbreak. Much as Charles didn't want it to be so, he knew the lure of adventure would be too great a pull for the men who had made their new homes on the other side of the planet. They would return to fight for the Motherland and throw their hats into the ring. It didn't fill Charles with any hope for the future.

They boarded a train for Rouen, the men all singing jolly songs and discussing the way the war might go. In the distance, if you listened quite hard you could hear the distant thunder of war, Charles had seen the resulting carnage that artillery could and, very often, did. As the train moved its way through France, the young men he had apparently taken charge of, came round and asked him about war. What was it like? Would he mind if they stuck by him to ensure they were ok? It saddened Charles to think they thought he might be some kind of saviour or even knowledgeable enough to know. All he felt was worry, he wanted to do his bit, be brave and strong, but, more than that, he wanted to go home, back to Colchester and visit 'Becca. He wondered how William was getting on with his training. It didn't seem a long time to take it all in, life as an infantryman was tough but then so was the comradeship. Each man knew he had to watch his mate's back, that way no harm could come to them; allegedly.

The silhouette of a huge spire of the church of a town and the slowing of the train told them that they were nearing their destination. The train stopped outside the town and the huge doors of the cattle trucks slid open. Dawn was breaking and each man had to adjust his eyes to the light and raised a hand to shield their eyes from the torches being shone.

"Hussars and cavalry. Any hussars or cavalry in this carriage step forward." Charles stood and brushed himself down

"Here, I'm a Hussar, as are all these men, I think. What do you want us to do?"

"You in charge?" Said the voice behind the light, "If so gather your things and come with me."

Charles picked his backpack, and pulled a couple of the lads to their feet as they collected all their things and jumped down to the trackside. Other men handed them their rifles, once slung over their shoulders they followed Charles and the other men towards the back of the train. Finally, they came across the back of the train and there were 10 horses, all looked tired and grumpy, and there were saddles and bridles just dumped in a pile.

"You men need these horses sorted and I will be back in half an hour, once the train has gone further into town to the station." Charles looked at the mess in front of him, the realisation that there were replacement horses and men hadn't occurred to him until this moment.

"Ok lads listen in. Go get a horse and bring it to me, one each. Dump your stuff over there for now." And he pointed towards a hump on the ground. The men took off all the gear they had just spent an age getting together, and putting on, and placed it in a tidy pile. Then they went to look at the horses, it didn't take long.

Charles walked down the line and gave each man a reassuring smile and each horse a pat on its neck and a little rub of their forelock, the horses all pushed his hand and tried to manipulate an ear scratch from this man. The horses needed a brush to clear the dust and straw from their dull but short coats. Charles checked a couple and recognised a hunting horse easily enough, he wondered if they were from the same hunt,? donated to the Army and dispatched, never to be seen again. He knew there had been more than one tear as these fine animals left their owners, sometimes willingly, but not always.

"Lads, just give them a hug, let them know you like horses. They don't know you from Adam, but a few kind words will help them, remember they know less than you".

As he stood in the shadows at the end of the train, just outside the station he could see two men walking back towards him.

"Are you the Cavalry?" said a burley Warrant Officer

"Yes Sir. 20th Hussars, I'm just returning from England and these lads are replacements going on to the Regiment Sir"

"Well son, your Regiment is on the move. You'll be pleased to know they are about 25 miles away. He produced a map and stuck a podgy finger on a point.

"This is where we are, that town yonder is Valenciennes, and your lot, according to these here notes, are at a place called Maubeuge and that's about 4 hours riding at a walk – trot. I have marked the map for you in pencil, you can read a map can't you? Over there is water for your canteens and some water bags for the horses. We don't have any fodder to spare, but the horses have all been fed in the night so they should be ok 'til you find your own mob. Any questions? Funny I thought there would be an NCO with the replacements."

One of the men overheard and said

"There was a Corporal Ross with us Sir, but he was arrested at the docks for being drunk and he missed the boat, Sir"

The warrant officer shook his head, "He'll be in the for the chop then" was all he said as he handed the map to Charles.

"Now there's some food made up and coffee if you're quick, but you need to be getting on with it, so pull your fingers out."

Each man grabbed a sausage butty and a mug of warm coffee, it was strong and bitter but with some sugar in it, it was delicious. Within ten minutes the men had all stuffed their sandwiches down and slugged the coffee, it was time to go.

"Form up into a ride of threes and a spare at the front with me, get a move on and let's go." The men quickly formed up into a squad and with a "Walk March" from Charles at the front they were on their way, back to the war.

The horses were frisky and jumpy, but the basic training of the men ensured there were no major problems. In time, they cleared all the built up areas. A good pace at walk helped loosen all the joints, it had been a very long journey to this point, but now there was no sign of the war or, indeed, anything other than a late autumn day. The larks were high in a sky devoid of clouds and a meadowlark sang its shrill song totally out of sight. The men talked and the occasional laugh came to the front. Charles would quieten them as he needed, but he didn't want to be a killjoy, he had seen enough of those in his time in uniform. After an hour, he decided to let the horses have a run, the men needed a distraction and, after all, they were going somewhere and not out on a Sunday hack. Ahead, there was a long field and he thought it would shake the cobwebs from his own riding as much as the new men behind him.

"Make sure everything is secure, I don't want to lose stuff, tighten your girths a hole and get your arses out of the saddle, no more weight on the horses back than necessary." He checked that everyone was ready and said "Stay in this formation, it's not a race so keep hold of your horse, but lets give them a 'pipe cleaner'. Ride will advance to trot, trrrott march." The resulting carnage left him speechless. Within ten seconds of the first horse trotting, there was a huge fart and a buck from the horse next to him. The rider hit the floor before knew he was off, and the horse, now free and loose, galloped off. The chain reaction was immediate, the next two horses reared as their riders pulled too hard on the bits that were ill fitted, and then they too were away at the gallop. Panic spread along the line and all the horses were running. Charles sat strong and pushed his bum deep into his saddle, the corners of his mouth raised subconsciously as he tried to suppress a laugh. As he looked around there were no more than three men still with him, the rest of his Troop had shell burst in different directions and, all around him, there were scenes of chaos and much as he should have been furious at the sheer incompetence of his colleagues, he was increasingly starting to laugh until eventually he didn't try to hold it in and with a quiet hand, he stopped his mount and broke down in fits of laughter. Without any doubt, it was a 'right mess.' The remaining mounted men gathered around him, seeing him laugh they too let the situation get the better of them. These three had all been riders before joining up, two had been hunt staff and one a professional jockey, the other had been groom to various people in their life before the Army. They were competent riders and the utter carnage before them taught them all a quick lesson in life, sit tight, because you just never know what will happen next.

Fortunately, no one was badly hurt, and, after a crazy ten minutes, all the horses had started to gather themselves into a small herd, the riders, swearing vengeance, were told to stand still and wait until the more experienced horsemen around them had collected their mounts. Charles took this opportunity to pass on some valuable information and basic instruction to the crestfallen soldiers.

"Listen in, all of you. That shows me that you men need to think on about what you can do and what you think you can. This isn't a training school now lads, it's real and if you get it wrong out here, the chances are old Fritz will see you away and that's bad enough. But worse than you getting clobbered, is me getting clobbered because we have to depend on each other to make sure we all pull through. The fact that you are replacements shows that we have already got it wrong more than once. So, let's stay calm, not get angry with your horse, if I see any man hit his horse or punish it in anyway I'll have you on a fizzer as soon as we get back. For the love of God, get it right and think. Now go and gather your horse and mount it quietly, no fuss. They are as scared as you are and they have no idea who you are either, but they do now know they can get you off so sit tight, they will try again. Be careful to pat them on the neck and let them know you're a team now."

The men walked slowly back to their horses. One or two swapped. Riding is as much about confidence as it is skill, and once you've been scared once, it's easy to scare you again. With luck, it wouldn't be a long ride, but, the other side of that was that the Germans could be closer than anyone liked. Truth was Charles didn't know where they were and, in fact, wasn't all that sure he knew where he was. They had skirted the town and left it behind at least an hour ago and there in the distance was another church spire. He was reminded of the origins of point to point racing, and knew that with the Regiment he would have made much better time, but he wasn't a natural leader, he much preferred to be a follower.

He had been told he was a good soldier but right now he didn't feel like it. He wished very much that he could let someone else take charge but that wasn't going to happen. He had the responsibility to make sure these men got to the Regiment and the sooner they got together, the sooner he could go back to being a basic 'Tommy', he was a very reluctant leader indeed.

In time, all riders and horses were reunited, and all the gear that had been dropped was now collected and the ride resembled something the Army might call a troop.

"Right then, let's try not to fall on our arses shall we, 'Walk March." The group of horsemen walked, and in a few minutes, were able to trot. This was good enough, they would cover plenty of ground over an hour, but there would be some very sore bottoms tomorrow. Saddle sore is a dreadful ailment but everyone suffers it initially.

They rode until they reached a large village, and, as if by pure planning rather than the complete luck, which, in truth, was what it was, they came to a halt in front of a barrier manned by a Tommy.

"Who you looking for lads?" he called.

"20th Hussars mate. Have you seen any?"

"Right up this street to the crossroad, turn right to the village square and over by the water pump, you'll find your mates feeding their horses."

It was music to Charles' ears as he said quietly "Now look lively and smart, the men will be watching if you're any good. The Sgt Maj will be looking for fodder, and believe me, with some of you, he'll find it"

They marched up the road and turned right at the crossroads into the town square there was a shout,

"Atherton, stand still on that horse. Who the hell have you dragged back? Are they soldiers?"

It was the Sgt Maj, it would be.

"Hello Sir, reporting back from pass to duty Sir. These men are replacements, as indeed are the horses, I picked them up at the port Sir."

As he dismounted, his mates came from all directions to see the new boys

"Where's their NCO?"

"In 'Pokey' Sir, he was drunk at the dockside so they embarked alone. Good job I was on the same boat or they might never have found us Sir."

Everyone dismounted almost in a smart and coordinated way, one man caught his heel in the stirrup and fell on his arse, much to the amusement of everyone, except the Sgt Maj. A group from 'A' Squadron stood and gawped at the new arrivals. It was always a mistake to stand idle when the Sgt Maj was around.

"You men over there, get some food and water for these horses, you new men, fall in over there and let's get you sorted out."

The horses were untacked and the parade formed up and waited for the Adjutant to come and allocate them to the different sections. Charles went to the main office to report back for duty. It seemed a lot longer than the 8 days he had been away.

The Unit had been stood down for a weekend to regroup and sort out kit exchange. Some of the horses looked worse for wear, and feed, although not overly scarce, was restricted. Fodder was taking up so much room on the ships that questions were being asked up at command level as to the exact requirements. The men looked tired, they had been busy since they had stopped the initial German advance and even turned them, but now the Germans had a second plan, if they couldn't get to Paris they would grab the ports further North in Calais and Dunkirk.

This single change in tack changed the whole pattern of the war. Instead of it being a very mobile war it would stagnate and become a war more of attrition than mobility. Artillery, and not Cavalry, would be king and the poor bloody Infantry would, once again, be exposed to the horrors of a modern war. Shells, not swords and lances, would be the killer. The German plan to rush North would be helped by their plan to hold onto ground they had previously taken, with no regard for its natural inhabitants. These poor souls would be displaced and join the massive human migration of war torn refugees. The alternative was to stay in towns that would become battle grounds and the buildings would be legitimate targets for the artillery. The French would once again bear the brunt of a war fought on their land by the invading Germans, the destruction would be devastating to anyone still living in the houses and shops. Regardless, the French locals maintained a spirit not shared by the Army, they remained defiant and stubborn, they tolerated the invasion of their property hoping that in time victory would be theirs and then the retribution and revenge would be let loose with all the fury only a defeated country could muster.

Charles listened to the reports from the previous week, promotion to Lance Corporal was mentioned, but he wasn't really that bothered, he was back with his mates who regaled him with tales of daring do and, in turn, he told them of his new sweetheart, Rebecca. The mail had caught up with the

20th, there were lots and lots of bags of mail. Over the past couple of days, each and every man had been handed mail. Some, who found it difficult to read, handed their letters over to trusted mates to read for them. Amazing news had been shared this way, the news of newborn children to long absent fathers on duty, news of new recruits joining up to help the cause, and, in Charlie's case, the news of a heart swollen with new found affection. He read the letters time and again, he had to go back to the Quarter Master's to pick up his gear. It was the last time he would be parted from it as the new directive was all kit was to be carried at all times regardless of leave or duty. From now on his rifle and uniform stayed with him no matter what. He wanted to go to the stable block to greet his trusted horse and he would have sworn he could hear the whinnying from his bereft chum.

"Aye, up Charlie lad, thank Christ you're back. This bastard thing has nearly killed two men in the last week, the Adj was going to shoot him! He's in the veterinary lines but he is fine, he's not an easy ride, that bugger, but everyone said you had a hex over him. He has a cut to his hind right from some wire he was caught in when he threw Corporal Grieves and buggered off. He slipped into a fence and has a bloody great cut up the length of his leg. The Veterinary has stitched it though and he's going mad to be out so, for the sake of us all, go and see him."

Charles felt his heart sink, Apollo was a fantastic mount but if the rider was at all unsympathetic, he could, and would, be a horror to ride. To the best of Charles' knowledge, no one else had sat on him for two years, so a new rider would have to rise to the challenge and Grieves was a cracking jockey, so he would have been up to the task.

As Charles went around to the vet lines, Apollo was biting the top of the stable door and weaving from side to side, he was fed up. Charles took Apollo's massive head in his hands and scratched his cheek. The horse sucked in the air through his huge nostrils and calmed instantly at the smell he breathed in, unison in perfect harmony, man and horse, friends. Charles went in to the stable to see the damage, it wasn't as bad as he had feared. The laceration was long but not deep, the stitches were tidy and the wound was dry.

"Are they good enough for you?" It was the voice of Major Leavis the Vet. Charles sprung up and stuttered

"Oh Sir, sorry Sir I didn't mean for anyone to be here."

The Vet laughed, he was being cruel and teasing the lad,

"He's pleased to see you. I take it he is your mount, he damn near killed me but you seem to have the gift over him. Atherton isn't it? I was told he was particular to you, well what do you think of him? Nice enough job or would you like a second opinion?" He was still teasing poor Charles, who was struggling to think of an answer.

"Don't fret Atherton, he will be fine. Tomorrow, seeing as you're back, you can walk him out on a long line, those stitches have been in for more than 5 days so he can have a wander around. You can look after him from now on, he is a danger to himself but, more worrying is my staff, so from here on in you can look after him. I will square that away with the Adjt and your Squadron Commander. Which Squadron are you in?"

"'B' Squadron Sir. I'm sorry he's been awkward, he can be a handful Sir, he doesn't mean anything by it though, the stitches are grand Sir, by the way." He smiled as he said the last bit, now he felt he could be a bit cheeky but wasn't going to push his luck. "When are they due out Sir? He needs to be exercised soon; he's like a bottle of Dandelion and Burdock pop Sir, all fizzed up. He's getting fat stood in here."

The Major smiled, he liked this lad, he clearly had a way with horses, he looked at the wild animal from yesterday and all he could see was a placid, calm Blackpool donkey looking back at him, the transformation was remarkable.

"Well let's see how he gets on tomorrow. As far as I am aware, we are staying here for a couple of days longer, at least HQ and support lines are, so that includes you and that devil horse of yours. Let's see how he gets on shall we? Oh and cut his ration back a bit, don't want fat horses and riders do we! He gently poked Charles in the tummy with his cane and they both laughed. Charles didn't have a pick on him, but the point wasn't lost on him, idle is as idle does. Don't be idle.

Charles finished with Apollo, who seemed much happier to have his mate back, and went back to 'B' Squadron lines., The usual suspects were there waiting for him, Sgt Blackie had told the lads he was back, and they had sorted a space in the barn that was serving as their accommodation. It wasn't much, but it was dry and there was plenty of straw for the sleeping mats they called a bed.

The water was on for a brew and for Charles it really did feel as though he was amongst family. His first job was to clean his rifle, he looked at it with dread, there was even a spot of rust. He was fastidious about his rifle and sword. His sword was in a much better condition as it had been wrapped in sackcloth with a rub of gun oil along its long blade. He sat with a steaming cup of tea and let the world catch up with him as he stripped his rifle down to its component parts, he laid them out on a clean piece of material and oiled a cloth ready to clean each piece of gun metal.

It transpired that the lads and the Regiment had been through a bit of a grinder over the last week, mainly as support for the Scots Greys, the action had been swift and decisive but it had come with a cost.

"Sid Hoyles and Bernard Hatheridge from 'A' both copped it on the same day, Alf Davies is missing and George Tittington hasn't been seen for a week or so, but its 'C' Squadron who have been in the thick of it. Mister Dodds and 6 men from the section he was leading all killed by a bloody great shell, all the horses as well. We were in the rear so didn't really have any part of the action, but the lads are proper shaken up so those lads you brought back with you are going to be welcome. Did you know 4 of them aren't for us? They're for the Scots, don't know why you brought them here?"

Charles looked up from his cleaning, he had scratched the rust off with his finger nail and oiled the working parts so they were smooth and easy to move. Outside it was starting to go dark, the dusk had closed in quickly and the light inside the barn had dimmed considerably.

"The Scots? But they all said they were for the 20th Hussars, why didn't they say something? I never even noticed their cap badges, have they gone then?"

"Knowing you Charlie, they probably didn't dare say, and yes they went about an hour ago. The Scots Greys are about 15 miles further up the line, they have had a lot of casualties but they've been in the thick of it for the whole fortnight. They're welcome to it."

There was a 'click, clack, click, clack' as the beautifully cleaned and oiled working parts of the Lee-Enfield 303 smoothly worked in unison. Once more, the rifle reassembled, was an engineering masterclass in efficiency of movement.

CHAPTER 31

Back to war

The next morning, the men woke to torrential rain. The noise that they awoke to was of the two squadrons getting ready to go out on patrol. Charles and the rest of 'B' Squadron were stood down for the day, and a game of football arranged. Charles wanted to spend some time sorting his kit for, although he had only been at home for a week, his gear had been thrown around in a stores wagon, his saddle and tack hadn't been cleaned and he wanted to catch up. First on the list was a letter back home.

No one heard them, no one saw them, but they were there. First one man, then two and then ten. They had crept round the back of the Chateau behind the veterinary lines, fortune had dictated that at that precise moment no one was there. The band of Germans, separated from the rest of their Army and hopelessly lost, hungry and with an all-consuming thirst, had been dodging their enemy for nearly a week. They had stolen what they could, from where they could, but there was no hiding what they were, either deserters or vicious renegades, it was all in the eye of the beholder really. Here, now, they were dangerous as they broke into the stable block to see if there was any food or drink.

If it hadn't been for the horses they would have been clear and away before anyone knew they had even been there, but the animals, much like the men that rode them had heightened senses for danger and they could smell Germans a mile away.

The first horse to be disturbed was stuck fast in the stable with a Nasty abscess from a shoe nail, clumsily hammered into the wrong part of the hoof by a novice farrier. He had learned his lesson the painful way as the horse hoofed him out of the forge, but the price had already been paid by the poor horse. Within a few hours the swelling had started and before the day was out he was lame, the abscess formed and was burst by the Vet. The relief was immediate, but the hole needed time to heal, so he was on box rest with a poultice of oats on his hoof. Another couple of days would see him right. He was disturbed and kicked the door with his good hoof this started a chain reaction and the other two sick horses including Apollo, plus five new arrivals waiting to be vet checked prior to issue, started to whinny and stamp. This wasn't necessarily a new thing, the horses did much the same if there was a rat in the box, in short order the rat would be killed by a stamp and often kicked out onto the walkway to be found by one of the grooms at sweep or feeding time, but this was different, more insistent and it caught the attention of Private Arthur Mills.

Arthur Mills wasn't brave, he wasn't even a very good soldier. He was unkempt and scruffy, he didn't have a picking on him. More meat on a butcher's pencil type of chap; Thin scrawny neck and long skinny legs, handsome hadn't marked him as his own, but he had a love of horses that few, if any, surpassed. He was a true 'nags man'. He had gypsy blood in him and when he sat on a horse he looked like a bag of coal tied in the middle, but nothing ever bettered him, he could get a tune out of a pig. He was a natural rider, careful with his hands and with his long thin legs he could literally wrap them around a horse's sides. He was what is now known as a 'horse whisperer' and, as a groomsman he had found his true calling in life, but now he was curious and as the saying goes, it killed the cat.

The noise he heard wasn't loud, it was just in the wrong place. The horses were anxious and he could feel it, something just felt wrong and, being gifted with the Romany senses, he reached for his rifle. Suddenly there was a commotion, a sudden violent outburst as someone was heartily kicked by one of the horses, and in a flash, there was a gunshot but the damage had been done, a leg broken mid-thigh and the resulting scream of pain. Arthur was there, he had one up the spout and from the outside there was the sound of an alarm being raised,

"Germans in the camp. Stand to, Stand to."

Arthur came around the edge of a wall, he could see down the length of the stable block, purpose built for the Chateau's former owners riding and draught horses.

There was an awful racket coming from the end stable and, as Arthur gave way to his senses, he ran towards the noise. There in the straw stood a horse, and under the horse, muttering all the curses in the Germanic dictionary, lay a broken man. He had been kicked towards the back of the box and from his right leg protruded a white bone as thick as a man's wrist. The gunshot had missed the horse and, although he was frightened by the noise of the shot, he stood like a sentry over his conquered foe.

"Hands up Fritz, right up in the air where I can see them." Arthur was shouting and spittle was dripping down his quivering lips, he was scared to death but as angry as he had ever been that a German tried to shoot his horse. He did think about shooting the German, but wasn't sure that he would miss the horse, so he shouted some more and gesticulated with the end of his .303 for the German to raise his hands high in the air.

By this time, Charles and the rest of the men left behind, were running towards the edge of the stables and house, no defensive line had been established because the Germans were miles ahead up the road, no allowance had been made for stragglers. Charles heard the shouting from the stables and in the chaos, he chose to see what was going on. As he entered the stable, he could see Arthur in a muck sweat and raging.

"Arthur, are you hurt? What's going on chum? Steady with that rifle, it might go off. It's ok mate I'm here." He walked slowly and quietly, he had seen what fear could make a man do and he had no doubt of Arthur's ability to shoot someone by accident.

"In here Charlie, there's Fritz all broken, should I shoot him?"

"No, wait, let me see." He walked towards the stable box and there he saw the terrified, and in great shock, the diminutive and shaking figure of a German. Hands in the air but desperately trying to hold his obviously broken leg.

"Shhhh, calm down Arthur, this chap's got a broken leg. Let's get him out before he gets trodden on. You take the horse and tie him over there on the upright, calm him down Arthur, he's scared and we don't need a scared horse in the stables, you know it'll set the others off."

As Arthur raised his rifle, the magazine fell off onto the floor, but he had been given something to do so he casually picked up the magazine and put it away as if it happened all the time. He took the horse by the rope head collar and walked him out, he stroked his neck and cooed words of comfort for the horse without ever looking back at the German casualty.

Charles knew this was a moment of danger, so he held his hand out to show the German to stay still. The pistol that the German had let a shot off with, was about 3 feet away from the German's hand, but he had no interest in a gun, he wanted someone to stop the pain in his shattered leg. Charles reached down and picked up the 'Luger' and put it away, he had no idea if it was set to fire or safe, and, seeing as he hadn't ever seen one before, thought it best to put it somewhere safe for the time being. He called out for a medic, there were some attached to the Unit, and, very quickly, one appeared at the stable entrance to administer some first aid.

Outside, there was a volley of shots, in the woods two Germans fell, both dead. The others ran into the cover of the woods and lay behind whatever protection they could find. As bullets smashed through the tree branches, they had choices, they could run, fight or surrender. There were seven of the original ten left, and, suddenly, they all felt a long way from their own side. Surrender seemed like the best alternative. They were hungry, cold and wet so, with heavy hearts, they hoped the British would be honourable and accept their surrender.

Back in the stable the Vet had arrived and the stretcher bearers had managed to squeeze past the mass of interested men in the doorway.

"Make way there, stand aside and let us through."

Major Leavis was looking at the prostrate man, who was

now clearly in shock and with each clumsy movement the pain would make him convulse and yell out.

"We need to splint that leg. There is a real chance if we move him he'll sever the artery and bleed to death. Either that, or I can shoot him, that's what I would do with a horse who'd broke his femur." He laughed at his own joke, it made Charles feel easier because, for a moment, he thought that he had meant it.

The bearers, both medics from the Royal Army Medical Corps, had received good training in first aid and agreed that it would be better, given the circumstances, to splint the leg. One pulled out a syrette of morphine and jabbed it into the poor German's good leg

"That'll help when we pull the leg straight, but we need to be getting on with it."

Two pieces of wood were found and tidied up at the edges. They were longer than the German's leg and, as he looked on, Major Leavis patted him reassuringly on the shoulder. The medics quickly manoeuvred the makeshift splints into place.

"Do you want some traction on that leg? I'm not sure I can apply enough to get it straight but it might make it a bit easier on the far side of the trip."

There was a brief conflab and the overall decision was to leave it be and just splint it as straight as they could. By now, the German was drunk with the effects of the morphine, so they quickly rolled him on his side and fixed the splint with bandages. Once this was complete, they tipped the stretcher and placed it against his back before they rolled the patient and stretcher onto its legs. Despite the analgesia and a firm hand to squeeze, Fritz screamed out as his leg couldn't resist gravity and his knee and leg straightened. There were beads of sweat on his brow and, as the medics strapped his broken leg to his good leg, he nodded that it was easier and said

"Danke, vielen danke"

"What's he say?" Asked one chap.

Major Leavis, ever a man of the world, said "He's saying thank you, although I still think a one on one with the Mess revolver might have been quicker for the poor blighter."

CHAPTER 32

Catch them and kill them

There was a parade in the afternoon, rumour was that there was a push about to start. All the patrols had returned by lunchtime and the general atmosphere was one of joviality. The mail had all caught up, the Unit had been rested for a few days, and the excitement of catching a real German had been credited to Arthur Mills, no one mentioned the incident with the rifle and magazine falling off.

As the whole Regiment paraded at 14:00 hrs there was a call to 'attention'- no one was mounted as this was a briefing as much as a parade – but the surprise was the man giving the briefing. As the parade came to attention and formed into a three sided square, from behind the building came the mounted group of the Commanding Officer, the Adjutant and the Commander of 3rd Cavalry Brigade, Brigadier-General Hubert Gough, there was a gasp from some quarters this was the main man, the big chief.

"Men of the 20th Hussars" he began, "You have already bathed your Regiment in glory and I am delighted to be able to meet you all today to congratulate you on the sterling effort you have already shown. Your diligence and determination has enabled all the units you have supported to, in the main, escape mauling from the enemy. It is because of the marvellous skills in horsemanship and professionalism of soldiering that you have made the difference. We have the Hun on the run! They are scurrying North to try and catch us with our breeches down and it is their intention to capture the ports in the north to use to their own ill-gotten gains. Well we won't let them.

As from today, you will be part of a bigger unit and will form part the 2nd Cavalry Division, with the addition of divisional troops from the Royal Horse Artillery and Royal Engineers. Shortly you will be joined by the 4th Cavalry Brigade to make sure we have the right amount of troops to win this war. I am very proud to be your Commander and I know that under the Commanding Officer, Lt Col Edwards, you will continue to provide the Army with a Cavalry they can proudly call their own, no longer will you be nobodies own. I can see by the determined look in your eyes that you are keen and ready to take the fight to the Hun, well you won't have to wait much longer. Once I am finished here you will be given your orders to ride north first to catch the Germans and then kill them. Good hunting and good luck. Keep up the good work and tally ho."

There was a shout for three cheers from the front and the General was roundly cheered as he turned his horse and walked away.

Once the commotion had calmed down the different Sections were called to order in different parts of the farm. Orders had been issued and now the whole Brigade would be heading north towards Belgium. The race to stop the Germans reaching the channel ports was being hampered by the Germans digging in and forming strongpoints to slow the advance, even trenches were reported.

The village of Vailly was the destination and it had been arranged that the whole Brigade would rendezvous there and the 20th would be the last to arrive. The town would be full of cavalry with the Greys and 12th Lancers getting there before hand. Between the Regiment and the town, was the river Ainse. The bridge had been destroyed by the Germans on their retreat, but the Royal Engineers had built a long pontoon bridge with boats as the supports. It was obvious that the cavalry wouldn't be able to ride over it so the whole regiment dismounted and walked.

Apollo was a lead horse and Charles was sat aboard a new mount, one of the replacement horses he had brought from the train. He patted Apollo on the head as the two horses exchanged pleasantries by taking a nip out of each other, as if riding and leading a horse wasn't hard enough without them misbehaving, it caused much laughter at Charles' expense. Most men would have left Apollo behind.

As soon as the Regiment had entered the town the Germans started to shell the bridge and gates. They were late because everyone had already crossed and the men were grateful for it, however the punch in the guts was that they shouldn't have crossed at all, instead they had to turn about and go back. The Infantry hadn't yet secured the heights and the town was a death trap if the horses and men remained. Such is war, communication is one of the first casualties, and so, with a huge amount of grumbling, everyone turned and set off back, only this time the German guns were ready and much more accurate.

The lead men of which Charles was one had it easiest, they ran rather than walked but always in order and never in panic. A shell smashed into the pontoon but didn't explode, it just drove a hole right through the bridge and boat beneath. Sam Eldridge was running behind Charles and he was thrown over the side by the next shell. It killed his horse and he was blown up, his legs gone and a huge piece of timber impaling him through his chest. He was dead before he hit the water below. The man behind caught the full force of the splinters but, although peppered with wood, he took the main damage and although his horse was badly shook up by the noise, he wasn't badly damaged and they pressed on so as not to hold up the men behind.

Once on the bank they jumped back onto their horses. Charles let Apollo go, he hoped that the horse would follow him as he rode to cover in some nearby trees. He did.

The clearing in the trees was long, but not very wide, and, as the new arrivals came past them, each team of horse and rider spoke to Charles to say thank the Lord. In total, 5 men and 7 horses were killed. The Colonel was furious that the butcher's bill had been so large for a mistake that should never have happened. More casualties of a ridiculous war.

CHAPTER 33

Splish Splash

As the wooded hills of France where left behind, the contrast to the long flatlands and flooded fields of Flanders was stark. All around on the journey was damaged or destroyed either when the Germans were advancing or, more recently, as they retreated. They had smashed water pumps, poisoned supplies and spoiled as best they could. It was saddening to see the locals who had lost most of what they had possessed but were only too pleased to share what little they did have. Beer, bread, chickens and paté were all shared, as was accommodation and fodder, as much as could be spared.

The Quarter Master had dumped all surplus equipment so that the pack wagons could keep up with the main column of riders. Much to the annoyance of the Signals Officer, his equipment had been deemed to be too heavy, and was dumped or swapped for food for both men and horses. All the picks and shovels had been left behind on the assumption they wouldn't be needed. Now it was becoming very clear they would be.

Although the ride was fairly quick, the Germans were always one step ahead. Each town that was occupied by the Germans was slow and costly in time and men. The Infantry had to catch up and then formulate an attack plan. All the while the Cavalry were idle, but this suited Charlie.

He was busy working with Apollo who was now stitch free and 'nowty'. So Charles had time to gently ride him then he rubbed liniment into his stiff legs. There was no doubt about it, he looked after that horse very well, it hadn't gone unnoticed by the senior men of the Regiment who would ask if Charles would "just look over this chap for me" quite regularly. Charles was always happy to oblige, he loved his horses. There were more replacements arriving, this time there were over 50 men and now there weren't enough horses to go round, so Charles had given his replacement horse over to the newly arrived men. There were changes in the Officers as well, some of the Senior Non Commissioned men had now received new Commissions, they were "good men who knew their jobs" said Bill Blackie who was surely due to be promoted. Eventually they were in Flanders proper, the lads couldn't understand much of what the locals said, but Charles and some of the other northerners seemed to have a grasp on some Flemish words.

By mid September, the rain was pretty well constant, just drizzle, but it left everything soaked if exposed for anytime. Autumn was showing her early colours and the weather was at best described as inclement.

Rumour was that the Germans were on the retreat and that a large bulge had been pushed into the German front just North of their positions in a place called Ypres or, as the Tommies called it, 'Wipers'. The Germans had stopped running and started digging trenches, building bunkers and pill boxes; there would be no more dashing charges on horseback for a while.

The good news for the troops was they were close by to a beer brewery. The Officers were able to make use of some of the spare accommodation and the troop lads were able to take advantage of a good bath, for most the first bath they had taken in the last month or more. To the replacements the smell of the men had been a bit of a shock, and although they all washed as often as they could, they never seemed to have time to wash their clothes apart from underwear and that would always be a cold wash. In the brewery huge vats of hot water were made ready and massive tanks normally used for washing hops and barley had been cleaned out and made ready for baths. To the side of the pump house there was a Unit of Pioneers who had set up a laundry unit, the plan being to use this facility for all the troops in the area. The owners of the beer house were much more appreciative of their British guests than the Germans who had tried to smash the equipment, but didn't have time before the local militia had harried them out of the area. Just men and boys with pitchforks and farm equipment had caused the Germans enough problems to make it more trouble than it was worth to stay and smash the beer barrels. This was the Belgian's beer, although they were happy to share and sell it to the British.

By the time 'B' Squadron were sent for their bath, the tanks had been filled with hot and steaming clean water.

"Right then, listen in. All shirts and blouses in a pile on the right. There are clean uniforms on the other side of the bath house. Dump your dirty ones here and pick up clean ones when you have cleaned up. There are warm hoses at the front of the bath. Make sure you all have a hose down before you get in, this water has to clean a lot of men today and your scruffy smelly carcasses are the first ones in, you lucky people. Don't dilly dally, get a clean up, then a couple of minutes soaking and then out. 'A' are in after you, they are getting sorted by the barbers, and then cleaning the horses along with 'C'. When you're finished you take over from 'A' and, in turn, they will take over from 'C'. In the end, we should end up with a sweet smelling Regiment. The Officers are last." The Sergeant Major shook his head, he knew this was going to be carnage, all these men having a mass bathing session and just letting their hair down for a couple of hours was just what the Medical Officer ordered

When Charles fell in with the rest of 'B' to march to the baths, the mood was one of jocular mischief. Jokes about Charles and his swimming prowess were the order of the day.

"Now then Charlie boy, no diving!" The laughter was good to hear and Charles took it in the manner it was meant.

Stripped to the waist you could see the men had all lost weight, some of them didn't have much they could afford to lose, and the Medical Officer was keen to run his eye over everyone. It was a fine production line. Shirts in a pile then form up into a line so the M.O. could take a quick gander at the general state of each man, then the rest of the clothes off and folded along with boots and underwear. Then into the bath house and the steam, hoses of warm water felt delightful as the water played over their thin smelly bodies, all the while wild shrieks of laughter and lewd jokes that only a soldier would say before they climbed over into the hot water, this had the effect of pinking them like shrimps. Someone had found some carbolic soap and this was cut up into small soap blocks the lads were in heaven as they splashed about and scrubbed each other's backs. As Charles found a moment of quiet in the bedlam, he reflected on the last month, away to war, home to Rebecca, back to war, captured and released. He had killed and nearly been killed himself, he had witnessed death dealt most cruel and life saved by simple humanity and compassion to other men. He had been scared, elated, bored and full of regret. It had indeed been quite a month, just four weeks and his life would never be the same. Out of the corner of his eye he saw Sam Atherton; he held his head in his hands as if washing his face but anyone who looked, really looked could see the tears of a man at his wits end. Fear and elation are twins of emotion, Janus faced, and Sam had seen both, his horse killed beneath him by shrapnel, his friends smashed like putty and mush on the bridge just a few days before. Charles made his way slowly, he didn't want to draw attention to the fact Sam was in a bad place, but when he got there he splashed Sam with some water and, as the two men caught the eye of the other, a simple wink and a nod spoke a million words.

"No man is an island, entire of itself...any man's death diminishes me, because I am involved in mankind; and therefore never send to know for whom the bell tolls; it tolls for thee." *John Donn* was a man of knowledge, his phrasing couldn't have been more accurate. But today they were alive and sat in a bath together, friends, brothers in arms as ever it was.

In each bath there were twenty men and there were three baths. It sounded like a battle in there and on the outside of the building, the Officers and Senior NCOs listened and smiled, whilst they smoked and talked about how the men had done a fantastic job in the last month.

Once the baths had done, it was out and into a large store room filled with blankets that they could use as towels and, next to that, was another room with clean uniforms in sized piles. "Just pick a shirt and get dressed" said Sergeant Blackie "Then go and get your haircuts and get on with cleaning back with the horses, he needn't have bothered, the horses were all spotless; the two squadrons waiting for their turn in the baths had cracked the whip and got the job done, it meant the afternoon was free for drinking a beer, and that was never time wasted.

CHAPTER 34

Dig in lads

The next morning, the war was back on, no more rest was anticipated for a few weeks, so it was time to get back out on patrol and back to work. It was the best thing they could have done for everyone; each man found demons with both eyes closed and sleep was best taken with a wary eye on the next day.

'B' Squadron were dispatched to cover the area in a place with a familiar name, but a long way from its namesake, America. This town being the right flank of the Division; it was also the furthest point away from the headquarters and everyone felt very nervous about this. Charles was no exception. Bill Blackie was on edge, but he was always a bit keen when out and about on patrol, all along the line there were pockets of fighting with the Germans who had an uncanny knack of appearing from nowhere. These skirmishes were bloody, and often desperate, hand to hand affairs, sword against rifle and bayonet and revolver against bombs. Although the mounted troops were thought to have the upper hand or advantage, often the Germans would lay traps for the horses which were simple but extremely effective, wire laid at ground level would trip the unwary and dump the rider on the floor, unarmed and unseated they were easy pickings for a charging bayonet. Calthrops, which were evil three-legged spikes, were thrown like nails along the road to catch the unwary horse. The war was getting dirty and more desperate on a daily basis as men were being lost and killed by the hour. Blackie was right to be edgy, it might well keep him and his men alive.

The shelling was getting heavier; from behind them, the British Artillery were on song, firing shell after shell, their guns must have been red hot, but this was matched by the Germans who had spotters watching the movements of the British and rained shrapnel and high explosives onto them from miles away.

"It's getting a bit hot Sergeant, what do you think, should we take cover a bit?" Being both young, and an Officer, was a curse for the men who weren't natural at leadership. The 20th were lucky all the Officers had been around for a while before the war had started but this was a very different scenario than manoeuvres in Aldershot.

"Aye sir, I think it might be best if we got off the road a while. Over there is a farm we can take cover in that for a bit till it eases off." Bill Blackie was a legend in the Regiment, as honest as the day was long and as grumpy as a housewife, he was a man of his word and he had seen a lot of action, both in Egypt and Ireland. As the section took cover, the shelling followed them until the woods that lay in front of the farm provided them with a haven. There wasn't much of a wood but it offered some cover and the spotters couldn't see where the riders had gone.

It wasn't long before a rider came galloping along the road towards them, it was a messenger from HQ,

"Sir you're to return as quickly as possible, the enemy are about to attack and cut you off."

Bill Stanesby was already getting the men to tighten their girths, this was going to be a race, in a soothing yet firm voice he could be heard telling the lads "Sit tight, don't fall off and if you do then get into cover until nighttime then make your way back."

Charlie was ready, he could feel his heart pounding and, as if it was travelling down through his trousers and to the saddle, Apollo started to twitch and buck, nothing big but still a reason for Charlie to "sit up."

With a shout, the Squadron formed into a ride and with no audible shout, they were off at the gallop. The lead horses were fast, there was to be no overtaking, this wasn't the hunt, this was a military gallop, a charge without the enemy in front. The road ahead had been shelled pretty heavily since the ride had come the other way earlier, big holes were in the path of the horses and the lead horse, with Captain Jones on it, leapt as if *point to pointing*. The next two just followed, but behind one horse shied away and the rider had to hang on as it veered left onto the path and then it jumped the ditch. This started a chain reaction and some followed it and some followed the lead horses. Amazingly no one fell off. The only casualties were a couple of hats blown off in the wind, lost forever.

As the ride neared the town after a good long gallop, they could see another squadron further along the road and slightly up the hill in front, about half a mile ahead. Suddenly a volley of shells screamed overhead and landed almost amongst the men in front. Some fell but more horses were wounded and some killed. It was heartbreaking to see the men crawl towards their writhing horses, it was just six shells but the damage to horseman and horse was huge. It was Capt

Sandford who came out with Major Leavis. Between them they dispatched the wounded horses whilst the horrified men looked on at their friends' demise. More men were wounded by our own guns that day than the enemy. There was a lot of ill feeling towards the Artillery that afternoon and Bill Blackie spent more than a few minutes calming his men. "Woe betide any "Drop short arsehole" who finds himself in our company tonight" he said.

The next morning, it was ordered that the Unit dig in. The farm that had been good cover for the riders yesterday, was absolutely the wrong place to dig a trench due to it being the perfect place for the enemy to shell. It also happened to be next to the stream that, in winter, took on a different role and became a small river that flooded the fields all around the farm. Water that was usually directed away by the dykes would be stuck in the fields because all the dykes had been smashed, by the Belgians to slow the German advance. Now the Germans had finished the advance and, had indeed retreated, they would retreat no more, they had already started to dig huge deep trenches and dug outs; the simple difference was they held the higher ground. That, in itself, provided the British with problems; it was much harder to advance up hill to eject the enemy, but worse still was come the winter and the bad weather, all the rain water would run down the steady slope and make the British trench systems a quagmire of mud and misery.

The Unit found a suitable area to start digging, but then came the problem of tools, the QM having dumped them all to make the freight trucks lighter and allow them to keep up with the main body of cavalry; almost. The C.O. had spoken to the Quarter Master and, by all accounts, a significant bollocking had ensued, although there was sympathy for the Q.M., he was an old school cavalryman and digging trenches played no part in a highly mobile Unit's war. Well until now. People borrowed shovels from local farms and dug with whatever they could lay their hands on, quite literally knives and forks. The Royal Engineers had been extremely helpful and had laid it on hard to help. Within a couple of days, there was a trench that men could safely take cover, and although it wasn't the finished article, there was sufficient depth that a man could stand and not get his head shot off by the dreaded German snipers. Word was, there was a master of his craft that the British Tommies had named 'Wolfgang' and he was reckoned to be the best. He would kill you before you knew it, best to keep your head down the lads were told.

When the boys weren't digging, they were filling sandbags with soil to place along the top to add to the height. All along the trench there was a shelf for sentry duty men to keep a wary eye open for a sudden attack. This went on for days and days and pretty soon the whole Regiment had dug deep and struggled with blisters to both hands and feet. There was relief when a different regiment such as the Lancers got off their horses and replaced the Hussars. It wasn't that the top brass didn't care, they made sure that people were rotated regularly, but they didn't know just how hard physically it was for the men of the cavalry who had little or no experience of digging. The Germans had a plan, it was simple really, dig in and stay put; keep the ground they had already taken and stop the British from pushing the German lines back any further.

One night in mid-September, whilst on sentry duty, Charles heard a noise he hadn't ever heard before, it was a painful mournful bellow coming from out the back of the lines somewhere near the farm but not there. It went on for hours, just very quietly and, when the Duty Officer came on his rounds, and to stand Charlie down with a replacement, Charles pointed it out. "Would it be ok if I went to see what's making that noise Sir? It sounds awful pained and it must be playing on the lads' minds, it is mine Sir"

The Officer, who was a country lad, ruddy cheeks and strong farmer's hands, reckoned it was a beast or maybe a calf missing his mum. Most if not all, the cattle in the area had been taken by the Germans for food, just stolen really, not ever paid for unlike the British, who paid for everything.

"Yes Atherton, you go but be careful. I'll pass the word on that you're behind our lines and the password is 'Orange.' For Christ's sake don't forget it or they will shoot you. Go see and if you can quieten the poor creature down a bit."

Charles took his leave. He walked along the trench in the dark, his eyes had adapted well to the night and he could see quite a way without lights. He left the back trench and made his way along the wood line towards the farm. He could hear the animal still; its pitiful moan almost haunting, it made him think of a siren oddly, seeing as there was no sea and he was no sailor.

It took him more than twenty minutes to walk the half mile or so back towards the farm. It was a challenge in the dark, but he had no light so had to go steady, every now and again he would check behind him, more to see where he had come from than to see if there was anything there behind him. As he neared the farm, he could see a lamp, lit in the barn area roughly where the noise was coming from. He reached down and touched his knife, it was his own, not issued, and he had no idea what he was expecting to do with it but all the same he was reassured it was there.

As he rounded the barn, he could see the beast tied into a milking box, her udders were swollen and massive. There on the floor behind her, lay the farmer. Charles stood up and walked faster to look and see if he could see what the matter was, there was no sound, other than the cow who it was obvious, was in quite a bit of discomfort, more than anything from her swollen teats. Charles touched the farmer, he was cold and a bit stiff, his lips were blue and his eyes open; he was clearly dead. There was no wound to be seen or bruises to suggest the cow might have kicked out at him. There was a milking stool next to the cow and a bucket with some milk in, it was cold but the poor cow's udder was hot and full. He barely touched the teat and it yielded milk. Although he had seen enough cows milked, he hadn't ever tried it, now seemed an appropriate moment, the milk mightn't be any good but at least the poor cow would feel some relief. He settled onto the stool and blew warm air onto his hands as if he was about to medically examine someone. As he held the engorged teat gently in his hand the milk oozed out in almost a squirt, and Charlie smiled as the second teat was as productive as the first., It didn't take long before he had a rhythm going and the sound of milk splashing into the bucket became more fluid than wooden as the milk hit more milk than wood, and the bucket filled. To the side, there was a milk churn and within a few minutes, Charles was pouring a full bucket of warm creamy milk into it. Suddenly, Charles froze; there was a sound at the back of the shed. It was Bert Clarke and Bill Stanesby, his heart started again and with a long breath out he said

"You daft buggers nearly feart me to death. What are you doing here?"

"We were sent to see if you were ok by Lieutenant Mills, he was wondering where you had got to"

"I'll tell you where I've got to! This poor bloody animal is full to bursting and I've just taken a bucket of milk off her, Yon mon is dead, I think it must be his heart or something; he was proper dead when I got here. There's now't we can do for him but this poor girl, we might be able to help. Is there anyone in the farm? I did think about going to have a look but it's all dark, the only light is this one so I think he might live here alone, or maybe he's sent the lasses away before the Germans came."

Bill took a mug and dipped it into the warm milk, he looked at the other two and drank it, it was like nectar and he didn't stop until the mug was empty

"Oh good Lord, that's wonderful, here try some." He filled the mug again and offered it to Charles. He drank it and purred when it was drained. Once more it was filled and Bert Clarke drank his share. The spoils of war sometimes need a bit of finding, but the odd times you do find them, it can be wonderful or so they said to the men back at the trench when they returned, but not until they had all milked for about fifteen minutes each. Eventually, the cow's udder started to feel baggy and flaccid and, although none of them were farmers, each knew she was empty.

"What do we do now?" It was Clarke.

Charles said "We need to feed her and give her water like the horses, she needs bedding down, I don't mind I'll do it, you two can go back with that milk churn for the lads they'll be appreciative of that." And so, they bedded the cow down in straw and fed her a load of grass from the roll in the barn. She got stuck in so they assumed it was the right feed. Then thy struggled with a milk churn that must have been three quarters full.

When they got back towards the trench they were challenged by the guard, "Stand fast there. What's the password?"

"Orange" said Charles, the other two looked on at him as if he were finally mad.

"What?" said Bill Stanesby, "Orange? We weren't told a password! They would have shot us!"

The three men struggled to the dug out Command Post and the Duty Officer came out to see what the commotion was.

"It was a cow Sir. She was full to bursting and needed milking. The farmer's dead Sir, will we be able to go and bury him tomorrow? The cow will need milking again."

The Officer was about to have a rant until he was offered a mug of fresh milk, they hadn't had fresh milk for a month. He didn't say anything apart from "Of course, well done Atherton"

Next day, they woke to find the rain had stopped and there was a touch of late autumn warmth in the sun. Charles was summoned and quickly reported to the Adjutant.

"You a farmer before you joined Atherton?"

"No Sir, I worked in a cotton mill."

"How the devil did you know what to do with that cow? I have to say, everyone is very pleased that you did know by the way. Now what are your plans for the poor beast? We won't be here for much longer and I suspect we will be moving further up within the next few days. I have spoken to the Sergeant Major and it turns out we have a couple of farming stock lads in 'C' Troop. Maybe it might be easier if they did the milking in future; let you get back to the Troop. I'll arrange for one of them to come and see you and then you can hand the poor animal over to them. I say again though bloody good job, you did a good Christian thing helping that beast, and when you fall out, go back and bury the farmer with the Chaplain and some men. I don't mind telling you Atherton, that we are looking for a stripe for that arm, you're just the ticket. Now fall out and carry on."

Charles turned smartly to the right, and marched the obligatory three marching paces. He was then deemed to have 'fallen out'. He opened the door and left the room but couldn't help feeling that something had been taken from him, he shouldn't have minded, but it was there in his head, he did.

"Heyup Charlie" It was Seth Pickersgill who was one of the lads from 'C' Troop, "I hear you've got a cow in trouble? I don't know, you lads from Bolton, you'll do owt." Charlie laughed and punched Seth on the arm, "Bugger off you dirty sod, I found a cow at the farm, she was tied up and in a rotten state, bless her, she was full to the top with milk. I did my best but you're a farmer not me. I'm sure you will make a better job of sorting her out, I don't know owt about cattle." He liked Seth, they had done some tent pegging together in the past before the war had started; he was quite good.

"Are you here to take her off my hands then Seth? I have to go and dig a hole for the farmer who owned her, he's dead. I'm off to find the Chaplain, then I'm going up to the farm, are you coming with me?"

It turned out he was, and so were some of the other lads who would form a burial party.

When they arrived, it was the first chance Charles had to take a look around, before he did though, he introduced Seth to his new cow, she was ready for milking again. Seth said once she had been drained she needed to go back out into the paddock at the rear of the farm, this paddock hadn't had any shelling and was fairly well covered from any because it was on the leeward side of the small incline of the valley. Seth took his new command and Charles and the others went to look for a good place to dig a grave. In one of the out buildings they found a stock of farm tools, shovels, spades and forks as well as a couple of wheelbarrows, but one had a wonky wheel where a spoke was missing, so they left that one. Armed with several tools they set about digging a suitable grave for the dead farmer.

One of the lads made a cross from some good timber and within the hour a deep hole had been dug. The farmer had been wrapped in a tarpaulin and this had been stitched by one of the saddlers with some good strong thread, the last bit to be closed was over the poor man's face, it didn't look peaceful, it looked pained as if he really wasn't ready to go. Once it was all closed, the Padre said some Christian words and the body was lowered into the ground. Then they filled it and packed it tight, there was already some water in the bottom where the water table was so they made sure he was well stuck to the bottom.

When the makeshift service was over, the cross was hammered into place and some stones made as a frame around the grave. All in all, it looked very smart, and very military.

Seth called the burial party over and they all drank their fill of milk, it was still warm and that was appreciated because there was a chill in the air, it wasn't hard to imagine that winter was around the corner. The nights had a distinct frost and most of the men were wearing a scarf when on sentry duty. The horses were well back, about 3 miles away, so the troops didn't even have the work of them to warm them up. Digging trenches was hard enough, and that certainly warmed them through. It was once you had stopped that the chill hit you. Now there was fresh milk and the cooks had made a huge boiler full of porridge for breakfast, some dried fruit and jam and it was a wonderful treat for the whole Regiment.

It was today that they would move back, it was today they would be reunited with their horses and it was today they would meet the Indians.

CHAPTER 35

I can hear you

The noise I could hear was strangely familiar. I hadn't heard a cardiac monitor for nearly twenty years, but it was a sound that stayed within your memory.

There was another noise, it was voices, they sounded distant as if not connected properly to my ears. As I listened they became more focused, more recognisable, it was my lovely wife Di. She was asking someone a question but I didn't know who that person was. It was as if I was in a dream, but not quite, I was aware that I wasn't asleep but I couldn't open my eyes. I wasn't scared or concerned I was euphoric and everything was very comfortable, but I was confused.

"It's just too early to say, he might be like this for weeks but I can assure you he isn't in pain and he is comfortable." It was a man's voice, I didn't recognise it though.

Di held my hand and lifted it to her face, it was wet where she let her tears run over our clasped hands.

"He is still in a coma, we have reduced the sedative medication but it should still stop any convulsions. The initial operation was very successful, but the tumour is still there, and we are just waiting for the swelling to go down a bit more before we go in and remove the rest of it. He was very lucky."

I didn't feel lucky, I felt confused. I couldn't move my hand to reassure Di I was ok and although I could move my eyes, they were still closed so it felt like I was rolling my eyes rather than looking at something.

"He may well be able to hear us talking, so it's important that you talk to him, when you're not here we keep the radio on for him to hear in the background.

"What station is it tuned into? Please tell me it isn't Radio 2, he hates Radio 2 he is much happier listening to Radio 4."

The man laughed, "I don't know but I'll check, I quite like radio 4 myself actually."

I heard a door close. Where was I? What had happened? Who was that man? So many questions in my head.

I felt Di rub my lips with her finger, it felt smooth but I had no taste or sensation of swallowing, she was rubbing some Vaseline on my lips to keep them from cracking.

"Love if you can hear me, don't worry. You're in hospital you've had an operation on your head, its why you have been feeling odd and fainting, they found a growth and have removed some, but they need to go back and take the rest out. Not your brain just the tumour." She laughed at her own joke. I so desperately wanted to smile and tried with all my might to lift the corners of my mouth to show I could hear her.

"Jim's coming down tomorrow, he is staying for a few days, Scott and Steve will be here at the weekend and Mark is coming to see me today, just to make sure we have everything." As she spoke I could feel myself drifting away, back into a deep sleep, and as I did, I was sure I wrinkled my nose, it might have been a dream because I was asleep again. I didn't hear her say "I love you."

CHAPTER 36

Lancers and Indians

"Those poor beggars must be freezing." Charlie turned to see Ernie Miles walking towards him and pointing to a group of Indian soldiers who had taken a position to the right of them. "Indian Cavalry, I heard, and the 12th Lancers are over there to our left, poor beggars it must be a real change for them, this cold and rain."

The 20th Hussars and the 12th Lancers had been in close touch since day one of the war, there were even inter regimental games between the two, when time permitted. Jumping, tent pegging and different activities such as tug of war, agility riding and even football, but now no one seemed to have time.

There was activity daily, contact with the enemy and different patrols to see where the Germans had made strongholds. It was good to be back with the horses, but everyone could see it wasn't going to be for long, the war had virtually become stagnant and from one trench they dug another, safe in the knowledge that the Germans were doing the same just over there. "Over there" could be as little as a hundred yards, close enough to hear them talking at night but woe betide anyone who risked taking a look, the German snipers were deadly so the war of words remained unsighted.

Each Regiment allocated a Troop or Squadron to trench work, whilst the remainder would remain mounted. This would be rotated every three or four days, that way no one was disadvantaged by all the digging. As many as there could be had shovels and part of the daily work party was to fill sandbags with soil, thousands and thousands had to be filled and then placed in front and behind the trench parapet. The Engineers did as much as they could by way of education, but the mounted troops had no idea how to dig a trench. They were, without doubt, getting better at it and it did help keep them warm.

The cow had been moved to a safer location further back in the line. Charles hoped she was okay and being looked after and the others took the Micky out of him for even thinking about it; they were back to condensed milk in their tea though, so he knew she had gone.

That night there was a terrible din, the Indians were shouting and then there was a barrage of rapid rifle fire for quite a few minutes and the whole sector was brought to 'Stand to". Flares were fired into the dark night but no one could see anything, it almost started a panic and very quickly rumours started that the Germans had broken through. It took the seniors a quite a while to settle everyone's nerves and reassure them that the Germans hadn't. Next morning, there were no signs of the alleged attack and, as it turned out, it was just the Indians being a bit trigger happy and jumpy. No one could blame them it was always spooky at night and even shadows looked like the enemy, better to be safe than dead.

All along the front there was a race, this race had a different objective and a very different direction, it was down. Men were digging faster than the Navvies from Ireland, and with each spadeful it ensured that the war would last longer. The

Germans were being most industrious, they were digging a front line but further back, much further, they were digging deeper, more permanent trenches and making concrete bunkers and machine gun posts. They had no intention of giving this ground back and above them the German Air Force was providing a detailed map of where the British where and directing their artillery with devastating effect. Each day the front line of the British trench system was subjected to heavy, accurate, artillery fire and the casualties were mounting up. All along the line different regiments and units swapped the daily drudge of digging and avoiding the shrapnel. The 20th Hussars were spared nothing. Charles noticed the men he knew where becoming hardened, even the quietly spoken were almost ambivalent to the danger. There was an acceptance of their destiny; for most it was life beyond the war but it depended entirely on the turn of a card or the roll of the dice. Fate is a fickle partner and she could change a man's destiny in the blink of an eye.

Back in the communication area, the trenches were more like a series of fox holes for Command Posts. Some were connected by shallow trenches, but these would soon be excavated into deeper walkways and then, in time, trenches. Charles was sat reading a letter from home, it was full of the mundane daily events, Mae was growing, the menfolk were joining the Army as fast as the Army could get them in. Rebecca was in love and missed him terribly, then the questions as to his health and when he would be expected to have leave again, had he written? He smiled at the naivety of the communication between home and the front. He settled further into his seat and composed a reply;

Sept 26 1914 Belgium

Dear Elizabeth

Dearest Sister, I received your letter today and very glad of its company I am, let me tell you. Things here are jolly busy, and the Hun is taking a dreadful beating everyday but he has lots of men, it seems an awful sin to see them all fall but the Kaiser has pushed this Tommy to the edge and stand fast we will.

I had an adventure with a cow this last week but the story will wait until I return, needless to say we had fresh milk and very grateful we all were as well. The charging has briefly stopped and we are busy digging but the Boche are shelling us so it's best to keep one's head down lest it be dispatched from ones shoulders!

I miss sweet Rebecca and I have sent her a reply to her letter, if you see her I trust you might let her know. I am pleased Mae is keeping you on your toes, poor Emily must be done in what with Thomas being away at the camp and her working as well. Are you baby sitting? And does Tom get home much? He is better in England than here, the nights have turned very cold and the rain can be dreadful but today is sunny and I am listening to the birds singing, it is quiet.

Has William been in touch? His Regiment is away, I believe, so he might be getting stuck in. I pray he will be safe, being an infantryman is hard work. I know this because I've had a bash at it these last few days and weeks and its tough going. William will be good at it as long as he can stick it.

Our spirits are good and we are all in rude health, the outside fresh air is so much better than being in the towns.

Well 'Beth, I must sign off for now. I pray God keeps your health and please pass my best regards to all at St John's, remind them we need winter gloves!

Always your loving brother

Charles

He liked writing home, it reminded him of the things he was missing, Rebecca being the newest but he missed a lot. Things had changed when his mother died, he liked his life in the Army, but there still was no place like home.

He heard the clatter of hooves and took a chance peek, things were much safer here in the rear lines and as he looked, he could see a Squadron of Lancers in the near distance. They were going out on a reconnaissance patrol and the sun reflected of the lance heads. He still preferred the sword to the lance, although he had proven he was more than competent with the lance when tent pegging, and, indeed, was highly regarded by both the men in his own Regiment and the Lancers who they competed against. They all knew him now. As he looked, one of the men from the replacements group walked towards him, they nodded and as he walked past he stopped to talk just as a shell screamed from on high and exploded some fifty yards in front of the dug out he was occupying. Large stones and bits of gravel and dirt rained down on them. The man fell onto Charlie's lap, he had a large cut on the back of his head, the cloth cap he had on offered no protection whatsoever and, as he shook his head, the blood ran down the side of his face.

"I'm hit" he exclaimed.

Charlie grabbed a first field dressing from his pack and wrapped it around the wound, it had been a piece of stone that had clouted him on the skull, the cut was long and the bleeding profuse. Charles sat the man down, "Here hold onto this and press it against your head, it'll help stop the bleeding, are you hurt anywhere else?" He couldn't see any other wounds.

Once the man had come back to his senses, Charles said he would help him to the Medical Officer, there was no need to call a stretcher he could walk easily enough.

It was getting somewhat more hazardous in the makeshift trenches and although the digging continued, they didn't offer nearly the protection needed. This was highlighted when one of the more popular Officers was killed by a sniper. He wasn't considered in harm's way, and nobody heard the shot or saw where it came from, it was deadly and efficient and it left 'B' Squadron missing an Officer. The shot was attributed to 'Wolfgang' who had a deadly knack of shooting the most popular and efficient men. It had an upsetting effect on the men all around. This was considered as safe an area that the Regiment occupied, a consideration that was quickly redressed.

CHAPTER 37

Turfed out

It was felt that the Germans were pushing forward. The October weather had a distinct winter's feel and, away to the left of the Regiment, the fighting was heavy. All the men in the reserve trenches were called forward, it appeared that the Germans were making a bit of a push to overwhelm the British lines. Along the line away, there was an old convent and, although it had been mainly vacated by the nuns, a few remained to care for some of the wounded men before they were evacuated to the field hospitals. It appeared that, despite their good intentions, the nuns were in mortal danger as the German Artillery didn't accept the neutrality of religion and often sent shells whistling towards the building. God must have had his protective arms around the boundary though, because of all the shells that were fired at it, very few arrived and even fewer did any damage. This convent was a grand line marker for the British field maps, the line of trenches ran parallel to its boundary. In the remnants of the mid-morning mists, and with the Germans trying to break the British line, it became a rallying point for the 12th Lancers who, once they had resupplied their men with ammunition, were pushed ever further back by the advancing Germans. This retreat left the 20th in a very exposed position, almost on their own they had held the line and, gradually, the advancing

Germans had nearly surrounded them before they realised their predicament. With Germans firing machine guns from the convent all along the British line, it was decided that they too had to retire but to slow the advance down, the 4th Troop of 'B' Squadron would stay and fight until the very last minute. Although there was no panic there was anxious moments of goodbyes and good luck. There was no Officer to command them, as he had been killed by 'Wolfgang' earlier in the day, but Sergeant Bassinthwaite was a good Second in Command. He knew exactly what he had to do and the men all followed him without question.

As Charles and the rest of his troop gave the lads who were staying behind all their spare ammunition, they shook hands and said their farewells. With no more than a whistle they were mounted and away back. 4th Troop set about waiting and harassing the enemy. Each man had twice the allocated amount of ammo, all laid out on sandbags in front of them. As they looked over with steely determination in their eyes, they could see the advancing Germans who seemed unstoppable.

"Right then lads, we are in a bit of a pickle, so make sure you drop as many of the beggars as you can. On my command we give them the lot, don't stop shooting until you're either dead or there are no more Germans walking over that field, do you understand? When we have stopped them, I will blow my whistle for us all to run back. The machine gun is going to cover our withdrawal so stick close but for the love of god keep your heads down. Are we ready? I want a maximum effort." With that the men all faced their enemy, they were about to unleash the fury of hell on the Germans, this was fight or die, it was time. "Ready, Aim,

FIRE" there was a bristle of gunfire and the first line of German Infantry fell, there must have been twenty. Then again, the crack of rifle fire and down went another ten or so. Along the British trench the soldiers loaded and fired as if they were indeed Infantry, no one could have told the difference with the accuracy or rate of fire, it was a fantastic effort and the Germans fell time and again, to the point they were crawling towards the British trench rather than charging it. This had the effect of slowing the advance down to the snail's pace and with each second the Germans were slowed, the more distance the British retreat was able to cover. The first German grenade thrower was shot dead and his bomb exploded and killed more of his comrades, but the second got his bomb away and it flew end over end into the British trench then the next and another straight away. As they exploded they caused great damage to the men who were looking over the top and not at the grenades being thrown. The German Commander instructed his men to lay down heavy concentrated fire at the trench top, and, under the cover of this, he ordered his bayonet men to run to the saps that led to the trench. By doing this he knew he would be able to attack the sides of the British and as soon as they were in place he ordered his men to rush the trench. The battle in the pit didn't last long and although there were only about twenty men of the Hussars, the hundred and fifty Germans had been held long enough. The retreat had been successful, but the sacrifice of the 4th Troop hurt the Hussars deeply. The machine gun that was meant to cover their retreat back was now a scythe to the Germans who, without much care or thought, understood the battle was won and the advance would be easy. As they jumped over the bodies of the men they had just killed in the brutal hand to hand fighting, they were met with a blanket of machine gun fire from the angry and vengeful machine gunners. The bullets ripped into the Germans with an appetite only death can feed and man after man, row after row of Germans fell back into the trench, dead or desperately wounded. It stopped the advance in its footsteps.

By the time the new trenches had been started, the French had sent a Regiment of men to help and the new trench system was quickly made into a substantial defensive position.

Charles and the rest of 'B' Squadron were to be involved with the retaking of 'Wytschaete', or as the Tommies called it 'White Sheets." Little did he know the life changing events that would befall him in the next few days.

CHAPTER 38

Oh fragile life

Wytschaete is an exception to the flatlands of Flanders. Exceptional because there is a slight incline to the top of the series of hills that form the 'Messines Ridge' of no other fame than to the British, everyone else called them the 'hills' that connected Wytschaete to Mesenes. To call it a hill really gives it credit for, in actual fact, it rises about 275 feet from the lowest point. This series of small hills would become the bloodiest of the bloody battlefield in years to come but today, it was relatively quiet. The Germans had occupied it and the British were hell bent on its return to British hands as soon as possible. With the imminent attack, there was a build up of troops. Men of the London Scottish Regiment had arrived but, to support them, the remnants of the 4th Troop of 'B' Squadron were offered the opportunity to take a hateful revenge on the Germans for the loss of their comrades the day before. Charles had stuck his hand up immediately they had been asked who wanted a crack at the 'Hun', as indeed had the rest of the men and several from other Troops and Squadrons. They were all itching for a fight, and the chance to take the fight to the enemy on their beloved horses and climb out of the trenches they had started to loath, was an event not to be missed. Col Edwards the C.O had smiled at the volunteers; these men were his charge and he had great

200

pride in the sterling work they had done so far and, it had to be said, in extreme circumstances; He wasn't surprised by the show of hands.

"Men, Men; quieten down a bit. Pipe down and listen in." The men quickly hushed and he continued;

"No one blames you for taking the fight but remember I have a Regiment to maintain! What a to do if you all gallop off after the Hun and leave me here all alone? That wouldn't do now would it? I need a few men, maybe 50, to help the Infantry rout the enemy from the town, and harass them all the way to Berlin." There was a great holler of laughter from his spellbound audience.

"The first to be picked will be from 'B' Squadron, then if we need to send support, 'A' will back them up, the rest of us will stay here and shout them on. Sergeant Major, take them away and let's be seeing some activity eh?"

With a shout from the Sergeant Major the men knew the drill, first the Squadrons would go and collect their horses form the horse holders who had been bringing the mounts to the front from the paddocks away in the safe zone.

Charles called his old chum and namesake Sam Atherton over to have a chat. Sam had been feeling a bit queer and nervous for a few days but today was the tonic he needed.

"You're going to ride alongside me Sam, I could do with your settling presence if you wouldn't mind." Charles knew his efforts at comforting would be seen through immediately but it would do no harm.

"Charlie Atherton you are a scoundrel, but a good lad at heart. I know you are just trying to chivvy me along but, yes I'd be happier if you were with me when we set off. I am alright but it will steady my nerves a touch to know you're there."

They tacked up the horses, Apollo was as mad as hell, he was jumping on the spot and everyone gave him a bit of room as he kicked out backwards. Charles spoke to him and he settled, it was truly remarkable how he could settle these scared and fractious animals, and men.

The London Scottish had marched over from Ypres away to the North, they had men playing the bagpipes, Sam commented that they looked like a 'wild bunch of buggers' but the pipe music was stirring even though it frightened the horses.

The plan was to advance to a break point when the Infantry would press home the attack and the Cavalry would edge round towards the west of the town ready to pounce on the retreating Germans. As the men gathered, and the different Troop Commanders shouted their orders, it all fell into place and each man seemed to already understand what he needed to do.

Charles looked around him, at the men he had known for, well, a lifetime it seemed. Miles, Clarke, Stanesby and Sgt Blackie. Sam Atherton was with there at his side and, with Apollo in this kind of mood, that might be the safest place after actually sitting on him. The artillery had been letting loose a good amount of fire for about twenty minutes and boom after boom had crashed into the streets and buildings that fronted the advance. This approach gave the Scots a chance to advance right up the main road and engage with any enemy they found alive, they needn't have worried about a reception committee though, the Germans knew this attack was about to happen, after all there had been plenty of announcement with the bloody pipes and Artillery. Bill Blackie was grumbling, that in itself wasn't unusual, but the men had learned to trust his gut instinct, it had kept many of them alive to be here today.

"Those dozy buggers need to be getting on with it, not making all that song and dance and telling the bally Germans we're coming. Right you lot, stick with me and wheel around to the left, try to find some cover by those houses. When I give the order to charge, draw swords and run the bastards down, no mercy mind. If I see anyone giving best to the Hun I'll shoot you on the field, I lost some good friends yesterday, remember they gave us time to get away so we can do this today, make it count."

There was a battle lust beginning to spread and everyone could literally feel their dander rising.

The town was soon in a state of battle. Some of it was from distance but very quickly the machine guns on the German side were bypassed. The initial quietness as the constant rattle of machine-gun fire ceased was quite disturbing, as everyone in the line waited to see if there was an even more hideous method of destruction awaiting just around the corner. There were anxious times, and new developments were arriving on an almost daily basis, and on both sides. The rattle of gun fire was replaced with sporadic rifle fire and then the screams of men dying in hand to hand combat, knife against bayonet, spade against makeshift clubs, the results were ghastly and vicious. The Germans were in trouble, they had met their match in savage killing and quickly the need to retreat became obvious for them. The started slowly at first, just one or two men running away rather than an orderly retreat then, as these men were picked off by sharpshooters, almost as game in the field, the Germans started an organised retreat, four and five men at a time running back fifty yards and then stopping to give covering fire to the next four or five. And so this continued until they were at a place were there was maybe a hundred men ready to charge over the fields to the German lines. In close pursuit, at this point, were the London Scottish, all fired and charged with blood lust, wild undisciplined killers with military training. In some of the skirmishes, it had deteriorated into street fighting bare knuckle and dirty, the men from both London and with Scots backgrounds were well versed in this kind of combat. Headbuts and stabbing at groins, biting and gouging, the Germans were outclassed in every conflict and they were keen to get away.

Quietly, the cavalry stood in the shadows along the walls that surrounded the area before the woods that gave way to fields and the German lines down the hill. Each man and his horse wound as tight as a coiled spring ready to explode into action as soon as the word was given, the words "Draw Swords" tightened every sinew. Bill Blackie could see best; he was at point and, with a premeditated satisfaction, he knew his prey would be on the move any second, he was, as most times, correct. There they were, running. Their equipment was falling off them and hats, backpacks and all unnecessary weight was cast aside, they had been routed, perfect hunting for the cavalry, with a shout of "There they go the dirty beggars" the Officers gave the command and the modern day dogs of war were released.

"Troop will advance to contact, CHARGE." Charles thought there would be more words of command but none came, they would have been wasted and unnecessary the whole of 'B' Squadron was at the gallop. It was as in the hundreds of hours of sword drill they had done, 'Infantry to the left' lean over and stab with the right hand, hold tight whilst you followed your kill to the floor with the tip of the sword and then it would just slide out of the body ready for the next drill. In the past there had been sandbags to practice on, but the real thing was harder, sandbags didn't scream in terror as they realised their fate, and horses never shied away from sandbags. 'Infantry to the right' easier, to stab and follow, much better chance of a clean kill, aim for the throat and let the blade slide into the chest to do its evil work, or righteous depending on which side of the handle you were on.

Charles had taken two before he looked to see Sam with a blighter stuck on his blade, he had stabbed into the ribs and it had stuck fast, the desperate German had grabbed the blade and with a yank nearly unseated Sam. Fortune had favoured the aggressor today and as Charles dispatched the German with a vicious slice to the shoulder he too had to be quick to remove his blade before it became jammed, still the German wouldn't fall. He was a huge man barrel chested and a gnarled, angry face, furious that he had been attacked and determined to make sure the offender had his just returns. Bill Blackie shot him square in the forehead with his revolver and as he died the two swords were released.

"Lads, no more messing about, kill the bastards and move on." Although, in truth, the viciousness of the attack had claimed about sixty of the terrified German Infantry, there were more to dispatch.

There was no warning. It came as thunder does; the deliverance of high explosive at hundreds of miles an hour. If you're in the wrong place you'll pay the price, who decides the place is Madam fate. The first shell lifted a huge crater and an even bigger cloud of thick black smoke, it was a 'Jack

Johnson' a 15cm shell that, like its name sake, liked nothing better than to knock people out only, in this case it was often permanently. The second shell arrived before the first had even exploded, it was followed quickly by a third and fourth. This Artillery support had been called for by the Germans, willing to sacrifice some of their own men to kill as many British men and horses as possible.

As fate would have it, Sam Atherton had allowed himself to drift slightly to the right of Charles, he was no more than ten feet from the second shell when it exploded. It killed him and his horse instantly and, as Charles ducked instinctively to avoid the blast, he was punched in the back by a large piece of shrapnel, a big jagged lump of iron hit him just above the right kidney. It lifted him clean out of his saddle and as it smashed through his fragile frame it took with it bone and nerves, muscle and skin and shredded the lot. Fate is a fickle mistress and, as Charles lay critically wounded, it was but a blessing that he couldn't feel either of his legs or indeed see the huge disfiguring hole in his back. The shrapnel had cut through his leather ammunition strapping and through his uniform. His over the shoulder strap dangled in the wind, and as he flayed around briefly on the floor before consciousness left him he was aware of the warm blood leaving his body. There was no pain.

Apollo, was totally uninjured and apart from being terrified at the sudden dismounting of his rider, who he then stood on, he just trotted back towards the rest of the horses. It was Corporal Stanesby who caught him and realised he was missing his rider. For now, all was quiet. Only four shells had landed, but six men were down, three horses killed and two more wounded which would need to be dispatched. The pitiful whinnying of the wounded horses was an anathema to the Cavalryman but the wounds were severe and brutal. One had a leg missing and, as he tried to stand on three legs, Bill Blackie shot him dead. The rider had died already. The blessings were few and far between but at least they didn't have to remove a hoof, as in the past before this war, when young Officers would gamble horses away and when they lost one claim it had been killed out hunting., These men would be issued with another horse but the QuarterMasters soon cottoned on and from that day, all horses had a number branded into a hoof. This hoof had to be handed back to the QM before a new horse would be issued. But this war had seen enough destruction and everyone knew there was a lot more to come, so leave the poor animal alone once it was dead. Stanesby looked around the area to see if he could see Charles, the place was a slaughter house there were dead bodies all around, mostly German but there, in the near distance he spotted Charles, he looked dead, he wasn't moving and was in a pool of fresh blood.

"Over there, that's Charlie Atherton, on the floor. He's dead." As he dismounted to see his friend and remove his identification tag, Charles was still warm, his life blood was oozing into the Flemish soil, then he frowned. "He's not dead! Stretcher bearer, over here, over here." Charles couldn't really hear what was being said it was all mumbles and he drifted in and out of consciousness. He was aware he was being lifted onto a stretcher but there was no pain, no feeling of anything. His eyes were half closed with swelling, this had been caused by the concussion of the nearby exploding shell and his ears were ringing, so apart from the awareness of voices, he didn't really know who or what was with him.

Had he known, he would have realised the effort that was being made to try to keep him alive, first the other men of his Troop, his friends, had covered him to make sure he didn't get cold. Then, stretcher bearers had lifted him and taken him carefully back to the Regimental Aid Post. Built in an old farm building, the Regimental Aid Post was manned by eight stretcher bearers and the Medical Officer. This was the first real opportunity the Medical Service had a chance to see the wounds properly. The Doctor, a Captain in the Royal Army Medical Corps, was waiting to see him, it was a clear case that he was badly injured. The doctor gave him some morphine and, once this had taken some effect, he rolled Charlie onto his side so he could examine the wound on his back and flank. They cut his uniform away with a penknife and it quickly became obvious that Charles Atherton had been both incredibly lucky and desperately unlucky, in that the bones in his spine had been exposed and therefor infection would very probably kill him. His injuries were severe, much too serious to treat properly here, he would need evacuation to a Base or General hospital, these units had been set up well behind the conflict line, some hundreds of miles away from the fighting.

The next stage of his journey might have killed him quicker than the predicted infection.

The trip in the field ambulance was thoroughly unpleasant until they reached the roads, the high chance of him bleeding from the now packed wounds would prove a constant threat that he would make it; and yet, despite all the odds he was a fighter, and a very fit, muscular fighter at that. The initial bleeding had been profuse, partially fuelled by the huge amount of adrenaline flowing through his terrified body. Each soldier had their point of fear, most hid it, some couldn't, and yet more used it as motivation to fight harder. The one undeniable was they were all scared, it was how you used the fear that made the difference between living and dying. When Charles had been seen by the doctor and pain killing medication administered, his wounds had been cleaned and the large hole where the jagged iron shard had made its mark was packed with a dressing. Then they liberally sprinkled wound powder on top of all the dressings and then a large field dressing was applied to cover the whole area. This was tied around his body and, in itself, could hold about a pint of blood before it dripped onto the floor.

The adrenaline had all gone now and Charles' body was calm. It had been traumatised and violated, abused and, in part, destroyed but, inside the man, his soul and spirit held firm and gave him hope to survive. He still lapsed into unconsciousness but when able he was happy to answer questions; the problem was he was deaf and the voices he was hearing were still badly muffled. A kind face appeared over him, it was a man from the Medical Corps. He cupped Charles' face in both hands to hold his head still and as Charles looked into his eyes he mouthed "go to sleep and rest." Charles understood him and with the understanding came a moment of hope; maybe he wasn't going to die today after all.

CHAPTER 39

Ambulance train to Rouen

When he opened his swollen eyes, the medic had gone. In his place was a young lady, a nurse he thought. She was tending to a man who had lost everything, first he had been shot in the chest, and then when he had survived the horrors of fighting and being shot, he had eventually arrived here on the train. The journey had taken its toll though and, in the end, his weary and worn out heart had just given up. He had been talking to the nurse when he died, he knew he was going to die; and asked if she would pass a message to his father. "Just tell him I did my best and my duty, please; he will understand." With those last few precious words, he squeezed his confidant's hand gently and smiled before he let the darkness of eternal sleep wash over him. It had been a peaceful ending to a very unpleasant few hours.

The nurse wiped a tear from her eye and stroked his dead face one last time before she called two burley stretcher bearers to take him away to the back carriage with the other five dead. She covered his face with the blanket and noticed Charles looking at her. His hearing had improved no end and the gentle rocking of the ambulance train was as soporific as it was nauseating.

"Hello Private Atherton. So, you're awake then. Can you hear me?" She spoke with a very posh accent and was just on the plump side of slim, her uniform fitted where it touched her and was baggy everywhere else. He nodded and then the pain hit him, just where his kidney was on the right side of his back; it was excruciating and as he screwed his face into a pained grimace. She threaded a needle into his arm with such skill he barely felt it.

"This will help the pain, you must lie still. You have a nasty wound to your back." He tried to speak but it sounded very strange to his own ears

"Can you loosen my boots please Miss? They feel very tight and I can't feel my toes."

She looked at his frightened face and reassured him with a simple sweet smile

"Oh, I'll see what I can do to help" and as she lifted the blanket to untie his laces a touch, she realised he had no boots on, just socks. His boots were there under his travel cot-come- stretcher. She touched his warm feet and said "There is that better?"

"No not really Miss, they feel very tight."

"Can you wiggle your toes for me Private Atherton?"

As he tried, there was no movement whatsoever in either foot.

"There, that's a good man. Well done, that should feel better shortly and the medicine I have given you will help with the pain. You can go back to sleep, and rest; we are a long way from Rouen and won't get there until tonight, or maybe even the morning, depending on the tracks, so go back to sleep for now."

He nodded again, through the fog of opiates he felt heavenly, he was sure she had said his toes had moved which was odd, he hadn't been trying to move them.

She held his hand for a moment and reassured him again with a smile and those kind grey eyes with happy lines like sunrays spreading from the edges all framed by a white veil sat on top of her head.

"Thank you Miss. I'm feeling very tired and if I can just have a nap I'm sure I'll feel better. Do you have a name or do you prefer Miss?"

"No, you daft lad, of course I have a name, but Matron will have my guts for garters if she hears you calling me it! My Christian name is Doris, but please call me Nurse Thompson." She winked at him, and he smiled as he thought how forward she was, not at all like his Rebecca, but he liked her all the same. As he slept he dreamed. The dream of a drugged man is restless and often volatile, and this one would prove to be just such a dream.

It started quietly, in the stables with his mates playing cards, he looked at his hand, it was a good score for cribbage. When he placed the cards on the table, he was shocked to see a skeletal hand take them from him. As he looked up, the skeleton was a dead German, he recognised him but didn't know his name, it was the man from the chateau who had broken his leg. Charles opened his eyes wide, he was terrified, he stifled a scream as he realised he was on the train still. The train was stopped at a siding outside the town of Rouen.

Through the window he could see the magnificent spire of a distant church, he missed Saint John's church back home, it made him realise he had asked from his Lord much more than he had offered in prayer and he closed his eyes briefly to ask forgiveness for his apathy and failure as a God fearing man.

Nurse Thompson was in the carriage, she was busy filling in the final reports for the men in her charge. Charles hadn't seen any other nurses, but he had been told by one of the Orderlies that there were five nurses and about 15 male Orderly Medical Staff who did most of the mundane work. There was a Medical Officer and a matron but Charles had no recollection of seeing her.

Nurse Thompson finally came to his cot side, he was the second one up from the floor, the middle cot. There was a bed above his head and an empty cot below his where the poor fellow had died on the journey. There was a metallic smell of blood in his nose and the chemical smell of disinfectant in the air. The upper beds had to contend with cigarette smoke as well which swirled in the ceiling before being sucked out of the rotating vents in the roof. The atmosphere was heady and although there were electric lights all along the carriage, they were dim compared to daylight. Dawn had broken and the mist from the river below obscured the main ground level features of the town, but the spire rose like a beacon of hope for Christian men, and the others who found God when the war found them. Charles had quite gotten used to hearing the cry for 'Mother' and 'Dear God'; he had cried them himself overnight.

The pain had returned to his back, the padding was firm and felt like a lump where there shouldn't be a lump. He was laid, as much as possible, on his left side but, occasionally, he was allowed to roll onto his back and although the train journey had only lasted about 14 hours, it seemed much longer. He was disorientated and had a devilish thirst, he asked Nurse Thompson for a drink of water.

"You'll be being taken off the train shortly Private, we are here all bar the station. I'll let you wet your lips but let the Doctor see you at the hospital before you have a proper drink." She soaked a cloth in some cold water, it wasn't fresh, it had been in the steel bowl for a couple of hours, but it was clean. He sucked the wetted cloth she offered and as the moisture wet his dry cracked tongue, he was caught by a bout of nausea and was nearly sick. She felt his forehead with the back of her hand, he was burning up and had an obvious fever. Privately, she was surprised he had lasted this long but she smiled as she wiped his head with the cool cloth. The swelling around his eyes had gone down a bit so he didn't look quite so cherubic or plump, and she could see his eyes for the first time, he wasn't dead but he was close, the shine had disappeared from his normally bright eyes.

"How are those toes feeling? Can you move your foot for me again?" He tried and, once again, she said what a good job he had done but he knew; he knew his feet hadn't moved, he couldn't feel them any longer or his legs. He had confirmed this himself by sticking his finger into his left leg, he had nipped the skin but felt nothing, he knew he was paralysed but didn't want to accept it, he wouldn't accept it.

"Where are they taking us Nurse?"

"You're going to the hospital, it's a big General Hospital where there are better, more modern facilities to help you recover."

He was, in fact going, to a General Hospital in some grand buildings near the racecourse, but there were quite a few more than this one, large, hospital and different casualties categories would be sent to more specialised hospitals to stabilise their conditions before their onward journey to Britain for recuperation.

CHAPTER 40

Fresh linen and new friends

The road trip in the ambulance was terrible, it rocked on the roads and each bump in the road caused Charles to wince in pain. To make matters worse, the other two casualties in his ambulance were being sick so the smell of sweet vomit clawed at his throat and nose. The heater was on but it was still very chilly in the back, worse for the driver who had no cover or windows to shelter him from the rain.

The General Hospital was about a twenty-minute drive away from the train yard where he had been unloaded, he had kissed Doris Thompson's hand as she said her goodbyes.

"Thank you, Nurse, you are an angel and I am sorry if I was weak, you have been wonderful." She waved him away with a blush, her work was about to begin, all the carriages needed disinfecting and washing, all the floors needed mopping and the blood cleaned away. Then back to the train for some sleep whilst they traveled back for more casualties in the morning. "Goodbye Private, good luck and get better soon." She didn't hold out much hope for him, his fever was worse and his wound had bled overnight but she had to concede he had a spirit she only saw in brave men and the world needed brave men.

By the time the motor ambulance had arrived at the hospital, there was a greeting party. A Medical Officer, who cast an eye over the casualties as they were unloaded; he then dictated where they went and to which ward. A number of nurses of the hospital, all ready to redress or undress wounds so they could be seen quickly by the Doctor, and an Admin Sergeant Major, with his Orderlies, who transported the casualty to the right ward or department.

Charles was seen fairly quickly but he was held over; he had two problems that needed consideration. He had an open wound and a fever. The wound wasn't considered dangerous to other patients, but the fever could be contagious, so he was sent to an isolation ward for a checkup. The wound surgeon would visit him there later in the day.

Charles was more awake than he had been for the past couple of days, the memory of what had happened was haunting. Sam hadn't been a particularly close friend, he was a good mate, but to see him just disappear like that was terrible, his horse hadn't faired any better.

Now, just two days later, he was here in Rouen, so far away from the battle and worse for him, so far away from his mates; he felt very alone. There was hustle and bustle all around as the new casualties had arrived and were in the process of documentation and allocation to different areas of the hospital. The smell of carbolic permeated the air and although he was still on the transport stretcher his bed was made and ready.

"The Doctor will want to look at your wound before we get rid of that filthy uniform." Charles hadn't heard the Nurse and Orderly approach, they were behind his head but, as they came into view once more, he was greeted with a smiling face. They looked at his tag, tied onto his lapel it had his name, Unit and wound priority written on it.

"We need to get you cleaned up a bit then the surgeon will have a look at your wound. Let's be having you then and get that jacket blouse off." It wasn't until then that Charles realised he had lost his ammunition belt that normally sat across his shoulder and chest. His boots were on the end of the stretcher and as he looked he realised he wasn't easily sat up because his legs didn't work.

The two nurses hooked an arm under his armpits and with a one, two, three hitched him more upright. It was the first time since he had been wounded that he was able to look people in the eye in the right plane, he felt a bit dizzy.

"Catch your breath soldier, it's going to be a bit uncomfortable whilst we sort you out." It was the male Orderly who spoke, he had a soft voice with a northern accent.

"Where you from?" asked Charles.

"Accrington" said the orderly "You?"

"Farnworth, near Bolton, do you know it?"

"Aye, I did some training in Bolton Royal before I joined up." As they chatted, the Nurse helped undress Charles. First, they put his boots on the floor and then his socks in his boots, so as not to lose them, then they started to maul about with his breeches and 'puttees'- the long bandage like strip that covered his boots and lower calf almost up to his knee. Normally, they would unwrap them but they just cut Charles' off with a pair of shears His lower half was soon exposed and a rug covered his dignity, it was about the last time he would be afforded any. His top was shredded and matted with blood. The bandage and field dressing had done their job and stopped the bleeding, but it was obvious as soon as the area of the wound was exposed that it had stuck fast to his flesh.

If Charles had no feeling in his legs, he had plenty in his back and as the Nurse tried to unreel the dressing, the pain that shot through him was as electric. He let out a yell of agony and instantly apologised, he didn't wish to come across as awkward or a 'difficult sort' but there had to be a way they could minimise the pain. He asked them, "Please go steady, that's very sore."

"It has to come off, and we shouldn't really soak it because that might make it bleed again. I'll go slowly" said the Nurse as she cut the strands off the field dressing and carefully peeled the dressing away from the padding that lay underneath. She was surprised at the depth of the packed in swabbing, she would have to chance it and wet this under layer. It would be far too painful to lift it off without.

After an eternity wracked in pain and soaked with sweat, it was decided that the best way to remove this dressing was for Charlie to soak in a salt bath, he felt dreadful and just wanted to sleep. He could feel his heart pounding and despite an injection of morphine it was taking its toll on his young body. There was an infection brewing inside of his tired and abused frame; it made the imminent dressing change more important, it quite literally was becoming a case of life and death.

The bath was a real one, a proper porcelain bath, he hadn't had one in a proper bath since he had left for France.

The Nurse poured salt into the warm, almost hot, water, this poor lad needed a rest but she knew the surgeon would be on the ward within the hour so the dressing had to be removed and the area given a good clean. These wounds looked far worse on arrival, what with all the dried blood from the journey, and, if she was honest, she felt cross that the nurses further up the line didn't clean them a bit more, but she was grateful that the lad was here. Some of those poor lads were in a terrible state and more than enough died either en route or within a few hours of getting to the wards, their poor hearts couldn't take any more suffering. She swished the water to make sure the salt had dissolved.

On a trolley set up next to her, was a new set of dressings, she knew the wound would bleed when it was cleaned, so there was plenty of gauze and lint to catch any blood. The new steriliser equipment had been working overtime but the wounds where they had used the sterilised instruments had shown great improvement and the infections seen were much less than expected. The steel dishes they used made it so much easier and as she carried the dressing pack to the trolley, Charles was about to be helped in the bath.

He knew he had no feeling in his legs but it came as a real surprise when he realised he had no use of them either. Two burley medical staff helped him stand, but it was less standing than lifting and, as they tested the water again to make sure it wasn't too hot, and as they lowered him into the fresh warm water he was aware that not only was he shivering but he was also filthy. He didn't feel his feet getting wet, or his bum but he could feel the warm water around his thin stomach and as the water soaked into the dry crusty dressing. It loosened rapidly and without any pain it flopped out into the salty water, then the blood turned the water pink so he was lifted out and laid on his stomach on the clean dressing couch. A new, clean dressing was placed over the top and as he dried slowly he could feel his temperature slowly drop, it made him feel much brighter.

The Medical Officer was a Lieutenant Colonel MacDonald. He had trained in Edinburgh as a Doctor before becoming a Surgeon and joining the army some 10 years ago. He was a soldier's man., He understood soldiers and their ways, in general they were tough and gritty but, as in all walks of life, there was the 'skivers' and malingerers he made short work of those, quite often with a very unpleasant enema. He found it to be very effective in reducing false claims of sickness.

He nodded at the Nursing Sister, a Nursing Officer in the Queen Alexandra's Imperial Military Nursing Service, or the QAIMNS as they were mainly referred to. She lifted the towel from Charles' back wound. It was a ghastly, jagged wound, deep and destructive. The soft tissue had all been ripped away exposing the deep tissues that connected the bones of his spine to the muscles that made it work. The bleeding had stopped and the wound looked unnervingly clean.

"Gloves" it was all he said, all he needed to say, and a pair of very thin rubber gloves appeared, he used talcum powder on his hands as he pushed his long slender fingers into the glove.

"Now Lad, it looks like the Hun has had a piece of your back away here. I'm just going to have a closer look then we can have a chat. If it hurts just let me know."

Charles nodded, he was very nervous and more than a bit scared, he wasn't the bravest but he wasn't soft either, he would do his best to endure.

As Colonel MacDonald looked deep into the wound the first thing he noticed was the pulsing artery that ran down the spine, it was quite intact and fully functioning but dangerously exposed. There, next to the white bones of his spine sat a huge splinter of iron, an ugly spike that had broken away from the large piece of destructive shrapnel as it passed through the soft skin and muscle. He knew it would need to be removed but it was sat frighteningly close to the kidney, which was still oozing blood. He didn't take long looking into the cavernous hole, he looked up and scratched his nose, he knew this was a serious injury. It was time to look at the paralysis of the soldier's legs, he was fairly sure he knew what was causing it but he needed to look at the surgery on the wound before he tackled the paralysis.

"Now Private, it all looks a bit grim back there, but I need to get a splinter of iron from inside. It's not the worst I've seen so that's good. I need to pack the wound once I've debrided some of the dead flesh that will become infected if we don't get it sorted. Then this loss of movement in your legs, I'm fairly sure it's because you have had a thump on your spine. I think the movement will come back, but it might take a while. I'll operate today and clean everything but because you have a fever you will come back to this ward until I'm sure you don't have anything infectious. How does that sound lad?"

Charles was relieved he didn't let himself down by crying out, and, even more so, that it wasn't going to be long before he was on the mend. He felt better since his bath. He was just very tired again.

"Now lad, it seems as though you have lost quite a bit of blood over the last couple of days so we need to get you sorted. Sister here will make sure you are clean then off to the operating theatre and I'll see you there in about thirty minutes. Don't worry lad, we'll do a grand job, I promise." With that, he stood and left, calling back to the waiting entourage "half an hour mind, no longer.

Charles was washed and put into a nice clean bed, it had linen sheets, they were lovely, with real pillows as well.

Charles was given an injection of Morphine and Atropine into his numb leg and told it would make him drowsy, as if he needed anything to help him sleep. Within a few minutes, he was sound asleep, the first time for a long time that he had no dreams, just a deep empty void in total darkness that eluded most soldiers for most of their service lives.

He was wheeled to the operating theatre still soundly asleep. He had no recollection of the rubber mask they placed over his face or the pungent chemical smell of ether, and, in a few moments, he was anaesthetised ready for surgery.

When he woke, he was aware of a pain in his side. It was a small drain placed there to allow any blood or fluids to come out of the now smaller cavity. Most of the wound had been sewn together after they surgeon had debrided all the dead tissue and removed an ugly metal splinter that was 4 inches long. It had come to rest just under his right kidney and had, indeed, nicked the plump blood filled organ so it oozed blood continuously, not in any great volume, but enough to make Charles anaemic, which hadn't helped his general ability to fight the inevitable infection he was now suffering.

Whilst he was asleep, the nursing staff had cleaned him thoroughly; even his nails had been manicured and later he would have his head shorn close cut to help keep his vulnerable body clean. He had a thirst, he was desperate for a drink and as a Nurse came to see him he croaked in a broken voice "Please, can I have a sip of water?"

It was a new Nurse, he hadn't seen this lady before, and, as all the others before her, she had an incredibly beautiful face framed in a veil of white and a spotless clean uniform with a tippet of scarlet and grey.

"Hello there, Private Atherton. Come back to join us have you? You have been sleeping for a whole day. We thought you were never going to wake up. I'll tell the doctor you're awake, he's doing his rounds so you're just in time."

Colonel MacDonald came and sat on his bed. He placed his hand on Charlie's forehead, he nodded and smiled.

"Good man, you're doing well. I have a memento for you, a bloody great piece of German shell that was sitting near your spine. Its what's been causing your legs not to work and, although it might take a few weeks for them to work properly, I expect them to be working soon. You had a nasty temperature but we have cleaned you up and I've managed to close the wound after taking all the damaged skin and muscle away. You're dammed lucky to be alive lad, it was a close thing. Now, I want you to rest a while. We will start moving you around a bit, I don't want you getting a pneumonia, are you a smoker?"

Charles felt a tear fill his eyes, he didn't quite understand why he felt so emotional,

"No Sir, I haven't ever smoked, it's not great for my swimming."

"Good man, plenty of rest then and Sister will look after you. A few days on this ward then we might see about getting you back to Blighty, how does that sound?"

Charles thought about home, he was very relieved that he wasn't in too much pain, just a dull ache. His head was a bit wooly and his throat was as dry as straw, but he could take sips of water and, as he pulled the sheets and blankets over himself again, he found himself smiling at how lucky he had been. Fresh cotton sheets and pillows and good grub before a spot of time in Blighty. He considered being wounded as not the worst that could happen. He looked around the ward. Opposite him there was a chap with no leg.

He was sitting up in bed but he smiled at Charlie and said hello. His name was David Smith and he was a Scot from the Gordon Highlanders. He had a very pleasant manner and was happy when Charlie told him of his time with the Gordons. Smith remembered the poor chap that had been killed on horseback with Charlie a few weeks ago, and they knew one or two people from the swimming baths back in Colchester. In the next bed, was another Scot, Alistair Miller, or 'Windy' to his friends. He was from the London Scottish that had attacked Wytschaete, he had been badly shot up by a machine gun and had been hit three times in the stomach and chest. Although very badly wounded, he would live; and, despite the fact that he shat his uniform every time he coughed or laughed, he was happy. They would be mates for the time they shared the ward. Charles soon discovered that coughing and laughing were not comfortable pastimes, he held a sympathy for his new friend.

Once Charles had managed to drink and cure his dreadful thirst, he was allowed to sleep. He remembered his friends and said a prayer for their safe keeping and, as he signed off, he thanked God for his life, and Colonel MacDonald. Sleep was easy, but only as long as he stayed on his left side. It was as if he was being stabbed when he tried to move onto his right but the nurse gave him a pillow to wedge under his right buttock, this had the effect of keeping him on his left so he was at last comfortable; and with that, he fell into a dreamless a sleep that is as much as any soldier could ask, guiltless and confident his fight is right.

CHAPTER 41

The road to recovery is long

Over the next few days, Charles noticed his condition was improving rapidly. Yes he still had a drain in his side and yes it was still producing blood stained fluids, but he felt better. He was noticeably stronger and, if he tried, he could imagine he could feel, if not move, his toes. Well not all his toes, he wouldn't be able to tell if you were to ask which toes he could feel. Certainly, when the nurses tried to test him, he failed each and every time. They would touch his foot and he felt nothing then when they had taken their touch away he felt them. If he was asked to wriggle a toe, he simply couldn't but he was so sure they nearly moved each time.

The lads in the opposite beds were merciless in taking the mick, but it was all good honest banter and no offence was ever taken.

'Windy' hadn't faired so well, he had taken a turn for the worse and a lung had collapsed while he was asleep. If it hadn't been for 'Smithy' he would never have survived. As always, these things seemed to happen at night when the nursing staff would be busy doing menial tasks, such as sheet washing and stocking up on the important supplies. All this in between being hellish busy looking after the poor blighters who were in a much worse state than this end of the ward, and any new arrivals transferred in from the barges, which tended to carry the wounded throughout the day and arriving at tea time. Either way it was dark and often wet and always cold.

Windy had tried to cough, he woke with a fearful cry as he realised his breathing was nearly impossible. Fortunately Smith was awake and called for help. The nurses were magnificent, and within a very few minutes, there was a Doctor and nurses all around his bed. Charles couldn't see what they were doing but he could see that Windy was sitting up with a pillow in his stomach. After a few moments he heard him cry out, not in anguish, but in relief that he could draw the cold night air into his lungs once more. The electric lights made the area of the ward as if it was daylight, it had taken a bit of getting used to for Charles, they didn't have electric at home yet and at night they would sit with an oil lamp lighting the room it was dim but comfortable. 'Beth would either play the piano and sing with the boys, or she would be darning and humming to herself. Even when he had joined up, the lighting had been mainly gas lamps and since they had come to France, it had been summer, so no lighting was really needed. Certainly, this long exposure to electric lights had been a new thing for him.

As he looked over to Windy, he could see now the hullabaloo had finished, they had fitted a bottle to him, not dissimilar to the one Charles had but Windy had one that bubbled when he breathed out. Charles later learned it was called a chest drain and it would help the lung grow back into place. The three mates were due to be moved to their new ward tomorrow all of them had come in with high fevers and now that there was no sign of 'flu' or infection, they needed to be moved back to the general wards. Charles took a few minutes to call the Night Nurse over to thank her for the wonderful care she had administered to him. He had gotten on famously with the two Medical Orderlies as well and he shook their hands as they were about to leave for their beds in the morning.

He had filled in a postcard for home, it was a simple card heavily censored to give no information other than the essentials. As he signed it he read it and hoped that the section where it said 'I have been wounded' wouldn't scare his sister or Rebecca; he was sure they would pass the message on to Rebecca he hadn't written home for a while and since he had been wounded he hadn't received any mail, so he knew it was important to let them know he was alright. It would serve no purpose to tell them he was paralysed and had a huge wound in his back; besides if everything went to plan, he would be in 'Townleys' Hospital soon enough, and that was just up the road for them to visit. He decided he wouldn't build their hopes up, he might go to somewhere else, what if Townleys was full of injured soldiers?

As daylight broke the night, Charles was relieved to see his mate sat up and although he was in obvious pain, he was smiling, he was able to say to both Charles and Smithy

"That was a bit rough, I managed to shit myself, again." As the three men tried for all they were worth not to laugh, there was a huge bubble in Windy's bottle and he started coughing and laughing. Charles was very sore when they laughed but it did him the power of good, he wasn't so sure about Windy.

CHAPTER 42

Cowards are shot

It was another two days before and letters followed and finally caught up with Charles. Certainly, the card he had written home wouldn't have arrived there yet, so these must have crossed in transit. As he sat in bed, it cheered him to be able to close his eyes and imagine Rebecca writing in her front room back home. He was as shocked as he was surprised, and as surprised as he was glad, at the news the letter brought.

My Dearest Charles,

I trust to God that this letter finds you in rude health and fighting fit. We received a letter from you and it made me so proud to be known as 'your girl'. Things here are much the same, the horses are nearly all gone from the mill and Arthur Davies, the Drayman, asked to be remembered to you when I next wrote. He has lost his four in hand and I'm sure he won't mind me telling you he was as distraught as if his children had gone to war. Poor man has nothing now they have gone, and Mister Jenkins has replaced the draught with a lorry. They are teaching Arthur to drive it, but he was heard shouting "whoa" to the truck the other day. He had forgotten how to stop it and it bumped into the gate house at Kersley Mill!. We did laugh, all of us, including Mr Jenkins. He was very understanding; Poor Arthur was very embarrassed but no one was cross really.

I have some more news from this side, but it is rather delicate and concerns that brute Alf Green. It was in the Bolton Evening News that he has been shot. I then heard from a friend he was shot by firing squad for deserting. It turns out he had deserted before but, this time, they caught him without his uniform and no rifle. He had been made to join up by the Magistrate in Birmingham, else he would go to jail for being a ruffian and causing an affray. He was no good Charles, I wish he had never crossed my path. Still it's an end to bad rubbish and I'm sure his mates won't miss him, he was nothing but a coward and trouble from the start.

I saw Emily this morning, she says that Thomas is enjoying being at the camp, he had been promoted to Lance Corporal (I'm sure that means more to you than me) but it does mean he gets a bit more money. His duties keep him away from home during the week but he is home at the weekends so Mae sees plenty of her daddy and she is growing so quick, she'll be a young lady when you next see her.

Elizabeth is grand, she is so nice to me and my mother, we pop in for tea and mum makes cakes, it's a right little tea party!

Well my soldier, I will write again later in the week. God keep you safe and remember your girl misses you but glows with pride to know her man is soldiering on the front.

Ever your sweetheart

'Becca

He sat and read it again, twice. Alf Green shot by firing squad was justice served on a coward. He pondered if he would ever desert. He had seen men nearly go mad because of the shell fire and each time they failed, they were picked up by the rest of the lads and made sound again. Each man was a friend, and each friend knew the others were as scared as they were, but no one had run, well except maybe the group that had been taken prisoner. He felt sick that they wouldn't return to the fight. He was off like a shot when his chance came and, sat here with a pipe in his back, was as a result of him coming back to the war.

The move to the new ward had gone very smoothly. There was an ambulance train leaving for Blighty this afternoon and the hospital was quiet for a change. It was a moment of peace in a mad world of tragedy and destruction, the Nurses were dog tired and this was a chance for them to rest. There had been some new nurses arriving and the old girls had had a chance to sleep in their Mess. He didn't know the new nurses on his new ward yet, but they were all angels to him and the lads, God help the Hun if they ever harmed one of these ladies. He had heard that the Germans were committing atrocities all over Flanders and in France. He didn't have any time for bullies and, if he could, he would be back to his mates to sort the Hun out as soon as he was healed.

It was a terribly cold day, he had clean uniform on and he was sat in a chair. Windy was in the next bed now, and Smithy was due to go back to Blighty that afternoon. He would miss Smith, he was a good man and funny. At night he would sometimes hear him crying at the pain in his foot and then he would curse because he knew the foot to be gone and the pains were a constant reminder of the fact he would never run or play football again. The day helped put those thoughts to the back of his mind and he busied himself on a deadly pair of crutches, he fell over at least five times a day, and each time he would roar laughing at his predicament.

Windy had somehow got his hands on a pack of playing cards, but Charles didn't really know how to play other than cribbage. Smithy had been his partner at cards and he was good. He sighed, he would miss his new mate, a lot.

CHAPTER 43

Home, but a million miles away

It was the Colonel who came to give him the good news, news he had been hoping for but thought it might be impossible.

"Well there young Atherton, how are you getting on? Sister tells me you can sometimes feel your feet but it's all a bit hit and miss? Well I have some news for you, you're going back to Blighty to a hospital that specialises in the very problem you are suffering from. I'm sending you to the Royal Victoria Hospital, Edinburgh. It's a specialist neurological unit for cases just like you and, incidentally, where I trained, oh, a million years ago. There's a chap there called Professor Dylan Durant-Jones. I've written him a letter and he is more than happy to see you. Now I'm fired up to have you away tomorrow if we can get that drain out in a second or two without any problems."

Charles was quite taken aback, Edinburgh? He had hoped to be going back to Bolton but if this Professor could help him walk again that would fit the bill splendidly.

"Oh thank you Sir, that would be very good wouldn't it, do you think my legs will get better Sir? They are starting to get some feeling back, but I just never know if it's real or a bit like Smithy's foot pain Sir. Is it real or am I imagining it?"

The Colonel patted him on the shoulder and gave him a beaming smile, his big moustache twitching, it highlighted his kind face. "If anyone can sort those pins out laddie, its Durant-Jones. He's truly a magician and what you're feeling in your legs is good because it shows me that you have nerves working in that bruised old spine of yours. Each day they will get better and you will get stronger. And besides, we need to get you away because a little bird tells me that Sister here is taking a shine to you!"

"Colonel!!" It was Sister and she was puce with embarrassment. The Colonel laughed out with a good roar.

Charles wanted the world to swallow him, he hadn't ever thought anything like that. The Sister was a lady and well above his social standing he blushed purple fit to burst and the Colonel laughed again at his mischievous joke.

"Right let's have this drain out once and for all Sister. Captain Dodson will be along presently, if you can just make this brave young chap ready, we'll have it out in a jiffy." With that he stood and laughed again as he walked past the carnage he had created with one well aimed jibe.

"The wound looks good Sister, there's a bit of scabbing but that'll take no harm. Those stitches can come out today as well and a dry dressing please." Captain Dodson was a tall thin Doctor with black hair and small round spectacles. He spoke with a perfect Oxford accent and he was clearly a gentleman. He was new and had finished his training as a soldier only a few weeks before. A member of the Officer Cadets at the University in Oxford; he had been qualified as a doctor for exactly 16 weeks. He had seen more in a month than most post graduate doctors would see in 10 years and his surgical techniques had improved so rapidly that he was now taking the more simple cases himself. Once he had the confidence to treat medical and surgical conditions in a few more weeks, he would be posted to a Battalion as the Medical Officer. Colonel MacDonald would have liked to have him for longer. He had proved to be a huge asset and was clearly gifted as a surgeon, but everyone knew the Regiments needed more Medical Officers as more and more Battalions were being formed. He was resigned to losing Dodson and being stuck here at a base hospital; and although the top brass had been keen for him to take a Command, he was too old and dyed in the wool, Command wasn't for him.

Charles was dressed in his new tunic and trousers, his boots having been polished and, although he couldn't feel them on his feet, he knew he looked smart again. He was sat in a wheel chair and even though it hurt his side when he turned he liked being moved about a bit, it meant he could chivvy some of the lads further down the ward up a bit.

Windy was being evacuated back to Blighty as well. They would be leaving on the same train in the morning about 10:00hrs.

The weather was getting really cold, it was December and no one should be surprised it was freezing. Snow had fallen just the once and it had gone by lunchtime the next day, Charles thought about his mates on watch and hoped they had enough winter coats. Apollo would need extra rations, he was a devil for shivering off his condition and, in no time, he would be thin as a hat rack if they didn't keep his food going in. He didn't think he would be home for Christmas but if the weather carried on getting colder, he was sure the fighting would stop. No one would be able to move supplies or men and it made sense that they close the trenches till spring. To him that made perfect sense, it meant everyone could collect their casualties and equipment. The war wouldn't be over by Christmas but he wouldn't be part of it, he would be in Scotland learning to walk. After that he didn't know what the future held but he had bridges to cross and the best way is one at a time, that's what his mother had always told them, it sounded like good advice today.

CHAPTER 44

Scotland, the home of the haggis

The next day was a significant day for Charles, first he met one of the lads from his Unit, and then he was due to leave on the train to the dockside to be loaded onto a hospital ship to Blighty.

Stan Goodwin was from 'A' Troop and he had been injured in a skirmish on the Belgian border. He had been shot in the back whilst trying to escape an ambush. The Troop had been chasing some *Ulans* and were catching them when they rode into some woods. That's where the ambush was set up, a couple of horses had been killed and a few men had been injured, but the Troop had been quick to retreat and had escaped the worst of the ambush. The Germans had been too keen to fire and the lads weren't fully in the killing zone, so had managed to ride into the woods and separate 'toot sweet' so causing the machine guns a fair bit of confusion they had managed to turn their own guns on themselves whilst trying to follow the tracks of the rapidly retreating British. Stan had copped a loose round and it had smashed into his back, he managed to hang on till the Troop reassembled but had fallen off when they got back. He had taken a proper beating and he lost a lot of blood but sheer stubborn will had made him hang on.

He was able to give Charles the news of the Unit. In general, it had been really quiet in their sector, and the rumour was they would be heading back to the front up towards Ypres. But for now, they were in the background of any action. He had been really unlucky to get wounded, the Unit hadn't really suffered any losses since Charles was injured.

Charles was busy chatting when he heard a familiar voice and it made him look up in surprise.

"Atherton you skiving bugger, are you still injured?" It was the dulcet tones of Sergeant Bill Blackie.

Blackie wasn't injured, he had been tasked with bringing mail and some personal effects for Charles and Stan. He was going home on leave to Scotland and had managed to cadge a lift on the hospital ship. It meant he would have to work his passage by pushing a chair or carrying a stretcher, but he was more than happy if it meant he got a couple of extra days at home.

Charles was really pleased to see him, he shook hands and told him all about his wound and, unfortunately, his legs. Blackie filled him in with all the news from 'B' Squadron; the new arrivals and a couple of the chaps who had gone off to train to be machine gunners. Lieutenant Golding had been seconded to the Royal Flying Corps to learn to be a pilot. The main news though, was that the 20th Hussars had been virtually dismounted and would be spending more time in the trenches and less time charging around, at least for the foreseeable future. The horses were staying, but way back in the line. They would be used but much less than they had, it was happening to a lot of the mounted units, there just wasn't the need for fast Cavalry now the Germans had dug in. Truth was no one was going far.

Bill Blackie asked the Transport Orderly if he could stay with Charles, he might as well be useful to someone he knew, it was quickly agreed. Charles was a wheelchair case so was fairly easy to move. Bill piled his gear onto a trolley with Charles' stuff and, with a kiss for the Nursing Sisters and a heartfelt thanks to the Orderlies, he put his cap on and was on his way. There were fond farewells as the train steamed up, all along the platform Nurses and Doctors said their "good lucks" to the men they had so lovingly cared for. Some men cried openly, whether with relief that it was over or in deference to the wonderful care they had received, no one seemed to mind. A lot of the wounded were troubled by shock and their mental wellbeing had been helped greatly by the men and women of the hospital. So emotional outbursts weren't admonished, just a caring hand from quite often, the most unexpected, the other casualties. Colonel MacDonald waved and laughed his wards away, his job was done, until the afternoon when another train would come from the front and it would all start again.

The train to the docks was a happy place to be. Men, wounded so viciously and in many cases so disabling were at last going home. Their futures were uncertain but within the next 24 hours they would be in Blighty. For many their war was finished, but new challenges at home waited. A lot of them were without limbs, about half the men had lost a leg, some both, but they all remained cheery, it was one of the things that had been a constant comfort to Charles. The camaraderie and banter and the sheer unwillingness to moan about the hand they had been dealt was as refreshing as it was remarkable. With a spirit like that there could only possibly be one outcome to this war, the Germans could never win, not in a million years.

It didn't take long before the train arrived, and there waiting, was the Hospital Ship Salta. She was much bigger than Charles had expected, two large funnels with smoke turning out of the top. It didn't take very long to load everyone and, within the hour, they were at sea. They were bound for Le Havre to pick up more men but a change in orders meant they sailed less than half full back to Southampton.

Charles laughed, they couldn't be much further from Edinburgh if they had stayed in France. The train ride was going to take forever, but Bill was good company, and he was exceptionally relaxed chatting to Charles, he knew Charlie had been a good soldier and he had known him for more than two years so the rank difference wasn't really an issue.

Somehow, when they got back on dry land and after Bill had cleaned up from being ill with sea sickness, they were able to stay together on the ambulance train bound for the north. They would change at Doncaster and transfer onto a different train bound for Scotland. It would take them overnight to arrive but there was hot tea and sandwiches provided. Bill shouldn't really have been on the train, but somehow he managed to convince the nursing staff that Charles was in his care and it helped that he was happy to assist with any lifting so he was allowed to travel.

It was raining heavens hard all the way up north. The train rushed its way towards the darkened clouds. As night fell, Charles could see the hot embers from the boiler drift past his window and, if he looked towards the engine, he could see the red glow of the fire.

Sat towards the front of the first carriage afforded them the smoothest ride and, at various stops, different carriages were uncoupled and new ones attached, but it never interfered with the journey because their carriage never changed.

The elation of escaping France mixed with the weariness of all the travel was taking its toll on the various men. Some asleep would cry out as if in pain and others scream in terror only to be soothed by the Staff Nurses and Medics. No one was immune it seemed, and Charles had bad dreams as much as anyone, always the same one with the man and his skeletal hand playing cards. Bill Blackie had pulled up his collar, and whilst he smoked his pipe, it was the only give away he was awake, he was lost in a quiet place called solitude, it was a seldom visited place, and he welcomed the chance to spend some time there.

After what seemed a lifetime, the train pulled into some sidings on the south side of Edinburgh Waverley station. All along the sidings stood a line of ambulances ready to take the men from the train. The Loadmaster Clerk had a list with passenger names and to which hospital they were being sent.

Atherton was one of the first names on the list, he was allocated to an ambulance. He shook hands with Bill Blackie whose onward journey would be on Hobbs pony. It was a foul night, but the smile from Bill showed how pleased he was to be home. There was a tram service just at the station, he wouldn't have far to walk.

They loaded Charles onto the ambulance along with another man, who was blind and had a terrible facial wound. He was swathed in bandages and Charles couldn't help but feel a bit of a fraud in comparison he was only paralysed in his legs, the wound in his back ached terribly but there was no complaint. Not only was his companion blind, he had lost most of his jaw and the majority of his tongue, there would be no conversation on the way. An Orderly acted as Medic and guide for the poor fellow. He dribbled constantly and the escort dabbed his dressing as he spoke to him reassuringly.

"No long now Tam" he nodded to Charles "We will get there in about twenty minutes."

The wind whistled along the road and drove the rain headlong into them, sleet and snow would follow later in the day.

The daily bustle in Edinburgh started early and when they saw the line of ambulances leaving the sidings there was a spontaneous cheer and applause. Men took off their hats and waved them in appreciation of the service the passengers had given. This wasn't the first train to arrive and it wouldn't be the last but they cheered everyone they saw.

The facade of the hospital showed its grand history, it wasn't large, but it was an exquisite annex to a much larger hospital. Charles was delivered to a door where there was a Nurse waiting along with an Orderly, he was huge and broad shouldered, he had bushy curly hair and looked just a bit feral. But when he spoke, he was struck with a dreadful debilitating stammer, the reason he wasn't in the Army was he was nearly unable to talk. Despite his speech impediment, he was cheerful and as strong as a bear. He moved Charles with ease and, as the nurse spoke, Charles realised the ambulance had gone, taking with it the poor disfigured soldier to a different area of the hospital.

It didn't take long for the paperwork and a bed to be allocated, they had prepared most of the admin beforehand it was just the detail they were missing.

Charles was tired, his back was very sore and there was a bit of a discharge from the wound site. It quickly became obvious that it was infected. The choices were either to open the wound and let any infection out or pack it with EUSOL, the cure-all from Edinburgh along with Iodine . The decision was, seeing as he was going to stay anyway, to reopen the wound. The smell was nasty, and there was some concern as to what was lying under the sutured wound. The plan was to take Charles to the operating theatre to open the wound and there was space in the late afternoon. Charles hadn't eaten for quite a few hours so the Surgeon was happy that he could have gas and not vomit. It was also noted his fever had returned but he hadn't really noticed because he had been asleep for quite a bit of the journey.

Once changed out of his uniform, he was issued a set of hospital 'blues', which was a sort of uniform itself and identified the wearer as an inpatient of the hospital; he had a bath and changed into a theatre gown, a bit like a nightshirt but open at the back for ease of access. He lay on his bed sort of propped up so he could see what was going on. The ward was very busy with comings and goings and decorations being put up for Christmas, he hadn't thought there were so many wonderful colours of paper rings and, at the end of the ward, there lay a yule log. It was decorated already, and the thoughts of Christmas and the blokes left behind left him feeling a bit melancholy, he hoped the war was quiet and that common good sense would prevail for the Christian festival. It reminded him that the Indians were in the same trench and he wondered if they would celebrate along with the other soldiers. He didn't know much about the Indian religion but assumed they were Christians as well.

When they trolley came to take him to theatre, he was surprised at the routine. In France, they had carried him on a stretcher to the operating room but here there was a trolley with sheets and a blanket to cover him. The trolley had big pram wheels and pushing it was the large man with the stutter and huge beard. He was friendly and, although speech was impossible, when the occasional word came out it was thick with accent so Charles didn't understand it anyway. They just smiled and nodded a lot to each other, it seemed to work.

In the theatre, there was a chemical gas sort of smell, it permeated the area and you could smell it from outside the room. The wall on the opposite side had a huge window in it to allow light to flood into the room, and above was a gas lamp, with reflective mirrors to throw light down towards the operating trolley.

A man in a suit stepped towards Charles and spoke in a very quiet voice, he too had an accent but it was soft and gentle and Charles found it reassuring that this gentleman was the Anaesthetist. He said he would help Charles get to sleep with a rubber mask, all Charles had to do was breathe deeply. The operation would only take a few minutes and then they would wake him and take him back to his bed where he could sleep the effects off. As he placed the mask over Charlie's mouth and nose, he talked quietly and soothingly. Charles could smell the gas, it had a sharpness to its smell and as he breathed deep he could soon feel the effects, his head started to spin, and he lost focus, there was an echo in his ears almost like a gentle throbbing sound, it was the last thing he remembered.

As the surgeon cut into the newly formed flesh, he was revolted by the smell, but worse was the maggots. The wound looked extremely clean, and there was no dead tissue to remove. The fat white maggots had eaten all the rotten flesh. When he cleaned everything out he could see there had been a lot of healing gone on in the few weeks since the wound had happened. New muscle and tissue had started to form and, although the thought of maggot was disgusting, they had proved time and again to be of huge benefit to wound healing; but these had done their work and it was time for medicine and science to take over.

He washed the wound with an antiseptic solution of chlorinated lime and boric acid, this new antiseptic was being hailed as a miracle cure for infected wounds and was called EUSOL, invented in Edinburgh at the University, it had a distinctive if not unpleasant smell. Once the wound had been washed, it was dressed with absorbent gauze to help keep the wound area clean. There was no bleeding and, once it was all sorted, it looked perfect and ready to mend. Granted it might take a while but this patient had paralysis of the legs due to a bruised spine and it might take a few weeks for his leg function to return. Fortunately, the wound and subsequent paralysis hadn't caused any of his bodily functions to fail and he was able to toilet himself.

The anaesthetic mask was removed and Charles started to breath normal air. It didn't take long for him to start recovering and, with a now familiar thirst, he started to wake up.

It took a couple of hours until Charles woke properly and outside the window it was dark, he thought it was night but everyone was awake and although the bustle had quietened down, there were still plenty of people around. He waved at a Nurse, she was pretty with a plump face and freckles framed with a shock of red hair. Her apron was gleaming white and her hat hung along her hair and then onto her shoulders.

"Hello, nice to see you awake, how are you feeling?" She had a wonderful Scottish lilt to her voice as she spoke her words bounced they were so light, he was instantly charmed by her.

"I'm fine thank you, my back is a bit uncomfortable but it's nothing, did everything go alright? What time is it, and is there a chance I might have a drink please? I'm very thirsty"

"Aye laddie, I'll sort you a drink of water for now but if that stays down you can have a nice cup of tea in a wee while. Your operation went very well and Mr Cummings, who is your Surgeon, will see tomorrow on his rounds. By the way it's nearly tea time" she looked at her fob watch "It's a quarter to six in the evening. I have asked that they save you some food for your evening meal, but let's get you that water to start with."

The water was like nectar and he had no problems with sickness. The tea was perhaps the nicest he had ever tasted and, with a lump of sugar in it, he was sure it would be a waste if he was sick.

Dinner was saved, he was able to take a meal in his bed at the same time as supper was being served by a couple of ambulant patients in their bright blue hospital uniform.

"You ever had haggis? It's from the devils arse I think, but its filling, and a welcome change from 'Bully or Maconochie's" Charles laughed.

"Haggis? Never tried it, but I'll give it a go." It came with some boiled potatoes and a spoonful of some washed out vegetable which he couldn't describe. He loved the haggis, it tasted so spicy and reminded him of something he had eaten but couldn't remember what, but he was keen to have it again.

The next day he was visited by both Mr Cummings and Professor Durant-Jones. Both men were delighted with what they found. Cummings was a wizard with soft tissue injuries and after he told Charles what he had found; everyone was very happy that the wound was closing itself and being dressed on a daily basis. The Professor was full of stories about his protege Colonel MacDonald and had written back to the Colonel to explain what treatment Charles was receiving.

He soon settled to the ward life. One man from the Black Watch pushed him when he was in his wheelchair and soon he was having physical training chaps from the Army moving his legs for him. Every day, twice a day, he was wheeled to the gymnasium for his leg workout. He was sure he could feel his feet again and he could definitely feel his thighs, and maybe as far down as his knees.

It was on Christmas Eve he stood for the first time, yes he was aided by the hairy bearded man and one of the physical training staff from the gym, but as he stood for the first time to his full height of five foot six inches he felt like a giant. Then the blood drained from his head and he fainted onto the floor. It didn't deter him, not one bit.

Christmas Day was a wonderful time, first the Nurses gathered at midnight with lanterns and candles, they went around the whole hospital and sang Christmas carols. Then the Padre came and did a Christmas service in the chapel, Charles was very keen to go and felt quite overwhelmed at being in church again, he realised how much he missed it and what faith he had.

In France, there was a special football match on Christmas Day between foes that had sworn to kill each other. But, despite all their hatred, they were prepared to put their quarrel aside for the festive season. It wasn't well received by either side's hierarchy, but it went on anyway. The one thing all participants agreed on was the real hatred was saved for the war itself, and not the men in the opposite trench.

CHAPTER 45

Learn to walk and go home

Back in Edinburgh, there was a special dinner being served, it was a goose; it was being carved by Mr Cummings, it had all the trimmings and Charles sat at the table for his meal. He didn't see Rebecca and his sister Elizabeth walk down the ward. There was a huge cheer as the families were allowed in for visiting. None louder than the one for Charles and his sweetheart. Elizabeth was quite heady with all the men paying her compliments and there was even tea served for the guests by the inpatients. Later, there were more presents from a grateful nation and one very special one from Princess Mary, a fantastic brass tin filled with chocolates and a card; one for every soldier serving.

Charles felt like a fraud on a ward where there were seriously injured men, he was healing faster than a greyhound and with all the good food he was having to watch his weight, for the first time in his life his trousers were feeling a little tight, if he was ever to ride again he had better fit his trousers.

He sat holding Rebecca's hand. It was as intimate as he felt he could be in company, and she felt like a lady in fine clothes and a soldier to love. Elizabeth was being serenaded by a Scots chap who had taken a fancy to her, he was singing with a beautiful voice and when he finished the whole ward clapped and whistled. Elizabeth offered him her hand and he kissed it tenderly, he was a brute of a man with enormous shoulders and a broad chest, a striking moustache and huge eyebrows, Elizabeth thought he was the most handsome man she had ever seen. The Christmas spirit was flowing through a tormented group of men who had being in hell a few weeks or day before, it was truly humbling to see them so happy. Mr Cummings and Sister sat with all the Nurses and had a drink of sherry whilst they looked over these brave and broken men, most missing their blood families but sat celebrating with the most ferociously loyal family they could have. Today this was their family, and each group shared the delights of the day with the few visiting family members that had made the trip.

"How on earth did you get here? Who told you I was here in Edinburgh? Where are you staying and when do you go back?" Charles had so many questions.

Thomas had paid the rail fare and Elizabeth had been saving for a weekend at the Blackpool Lights, but had enough to pay for the bed and breakfast lodgings for two nights. Tom was on Christmas guard duty so, Emily and Mae had gone to her mother's in Runcorn. That left the two girls to fend for themselves, so here they were. It had been a great adventure. They had heard from a Captain Sanford that Charles had been transferred to this hospital, he had sent a telegram, at first, they had been too afraid to open it in case it was bad news, but it turned out to be wonderful news, and at Christmas as well.

Charles gave Elizabeth his savings book for the bank, his pay went directly into it apart from a few pennies he needed for polish and the occasional drink. He didn't drink beer and wasn't fond of wine so he tended to drink whatever was available. He was quite well off for a single soldier. He also gave his sister a five pound note, that should more than cover the trip.

"Pay our Tom the money he lent you, and say thank you from me. He's a grand lad our Tom."

Christmas went by quickly, and, along with the brass box from the Princess, it was memorable for the kiss he stole from his own best girl under the clock tower. He knew for certain then that the feeling was returning to his legs.

Boxing Day meant the long goodbyes and, with a tear in her eye Elizabeth said hers first. It had been smashing to see her brother looking so well, the movement and feeling in his legs was already much improved. The Professor had been using some form of electromagnet machine to improve the blood flow and nerve healing in his back, it was a very specialised piece of equipment, and Charles realised he had been extremely lucky to come to this hospital.

It had also heralded the news he was longing to hear,

"If we can get you standing on your own, we can transfer you nearer to home, you will be able to see that wee lassie of yours."

It would take a huge effort and a bit more time but he had a target. He was determined and he had an idea that might help, swimming.

"Sir, I have always been a strong swimmer, do you have access to a swimming pool?" It was a revelation.

"Why, yes laddie we do, that might be very useful. I'll speak to the physical training chaps and see if we can get that set up. That young man is a very good idea."

It didn't take long before they had him in a pool. It felt a bit odd at first, the change in temperature registered differently with his legs to his stomach. To his legs the water felt really quite warm, to his stomach it was extremely chilly but with the help of a man on each side he could manage to stand in the shallow end. It didn't take many minutes before he was stood on his own but the first effort at a step saw him swimming as he tumbled, like a circus act, head first into the chilly water. It wasn't all going to be easy.

CHAPTER 46

A New Year and a half

1915 was celebrated as only the Scots could, there was drink and festivities as if there was no war. In Edinburgh the bells rang out at the stroke of midnight to hail in the New Year. A million kisses were given and a million more promised. Charles watched it all from the balcony of the hospital which overlooked the city, in the near distance he could hear, and indeed see, the castle. It had seen its fair share of strife and conflict, but tonight it was a beacon of hope and fancy. Hope that this war might be near its end and fancy that once again the country would return to normality. The menfolk would march up Prince's Street in celebration of a quick victory over the dreaded Hun. The Kaiser, taught a hard lesson and Germany, once and for all, put in her place.

As Charles was delivered back to his bed by a man from the Black Watch, they spoke of their hopes and dreams. They had both seen the horrors of war and neither wanted to see it any more. 'Jock' had lost an arm to gangrene. It started as a wound to his hand, then his wrist, elbow and finally his whole arm had been amputated. He carried a contact smell of EUSOL with him as the dressings over his padded shoulder slowly did their work.

"It'll ne'r stop this year, until the Froggies start to put their shoulder into the fight."

'Jock' Stewart had a thick accent, he was a highlander who had joined the Army in 1910. He loved the life but was no fan of this war.

"They're canny them Germans, they have the machine gun working and the high land, we won't win this war anytime soon Charlie boy. My war's over, I'll ne'r be back to the front. Time for me to gan hame to settle, but I'll be dammed if I nay what I'll do."

Charles nodded, he agreed the war wouldn't end quickly, it was fantasy to think it would. He did differ with 'Jock' in that he hoped he would make it back to his mates, he was 20 years old and he had hopes for the future. These included Rebecca and a home, maybe in the hills outside of Bolton, with a small farm and animals. Everyone deserved a dream, but before all that, he had to survive and return home.

The swimming had done marvels for his recovery. He could now feel most of his legs and feet and, if he concentrated really hard, he could move his toes and sometimes even his ankles. There was little doubt he would recover, the wound in his back had all but closed and the new skin and everything around it looked clean and shiny, it was more of a dent in his back than a wound, it had healed lovely. Occasionally he would get a stab of pain in it but the Doctor had explained it was the nerves doing their work. He had terrible pins and needles in his legs and feet though; sometimes it drove him to distraction and the burning he felt as he touched his legs were just a further indication of the nerves coming together. He would recover sooner rather than later but the secret was not to rush it. "Nature has a way of slowing you down" said the Nurse, "you will get better when she says, not us". He liked Agnes, she was pretty and clever, she always seemed to

252

have time for anyone who wanted her. Not like some of the others who were always busy. Agnes just found time to talk. A lot of the lads had terrible nightmares and would wake crying or screaming, Agnes seemed to be the one they all called for, after their mothers.

"I hear word that you are leaving us Private Atherton? Going back to England I understand, by the weekend. Well I'll miss you and so will Jock, you two have become as thick as thieves, don't think I haven't noticed." She laughed at the innocent face Charles offered her, a clear statement of guilt hidden in innocence, a pointless exercise because she had their cards marked from day one.

When it came for him to leave, Charles was genuinely sad as he said his farewells to the rest of the inpatients and ward staff. The nurses hugged him and Agnes kissed his cheek. The gymnasium staff wished him well and handed him an envelope with his exercise routine for the new hospital.

Jock shook his hand a gentle, firm hand shake, more of affection than formality;

"Good luck Charlie, I'm glad we met, even under these dreadful circumstances. You'll soon get your legs back and I'll have a new arm. If you ever get back to Scotland you'll be welcome in the highlands, just tell them Jock Stewart is your friend, they'll find me."

He was still in a wheel chair and didn't have his independence, but he was alive and rapidly mending. He looked over his shoulder as he left the front door, back at the big stones, and he was sad when he saw all his mates waving him goodbye from the windows. In his heart he knew he would never be back here but he had felt at home with the Scots, even if it took a great deal of effort to understand most of them.

The motor ambulance pulled into the station and, as they drove down the entrance road, he could see last night's ambulance train in the sidings. It was being cleaned by the medical staff and had discharged all the casualties it had carried here. By now those men would be getting to their hospitals and being welcomed by the Nurses who would do it all again a million times and never complain. It was raining and freezing cold as Charles was loaded onto the train to England, he would be met at Manchester and hand his notes over to the staff there. The train let out a long mournful whistle and with a small judder and a powerful 'chuff, chuff' it started its journey south.

In his wildest dreams he would hope it would be like Edinburgh but, in reality, it was more like Bedlam. Manchester was in turmoil, there were trains on all the platforms, all with soldiers getting on and families saying goodbyes. There were shouts and whistles, tears and sobs, hats were waved and handkerchiefs dabbed as families said farewell. As that happened on one side of the station, he arrived at the other along with two more ambulance trains all carrying wounded. There was a long line of trucks and ambulances to take the offloaded men to their different hospitals, Charles was astonished to see how many there were.

At the front of the line, there was a simple wooden office with a Captain and a Sergeant directing the ambulance staff and medical orderlies as to where the particular ambulances were going.

It didn't take long to see men loaded and moved like cargo onto the waiting transport. Charles was put in a car, it wasn't an ambulance, and the chair he was in was whisked away, he hoped there would be one at the other end of the trip.

The drive to Bolton wasn't familiar, he couldn't remember a lot of the route as it differed from the tram route he used and he hadn't done that trip for about five years; he did feel very grand in a motorcar. There were two of them sat in the back, it was wonderful to hear such a local accent and the two men laughed at each other when they said how posh the other one sounded. Stan Johnson was from Bury and was serving with the Loyal North Lancashire's, he had been blown up by a shell and broken his arm, and collar bone as well as some ribs, none of which was healing too quickly.

As they approached Farnworth, Charles could see the mill at Kersley, he wondered if any of his old friends would be there still, he doubted it, apart from the old and cronkey, all the rest would be away in the Army as soon as they could.

They neared the hospital and there was a reception party waiting. As the door of the car opened, he was surprised to see a familiar face from the past, it was Megan Jones who was working as a Nurse. They had been to school together and she sang in the choir at St John's. When she saw him she beamed a smile, and gave him a hug as old friends might, it was a wonderful welcome home.

CHAPTER 47

Home and return

The hospital was an old workhouse and, in parts, felt and looked as if it still was.

He settled in quickly and soon had visitors from home. Even Mr Phipps from the mill came to see him. The news from Kersley Spinning Mill wasn't good. Lots of the lads had gone to join the new Kitchener's Army and some of the boys who joined early had already fallen in battle. There was a general mood of patriotism and a genuine pride in the boys who went, many of them were just that, boys, but there was also a feeling of melancholy in the huge cathedrals of cotton. The chimneys had hardly slowed their constant belching and the ladies had proved to be just as able. Mr Phipps was wise, he knew it would cause ruptions when the men returned but he was honest, and said the girls were easier to work with than a lot of the men. The war on the Homefront wasn't much spoken about, but the effort the people left behind had made was, frankly, unbelievable. Production of army uniforms had seen a huge order book fill faster than they could have imagined. Phipps had a son who had been commissioned into the Loyal North Lancs, he was just 18 years old, just a boy but his duty needed doing and a fine lad he was.

Within a couple of days, despite the dreadful weather, the swimming pool once more became the regular haunt of

Charles. He would spend as long as he could there, swimming interspersed with hot mugs of Bovril to keep him warm. He was swimming more than ever and, as a consequence, he could move freer and was stronger. The slight tummy he had gained soon disappeared and the tone in his legs grew tighter. It wasn't long before he could take a few steps in the water at neck depth. Within a fortnight he was walking into the shallow end. The trainer was determined to help, and the two of them put many more hours in than they perhaps should, but it was paying dividends. Outside in the foyer, there was a set of stairs that led to the balcony. It had a good strong hand rail and with a grip of the rail in his left hand and holding onto his trainer he took his first tentative steps. He fell down so often initially that they both thought perhaps they were rushing him, but he was as determined as ever so they tied a pillow to his bottom and he tried again. First on the flat to the payment booth, and then to the stairs. Charles would sit on the chair and quiver like a jelly as his legs grew used to standing and walking again. They fashioned a walking frame by the trainer holding a broom handle between his hands and Charles holding onto it for a bit of balance and stability. It didn't take long before the stumble became a walk, but there was no strength in his legs. Good food, beef tea and 'cow heel' pie, a speciality for Elizabeth, was the answer to that particular problem.

Next day, he had a hotpot of cow heel pie delivered to the ward, it was wrapped in a tea towel and as the smell wafted down the ward, he could feel his mouth water involuntarily, his wasn't the only one.

Within a week, the effects of all the training and good homemade food was producing great results. He was still a bit wobbly, especially on the stairs but his walking had improved both with and, now, without support. The wound on his back had completely healed and his gait was much more man, rather than chimp and although he was clearly still struggling, there was an air of optimism for a complete recovery. The other lasting issue was he sometimes struggled to hear things quite so clearly as he did and found he said "Pardon" far too often. It didn't take long for the other patients to nickname him 'Private Pardon' all said in good humour and taken the same. It was this banter that kept them sane. Often at night there would be a terrified scream as one of the lads dreamt his way out of certain death in the field. They just accepted it, and at night those dark moments were shared with a cup of tea and a cigarette. They all understood, it didn't need explanations.

January was a foul month in Farnworth. The dark nights carried cold winds and rain and each man thanked his luck that he was in a warm hospital bed, despite the horrendous wounds they had received, home was better than France.

Charles was allowed to walk out in his hospital uniform, he couldn't manage much but Rebecca would come to collect him in a wheel chair and push him around the grounds of the hospital. When Tom was off duty and was free to visit he would barrel down the ward and cheer Charles with a smile. He was able to take him further afield, they even managed the park where Charles had first met Sergeant Harris before he had joined up. The band was playing on the bandstand, but it was a freezing day and the crowd was a touch sparse.

"I'll be fit enough to go back soon Tom. I'm not sure how I feel about that, I want to go but don't at the same time. I miss the lads but by Christ its rough sometimes"

Tom understood, he saw the condition of the prisoners when they arrived at Leigh. They would be marched as if on show through the town from the station, surprisingly there was little or no resentment from anyone, either prisoner of war or civilian. They just recognised the travesty of the situation.

"We have to do our duty Charlie, you know better than any of us. Did you hear William is in hospital? He's not injured but he has an ear problem and keeps getting dizzy. There's a real chance they will invalid him out and, as yet, he's done nowt. Is there no chance of you getting a ticket?"

A ticket, the medical discharge equivalent of a golden wish. Charles was sure, if he tried he would be excused duty and discharged from the Army, but it had been his life choice to join and now it was a bit rough he couldn't see himself running away, no he would stick with his mates. He knew he would go back despite all the temptations here to stay. He thought he would be fit enough within a month and the Doctors had tended to agree. If he kept improving the way he was with his mobility, they could see no reason not to let him return. They all thought he was a brave lad, he wasn't so sure.

Over the next four weeks, he pushed himself harder and harder, the more he got better, the more he demanded greater improvement. He was able to walk and jog, he could do stairs both up and down. He was fit, his swimming had returned his shoulders to a huge width, his tunic was over tight up top and over big at his waist. More than anything physical though, he was bored. Yes, it was lovely to see Rebecca and Elizabeth nearly every day, and seeing Tom was just the ticket, but, deep inside, he knew his mates were in the shit and mud and he should be there with them, not here being mollycoddled.

The day came when he needed to talk to the Medical Officer about his return. It was mid-February and, as he marched into the Medical Officer's office, he halted and saluted.

"Now, Atherton. You ready to go back? No one would blame you if you wanted to stay a while longer. I hear you're doing very well in the pool and on the marches. I can't help but think you might be trying a bit hard but damn it all man I'm envious. A young fit chap like you doesn't want to held here like a songbird in a cage."

Charles stood and said,

"I'm fighting fit I think Sir. The lads will be needing a hand over there and I'm ready."

"Very well, the end of the week then, that should give me time to write your discharge and a chance for you to get some more cow heel delivered." He looked up and smiled, he had tried it and loved it.

"I hear your sister has volunteered to become an Auxiliary Nurse here. She will be a great asset to the nurses."

Charles had heard that to be the case, she was a natural carer and would fit in fantastically here in the hospital.

" She will be a great help Sir, I'm sure she will do well."

There was a lot to do. First and foremost he had to tell his family, and that included Rebecca. Then he had to go to the stores and get a new uniform, he spoke to the Orderly Sergeant about kit issue, there was a uniform store in the nearby territorial camp.

All the travel documentation was ready and he was issued with the right size uniform and equipment. He still had the more important parts of his original kit including his hat, buttons and boots. Rebecca was heartbroken at the news that Charles was going back. She understood the reasons and felt proud that he was her soldier boy but she wanted him to stay at home so badly, surely he had done enough, he had done his bit. They had a long talk whilst he tried hopelessly to sew his buttons onto his new tunic, she said it was pitiful to watch and took the job on for herself. It was so easy to see her sewing pedigree. Within half an hour they were all sewn on and perfect. Charles took his razor and shaved the inside of his wooden blouse, the 'old sweats' knew this trick to stop new shirts itching, he also ran the razor along the seams to make sure there were no threads that the dreaded 'chats' could hang onto. He had to explain the term chats as lice, Rebecca shuddered.

"They're a bit like nits that kids get in their hair, but the little blighters don't half bite and they make you itch badly. Might not be such a problem in the winter though."

Rebecca was tearful but stoic, she knew the truth was he was a soldier and he needed to be back with his mates, there would be time for them when the fighting was done, and he would come home. The fire flickered in the parlour of her house. He would have to leave soon, he needed to be back on the ward by 9pm. He had told no one about the numbness he still had in his foot, he needed to go.

When he got back to the ward, he spent a little time chatting to the lads in the ward and saying goodbye to those fellows who he had become fond of. Some of them would be invalided out and others might go back to some sort of administrative post in their Battalions but, as far as he could make out, none of them would ever go back to the front, not on this ward. They were a grand lot and he felt glad he had made their acquaintance. The familiarity of servicemen and the easy bond they formed was legendary.

Early next morning he was up, washed, and shaved. The fear he had in his gut was that he might back out of going. God knows there was enough reason he thought.

He took time to thank all the nurses from the night duty, and once breakfast had finished, he set off on his rounds to clear the hospital. First, he had to go to the gymnasium to say a heartfelt thanks to the physical training staff, without them he would still be bed bound of that he was sure. They shook hands and patted shoulders all bonhomie. From there he went to the Admin Office, where the Admin Sergeant issued him with an envelope. In it were his travel documents and a travel warrant to *London* on the train. From there he was to travel onwards to *Southampton* and from there he was to board a steamer to *Calais*. Once he had arrived in *Calais* there was a pass for transport to *Poperinge*. Here he would rendezvous with his Unit. It would take him 24 hours to get there and from then on, he would soon be back in the war.

CHAPTER 48

The Prodigal son returns

It had been a galling 24 hours. He hadn't slept much, just dozed on the different forms of transport. He thought back to the previous day. There had been tears, nearly his, but he had hung on to his emotions. Rebecca was stoic, Elizabeth less so but, funnily the one that tugged, was Tom. Brothers saying goodbye is a dreadful wrench, they hugged which was totally unexpected and completely the right thing to do.

He was then on a tram, from the tram a train, then onto a steamer, SS Stump, from there another motor bus then an Army truck from Calais to Poperinge. He had snoozed on every one. He felt he was as fresh as a daisy, despite not getting a lot of sleep. He thought it as much the relief of having said his farewells as getting here.

He had no rifle, no ammunition. In fact, he had only what he was wearing and, smart as he was, he did feel as if something was missing, most soldiers felt like that without their weapon, he would need a new one issuing today.

It was Bill Stanesby who stood grinning and shaking his head.

"Dear God, the Prodigal son returns. Charlie Atherton you daft bugger, what are you doing back? Thought you had a Blighty and we'd never see you again. You're a sight for sore eyes Charlie boy, a sight indeed. Come on there's tea on the brew and the lads will be surprised to see you. I'll take you to see the Sgt Maj first then let's get you sorted."

It was like coming home, he felt a deep comfort from seeing the boys. Poperinge hadn't been badly damaged by the war, just a few buildings knocked about, but hardly anything. His Regiment were billeted in an old hotel and surrounding buildings. They had been here for two weeks, they were due to move in the next few days.

The necessary paperwork and interviews were quickly sorted, he had a proper welcome from everyone with a genuine interest in how he had gotten himself back on his feet. The consensus of opinion was he must be dead, the wound he had suffered was a killer, everyone agreed. Even the Commanding Officer came to say hello in the Adjutant's office to welcome him back to his second family. To Charles he wasn't so sure they were second, he felt as at home with these men as he did in Farnworth.

"Right then, first things first. You need a rifle, we are being used as dismounted infantry for the foreseeable; all the horses have been taken way back, oh and yes that bloody thing of yours is ok, he near killed the farrier but he's well and has gone back with the others."

The Sergeant Major had known Charles all his military life. He was a Sergeant when Charles had joined and he had been in the same Squadron with him since 1913. He was all drill and polish with most men, but today, he lowered his voice and said "Charlie it's good to see you old son, welcome back" it was a gesture of friendship and kin. Totally unnecessary but completely perfect; the bond had been retied.

It wasn't long before the news got around that Charlie Atherton had come back and there was a gang of the old boys to greet him with handshakes and tea. Cake was produced first, then cigarettes and beer. A soldier's family is a coarse, sometimes uncouth group; it is a friendship forged in pain and suffering, and disgruntlement with most things, but together, they are bonded like brothers and no one would understand except, those who knew the feeling. Today Charles knew the feeling, he had returned to the fold.

February was a very wet month. The Battalion had moved up to Ypres, the ancient city with its beautiful architecture, in particular, the cloth hall and cathedral. Both buildings were huge, imposing themselves on the skyline but equally making themselves targets for the German Artillery. The cobbled square and streets were often manned by market stall holders who, despite the war, continued to supply their wares with hand made or home grown produce. Cafés and bars supplied a ready ration of locally brewed beers, in fact, two of the three commodities required for every soldier from any nation was available right there in Ypres. The little town would, in time, become so much more important to the British and her allies. Even as a monument to the British in their darkest days, Ypres resounded defiance.

Marching was tiresome and when at last the horses came back there was a feeling of relief. The whole Regiment had spent plenty of time in the trenches, either as back up for the tired troops, who were already there, or as replacements for large groups allowing them to fall back for some rest and recuperation.

Now, mounted once more in the role of cavalry, the men eased their way back into the saddle, the results were painful for a few days as they got used to riding again but it was as a Unit they suffered and the jokes were ruthless about the way men walked after getting off their horses.

CHAPTER 49

It's Touch and Go

In the background there was the incessant beeping of the monitor. The consultant, Mr Marshall had asked for the family to meet him at the hospital. My wife had feared the worst, after all there seemed to be no reason that I wouldn't wake up.

"We seem to think he's locked in. What we mean by that, is that his brain won't let him regain a conscious state. We haven't ever seen it in a patient with a tumour, only stroke victims seem to suffer from it and even then, only about 1%."

Mister Scott Marshall was a good Surgeon, he was young to be so senior but he had quite a bit of experience from his military career. He knew that there was a history of both my wife and myself being in the military, it helped when the humour turned a little dark.

"I think when we take the rest of the tumour out, we will turn a corner one way or another but you need to make the choice. On the one hand we might release him from this state but on the other we might not. We just don't know which way it will go. I have spoken with, and shared all his results with, as many of the top surgeons as I can ask, and we all agree, we just don't know. All his vital signs are good, but his EEG, the machine that measures brain activity, is frankly, well just weird. He is alive in his head Di and his brain is working overtime. Only after the operation we will know what the outcome will be. But the decision is yours. I think it's a gamble worth taking if it helps, for all it's worth. However, you need to sign the consent form. I'll leave you to talk amongst yourselves for a bit. There's no hurry, the last thing we want to do is rush this."

I could hear everything. In my head I was screaming 'do it!' She knew I was, I knew she did. My sister sat holding my hand, she was the last of my generation other than me, the rest had passed. My son was sat holding Di's hand they were very close, I guess 'spare mums' are.

"Well, he would want the operation, I'm sure he would; but I don't think I can decide on my own. He's your dad and your brother, you get a say."

In my head I was shouting "No they don't, you say it, I want the operation"

It didn't take them long, and, as Mr Marshall came back with a Nurse and a tray of coffee, the decision was made.

CHAPTER 50

Gallop for your life

For the next month, it was a rotation of reconnaissance on horseback and the daily grind in the trenches. It hadn't taken long for Charles to get back into the swing of things. Apollo was as much a belligerent mule as a horse, and seemed to resent the fact his rider had been absent for so long. But when it came to reconnaissance, he was sublime. On one occasion, the Troop was observing the German movements near Zillebeke and so engrossed in their activities that they missed the Ulan Squadron who had seen them and set off to engage with the troop. The first 'B' Squadron knew of the Ulans, was the dreadful sound of galloping horses coming from the woods behind them. When they turned, they were already within 50 yards. The Ulans had their long lances extended ready to strike and, but for an extremely rapid response from the 20th Hussars, it would have been a massacre. There was no time to load and shoot their rifles or sidearms, this was Cavalry verses Cavalry, the sword against the lance. This mini battle was straight from a different time, Waterloo and before that. Charles drew his sword and, in one movement, parried a lance over his head. Apollo moved as if he was on strings, just by mere leg pressure Charles was able to move him left and right. As the long spear was deflected overhead, it left the sword in the perfect position to strike and, as he dragged the blade from high to low, he slashed along the back of the passing German. The wound was long and deep, but the German was full of adrenaline. He turned on a sixpence, lowered his lance and directed it at Apollo, rather than his rider. Charles kicked hard, and Apollo launched forward at such a speed he nearly unseated his rider, with a swoosh through the air Charles plunged the tip of his sword deep into the belly of the charging German. The momentum of the charge ensured a deep, to the hilt, strike and as they crossed, the German dropped his lance and fell from his horse. If he hadn't he would have driven Charles backwards and they would have both been unseated, as it was, the weight of the stricken man pulled the sword free. There was no time to look at the outcome as another Ulan came forward, he was a huge ugly brute of a man and he sneered as he eyed up Charles for the fight. Charles had gathered his reins and his dander was up, he kicked on and once more felt the power of a British horse under him. He roared his defiance at the grinning killer opposite, there was a 40 yard charge and, almost like knights of the medieval days, they came towards one another. The German fell off his horse as his head exploded outwards, one of the lads had seen what was happening and taken aim with his carbine 303. The resulting death highlighted the futility of this crazy attitude that the Cavalry could compete. The days of charges and sword fights belonged in the history books this war was being fought with machine guns and artillery. The days of the horse would be very short, they didn't fare well against bullets or shells and shrapnel.

The retort of the rifle shot seemed to stop the fight momentarily, but these Germans were trained to be ruthless.

Their initial charge had passed the contact area and now they wheeled round to come back. The brief passage of time had ensured the 20th had time to see their escape route, they were hopelessly outnumbered, and it would be suicidal to try to stop and fight.

"On me, On me!" The Troop Officer, Lieutenant Hall, shouted and the 8 men gathered their horses and galloped after him. In close pursuit came the Germans, already at the gallop, it was a near impossible escape and as the first German struck with his lance, the deadly tip sliced into the back of the last Hussar. He was lucky, the point had struck his leather belt and it guided the tip upwards away from his kidney and into the soft flesh in his side. It was just a jab, and the lance was out as quickly as it had gone in and, although he felt the punch in his side, he didn't really register what it was. As the horses galloped towards the open field between the British and German lines, there were sharp shooters from both sides who took pot shots and the racing targets; no one was hit. Lt Hall had been the Regimental point to point champion only last year and he found a route that was flat and fast, firm under foot, whereas just to the side was boggy and wet. Ahead there was a barrier, it was a large hedge, easily 6 foot high and probably as wide. This was the way to escape, the Germans were heavily armed but the British were a light patrol, made for speed on top of the ground, fleet of foot and galloping for all they were worth, the hedge was their target. Charles was in the middle of the group, it was a wild race but quite sensibly the rider either side of him edged out slightly to give each other room. Apollo was all fire and fury he was locked on to the hedge from 20 yards out and from here on in Charles was a mere passenger. He heard himself say out loud so all could hear him, "Keep your leg on lads, ride them into the jump" he knew it was for his own peace of mind that he recited instruction, he did it quite a lot when under pressure.

The first two horses, Lt Hall and Sgt Blackie took off from under the hedge, both riders adopted a hunting seat as their horses sailed skywards, both horses scraped their front legs over the hedge, there was fear in the eyes of both men and horse but fortunately no one could see. Before they had even cleared the hedge the next three had taken off at full gallop, no one had checked their horses stride, there was no stride counting; it was a clear case of kick on and hold tight.

Apollo never touched a twig, his front legs were tucked up tight to his chest with Charles in perfect balance on top. Ernie Miles was next to him and he lost balance in mid air, he had been caught off balance as the horse took off. The horse did amazingly well to clear the hedge, in truth it was the maximum he could have jumped, and the saving of Miles was the fact the horse bellied out a bit on top of the hedge, it almost threw Miles forward and he was able to grab the rope that was around the horse's thick neck. As he landed however, he was steep, he needed to lean back, right back, to maintain his seat and he would have fallen arse over head if it hadn't been for Charles reaching over and grabbing him. It was like a scene from a Western but Charles was just able to steady Ernie before he took a fatal tumble. It was just a touch, but it was enough. No sooner had their three touched down when the next three landed, it was a masterclass in cross country riding and as the last three looked back they saw that the Germans had pulled up. The hedge was just too big for them with their lances and it was better to be able to fight another day, besides, they had done their job and scared the British away.

The hedge was renamed 'Hall's Hedge' from that day, it was even big enough to be seen on the military maps and at first people laughed when the tale of how they had escaped came to light but in the end, everyone believed them.

Private Taylor was the wounded Hussar. He was seen and sent to the hospital for stitches in what was a deep and ugly wound. Once everyone had told their tales of heroic daring do, the micky taking started. Everyone had heard that Charlie Atherton had taken a riding lesson whilst at the gallop, it was good humour and taken as such, but the truth was the men felt reassured to have such a competent rider who, despite being in dire peril, still kept his cool enough to talk his way through what was, by any stretch of anyone's imagination, a massive jump.

Ernie Miles took more than his fair share for nearly falling off, saved by the new riding master apparently; Bert Clarke had started it, he was in the last three to clear the fence and he had been able to see what had happened, it had been instinct of course, but Charles had certainly saved Miles from a desperate situation. Sgt Blackie came and cuffed Miles round the head for being such a "Dunderheed" but the whole troop laughed as mates do.

The next time they would be mounted would be some time away, it was time for them to go into the trenches and tomorrow they would hand their horses back to be moved to the rear.

The postman came, and all the men were summoned to form a square for the mail call.

"Form a square in Troops" Sgt Major Bell shouted, the whole Regiment had been formed into a square. 'A' formed the right leg and 'C' the left with 'B' forming the top and Head Quarters the bottom of the square. This type of parade was normally saved for special VIPs or big announcements and, as the Commanding Officer and his staff made their way to the middle, there was a murmur of wondering what was going on.

"Today, we saw action with 'B' having a clash with the Bosch. Lt Hall and his men proved without any shadow of doubt that the men of the 20th Hussars are a class above anything the others can produce in the field. I want to congratulate the men for a sterling effort and a job well done. Tomorrow we are moving to the communication trenches and will be in the line with our friends the 12th Lancers. I know you will be absolutely first class. Horses will be withdrawn this afternoon and we will be moved by omnibus through Ypres but Squadron Commanders will give you orders following this parade. Well I say afterwards, but we have a very special announcement to make. Today is very important to Private Charles Atherton. Step forward Atherton."

Charles was mortified, he thought he might be in bother for this morning's doings but, as he stepped forward into the square, the CO came over and shook his hand.

"Today, this young man turned 21 years old, and I know you will want to congratulate him in the usual manner, but first I'd like you to raise your voices in a rendition of 'For he's a jolly good fellow.'"

Charles blushed so much he thought he might faint. There were cards and letters for him saved by the Adjutant, a cake and, behind HQ Company there was a table with drinks. There weren't many things to celebrate, and even if there were there wasn't ever time, so today was a chance for them to have a couple of hours slack time. After a hundred handshakes, a lot of thank you's and smiles Charles was back with his Troop, no one had known a thing about it. It was Bill Stanesby who came and spoke to him first.

"Happy birthday Charlie, you kept that quiet."

"I didn't want any fuss, but that turned out differently than I thought."

"I heard you were splendid out there today, the lads know what you did but you're far too modest, it's what we all like about you man."

Drinks were taken, and the cake disappeared quickly. The men were fallen out into Troops for orders for the next day. Charles made his way to the Adjutant's office, he knocked on the door and was called in.

"Sir, I wanted to say thank you for the cake and things, that was a lovely surprise, thank you."

"You're welcome lad, it's not every day you're 21 is it! I hope you don't mind me keeping your letters for a couple of days, I didn't want to give anyone a chance to spoil it for you."

"No Sir, I don't mind at all, I'll get on now Sir, if you will excuse me, and thank you again Sir."

He saluted, turned smartly to the right and marched out. He felt 6 foot tall, which was, actually, a full 6 inches taller than he was.

CHAPTER 51

The Foul Trench

Next morning, the camp was alive with activity, there was an air of early spring and, for a change, it wasn't raining. First parade was 07:00 hours and as the men all gathered around, there came the familiar shout of "Fall In." The Regiment formed up on parade in full battle order. Rifles, ammunition pouches, sandbags and all the equipment for going into the trenches.

Formed in ranks of three they were turned North and on the command 'Quick march,' they set off towards Ypres. As they marched there was no fear or trepidation, the mood was light and cheerful and occasionally a song would ripple down the ranks. Looking on the observer would have been forgiven to think they were marching to a church service in Colchester rather than towards the raging guns of the war.

Charles marched alongside his chums, it was where he belonged, they all felt that was the case. As they rounded the corner they were met with a line of London buses still in their London livery. Charles hadn't really been a passenger on a bus, in the north it was all trams. The parade was halted, and each Troop climbed aboard a bus. It was a fool's game, and took an hour for everyone to be sorted. Then when the buses started their journey, it was woefully slow. So slow that a marching Regiment would have overtaken them. Horses and carts overtook them as did the Field Artillery and their limbers, they were the laughing stock and it didn't take long for the humour to turn to angry men and officers.

"Stop! Stop the bus." It was one of the Majors. As the buses came to a halt, there was a cheer, up went a cry of "everyone off the bus" and within ten minutes the parade had formed up again and they chose to march the rest of the ten miles. From miles away, they could see the imposing sight of the Cloth Hall and Cathedral, still standing in defiance of the German shelling. They were both smashed but stood upright, like a heavyweight boxer who has been beaten but won't give in, there was no referee to stop the fight though.

As they rounded the bend on the approach to the town of Ypres, they were met with joyous crowds of the remaining locals, mainly women and children, the men folk off to the war. It reminded them all of their arrival in France almost a year before, and flowers and kisses showered the marching men. The main difference being the tired, worn faces of the women and the tatty and worn clothes of the children, their appearance betrayed their demeanour. This was a beaten population, hanging on to hope of salvation by friends from far away. The might of the German Empire had been turned on them, innocent and unsuspecting, they had been brutally subjected to behaviour and acts that no Army should commit. This small population had seen their own Army then the French, the British and her allies march through this ancient town as salvationists, only to see them leave again to be replaced by others. Each time worn down by the stagnation of the trenches. The Ypres salient was a pustulating boil, the edges writhed and moved as if it was alive. The boundaries pushed first one way then back again with a counter attack.

It was a cauldron of bubbling hatred. The trenches here were deep and very permanent. The early British, and indeed French, ideas of temporary, shallow attacking trenches that provided little cover had been abandoned here. The Germans had dug deep and with their solid permanent trenches there was to be no withdrawal. They also built high bunkers and pill boxes, all in all this was a static battlefield where attrition was king. The British had stopped the German rush for the ports at Dunkirk and Calais, they had pushed them back to a new battle line and that line was now etched deep into the Flanders fields.

The Regiment stopped in the town square for a meal and drinks. Soon there was tea made and 'bully' shared, hard biscuits and soup, it wasn't a feast, but it was welcome fodder. The men had marched hard after the humiliation of the abortive bus trip. It wasn't the buses to blame for the smashed and crowded roads, but the pride a Regiment carries is strong and no one would embarrass the 'Nobodies Own'. The fresh faces gleamed in a fine sweat. Here, things were sorted and organised better, pack horses took the brunt of the weight instead of the men, the machine guns were loaded and not carried, the huge ammunition boxes were put on the back of carts, much to the relief of the men carrying them.

Men sat and smoked on the roadside, the Officers drank wine in the roadside cafés and ate much better food than the marching men. In fairness, that's how the men liked it, they were from a different class and much as they liked and respected their Officers, they didn't really want to break bread with them, well not all of them.

As they marched over the bridge that crossed the ancient moat on the road to Menin, few men knew that it had long been a pinch point for the defence of the city. Meninpoort to the locals, and Menin Gate to the advancing Armies of the British, would see more than 300,000 men cross it in the next few months as they made their way to the grinding machine that was the front.

The 20th were to take charge of a line of trenches next to the 12th Lancers, in the main they were communication trenches that were connected to the front line but sat a way back. Their arrival was greeted with cheers and whistles by the resting troops about to come out of the line. Word was the Germans had a plan to advance and close the salient, after all they had all but surrounded the area, so the British and her Commonwealth friends had Germans on three sides. If the Germans could only hear the determination of the men they faced, they wouldn't have ever tried.

"Where are we Sarge?" It was Ernie Miles, he had a particularly annoying tone to his voice, it was nasal and always sounded like he needed to sniff.

Bill Blackie, didn't really like "Sarge", he was old school and liked 'Sarn't'. Most of the men had known this for years, but Ernie never learned.

"Miles, I'm not a Sarge, are you being deliberately stupid? We lad, are near a place called *Halte* but don't ask me where that is, apart from between *Potijze* and *Hooge,* pronounced 'huge' in Welsh. Other than that, I don't know. What I do know is if you call me 'Sarge' again I might place one of these 'ere shovels around the back of your head!" It was a rare moment of angst and it was broken by a snigger from somewhere and quickly grew into a laugh, including Blackie, who wasn't given much to laughter as a rule.

There was quite a bit of shelling around the area, some made Charles duck slightly more than others, it was understandable.

The news that the Germans had used poison gas had disgusted every civilised human. It was a despicable act of barbarity and had caused outright panic in the trenches who had faced it a few days before. It would be the French and their colonial friends, the Algerians, who would first be exposed. They had 'stood to' in the late afternoon of the 22nd April when a sentry saw what they all believed was a smoke screen rolling towards them from no man's land. The whole Regiment had stood waiting for the German hoards to come thundering through the smoke but, as the supposed smoke drifted over the trench, the misidentification became horribly clear. The smell of bleach was the first sign that something was dreadfully wrong, then the men started coughing, their eyes burning like fire and then heaving and vomiting. Those men in dug outs were badly affected, these were the first men to die, a grim death in horrific conditions. They were killed like vermin and died a pitiful death. The cloud washed over all the trench systems and men, who were now struggling to draw breath and blinded by the screaming pain in their eyes, panicked and broke to run. The men behind in the rear trenches saw an apocalyptic panorama before them as men stumbled and fell as they tried to flee. The screams of agony and death carried all before it and soldiers not yet affected threw down their weapons and ran for their lives.

The brave Canadians tried to stand their ground but died, or were maimed and disabled as they tried to defend the impossible situation before them.

News of the gas attack had travelled quickly, mainly by necessity and not just soldiers' gossip and boast. They needed a defence against this abhorrent attack and one was quickly found and was already being tested in Blighty. In the meantime, a simple handkerchief soaked in urine would offer some protection, and much as it sounded rather vulgar no one would balk at the thought. Being gassed was far worse. As long as you used your own handkerchief.

Some of the shells didn't go bang they just fizzed and belched out their deadly contents, the Germans had discovered gas shells. Previously they had used large canisters to disperse the foul gas and it was carried on the breeze. Now they had found another way to deliver the torturous poison in the form of gas shells.

The shelling wasn't quite constant, there were long periods of quiet, but the men soon had a taste of gas and learned that their own pee smelled distinctly better than the bleach tainted air. It was a cause of much amusement amongst the men and if the consequences of non-compliance hadn't been so terrifying, it would have been a classic jape; but there was no joking, this was a deadly game and the outcome was that everyone drank, just a little bit more water than before. The *thought* of not being able to piss was nearly as bad as not being able to.

Life in the trench was dreadful, there were so many hideous things about living a subterranean life. Rats feasted on the dead, and that was as disturbing as anything.

Just seeing so many dead laying out in no man's land. The waft of the foul stench of death and rotting flesh was somehow sweet and clawing. Then the flies and bluebottles, fat on the blood of the fallen, whose bodies were swollen and distended. Some of these bodies lay no more than 10 feet away and often you could see a man transfixed as he watched the maggots crawl from the eye sockets of a fallen enemy or comrade, all shared the same fate. These men were buried as soon as was safe, but it wasn't always quick. The distance between the front line trench and the communication trenches wasn't as far as anyone liked, and room for field burials was scarce.

When it was quiet the songbirds were as active as ever and skylarks sang a trill song for all to hear. A moment of natural beauty that seemed irrepressible, at night you often heard the mournful cry of an owl or a lonesome dog who had perhaps lost its home and would howl its sadness. When they weren't trying to obliterate each other, the opposing sides shared the best nature could offer.

The long nights would soon start to shorten as summer approached. Dawn broke over the Western Front and the night's watch would see the sunrise over the ruined cathedral back in Ypres. For the first time in weeks it had stopped raining, it hadn't rained for three days now and the ground, although still sodden, showed signs it might firm up. If they ever got back to their horses, the Farriers would be busy; this was shoe pulling ground.

CHAPTER 52

Into thy mighty arms I fall

May 1915:

Dear Tom,

I am writing to you on the eve of May. April has been wet and miserable, but I am in the best of health and spirit. We have moved again, and the censor would remove any sign of where we are but it is a bit sticky, what with the Germans using poisoned shells. They make one's eyes water dreadfully and we have had them for an hour or so. They kill you if the dose is heavy enough and this had done in a few of our Infantry earlier in the week. I can tell you we are in the trenches and I have received the letters and a parcel. Please pass on my thanks to Rebecca. I will send you post cards until we get back from the front. Give my love to the girls.

As letters go it wasn't much but it was all he had time for. The call had gone out for men to volunteer to help dig a sap out into no-man's land. They had no idea how long they would be out, but it was going to break the monotony of being in this wet stinking bog. Ironically the front trench was slightly up hill from the communication trench where they were, so it would give them a chance to be on dry duck boards for a while and, with a bit of luck, their boots might dry.

It was Corporal Stanesby who suggested they go. Ernie Miles wanted to keep out of Sergeant Blackie's way for a bit and Bert Clarke couldn't really care less, he was fed up, so a change of scenery might be good for him. Charles was happy to do some digging, it was good for his back which had stiffened up because he had been stooped over quite a bit. They had to wait till nightfall before they could leave but they all agreed they would go. It meant they would have the next day off because they had pulled an extra duty.

They set off along the trench to the 'B' Company command dug out to offer their services.

It was 20:00 hrs and they had time for a brew before they left.

By 21:00 hrs the light was fading, dusk was well underway and along the line you could see candles and oil lamps being lit. Obviously they would have to remove as much of their excess kit as possible and travel light. Digging was hard work, it was agreed they could leave it in the Command Post.

They stood having a cigarette in the doorway as Sergeant Thomas put their stuff in the corner. The shelling was over towards the 12th Lancers' section of the trench and the constant 'crump, crump, fizz' of the incoming shells registered but didn't cause undue alarm, as they listened there was a different sound, more of a hissing than whooshing they all knew the sound but, before they could move it exploded amongst them.

There was a blinding flash, brilliant white and reds and black. The heat scorched their skin momentarily before it ripped through them as if they were made of paper mâché the power of the high explosive shell destroyed every cell in Miles and Clarke, they both disappeared in a pink gloopy mist. Bill Stanesby was cut in half, he died instantly and didn't register his death in his eyes, he had been looking at Charles the second he lost his life.

Charles could smell cordite and taste blood. His eyes had been spared but when he looked he almost wished they hadn't. He was mortally injured. His leg was clearly broken and at completely the wrong angle, his left leg had gone, his right one smashed to pulp and was smoking from the red-hot debris lodged in the soft tissues. He couldn't breathe, the weight on his collapsed chest was in part, to do with the trench wall pressing against him but more that he had lost a huge part of his right hand side. He looked at his left hand, it was hanging at an impossible angle and, with stunned eyes, he looked at his right hand. It was perfect, without even one blemish or wound. How was it possible that his body could be so massively damaged and yet this hand untouched? There was no pain, no feelings, he wasn't scared or worried, he knew he was going to die. His brain had been stunned into submission. He called Bill's name, he had been looking right at him, he had stood right there opposite him, and now he could see him on the floor, his eyes looking directly at Charles, there was nothing in those eyes, they were dead.

Charles tried to cry out, there was a hideous gurgling and he coughed, there was blood and lung tissue but no noise. He felt a hand touch him, it was a Medic. He couldn't hear anything bar a loud ringing in his ears, not like a bell though, more a constant high pitched tone. He felt the needle pierce his skin and remembered the soporific beauty of morphine, then again, another needle, and another. As he drifted into a long corridor of light he realised he would never awaken and, with a deep sigh he surrendered his last thoughts to the eternal heavenly darkness.

CHAPTER 53

Go back, it isn't your time

The anaesthetist heard the monitor first, it was a double blip, an extra heartbeat. Then there was another this was quickly followed by many others. The heart rate accelerated and as he looked at my face my eyelashes twitched.

"Is he light David?" It was Mr Marshall "He seems awfully mobile, his brain is pulsing a bit, what's his pressures doing?"

"Actually Scott, I'm more worried about his heart. He's throwing ectopics here and I think he might be heading towards VF, his pressures are up, all of them. I need you to stop for a minute, let me see if I can get this back under control."

The monitor told the whole theatre that my heart was in crisis and then the regular beating tone of the monitor stopped. It became a long constant tone, high pitched and as it dimmed in my conscious mind I saw him.

"Hello again Mike," it was Charles; and he was complete, no injuries, no age.

"It's time for me to rest, but it isn't your time yet. You can't pass yet, you have to live. I will always be there, in your heart and mind; but you have to live, fight it, go back."

I asked him "are you real or have I dreamt all this?" He smiled and said it was a release for him, but he couldn't explain. "In time you'll understand, it's just an Echo in Time"

As he drifted away I wanted to ask something, but I couldn't remember what, he dimmed until he disappeared. He smiled all the while, he was happy, content and ethereal.

CHAPTER 54

Living beats anything, so far

As I listened I could hear the beeping, I remember counting it in my head and I imagined a clock to count it by. I counted 20 beeps and multiplied it by 4, my heartbeat was 80.

My mouth was dry, really dry, and the light hurt my eyes as they slowly flickered open. The room was darkened, and I was able to make out silhouettes in the gloomy light. A Nurse stood there with her back to me, she was looking at a machine on a drip stand, and as I rolled my head to the right, I could see Di, she was there holding my hand. She smiled at me, it was beautiful. Her eyes were swollen from her tears and all she said was, "He's awake."

The Nurse turned and spoke to me, "Hello, can you hear me ok?" I went to nod my head but it was heavy and bandaged. The bandage covered my ears so it was a bit muffled.

"You are in ITU, your wife is here, you have had an operation on your head but you're fine now. Do you have any pain?"

"No, thank you." They were the first words I spoke.

A tear ran down my cheek, I was happy and sad in equal measures. I knew I was alive, but I also knew Charles had gone, perhaps forever.

Di wiped my cheek, and for some reason she kissed me on my hand, it was a reassuring feeling and I remember feeling safe.

"Can I have a sip of juice please, I'm very thirsty and my mouth tastes awful." The Nurse dipped a pink lollypop of sponge into some water, and placed it on my dry lips, water never tasted so good.

I had a million questions to ask, but I was weary and they would wait. I closed my eyes and heard the Nurse say

"You go to bed now Di, you've been here for hours, go and sleep he'll be ok, I'll look after him for the night. Come back in the morning I'm sure he will be more awake then."

In my head I said, 'yes go to get some rest love' but then I was asleep again and didn't finish my thoughts.

As I drifted into a restful and somewhat drugged sleep, I was aware of the beeping and of the emptiness in my brain. Charles had gone, as had the war. It was finished.

CHAPTER 55

Aftermath

As it turned out, the tumour was attached to a part of my brain that is responsible for memory and creativeness.

I explained my thoughts to everyone, I couldn't bring myself to call them dreams, they were far too real and tangible. I felt the feelings of the time, I did think perhaps I was maybe going mad.

Mr Marshall was enthralled, he said in one of the final outpatient's meetings,

"You know, there have been serious scientific studies to do with reincarnation. Some of the findings have been quite unbelievable. One woman was hypnotically regressed and was able to give very in-depth detail of a doorway in a building that no one had ever known about, it had been blocked up 150 years before, and she knew exactly where it was. Another man was part of a bomber crew in World War Two, the plane he was in was shot down and the whole crew perished. One night this chap had a dream that he was one of the crew that night. For no apparent reason he recognised his 'dream state' and was able to guide a salvage archeologist team right to the wreck in a swamp in Holland. He hadn't ever been to Holland before in this life and there inside the wreck were the remains of the 7 crewmen. Mike, these things remain unexplained, but I would be being naive in the extreme if I didn't accept that there are things we might never quite understand. I can tell you that the tumour was very deeply embedded in a part of your brain we know as the *medial temporal lobe.* There were long strands of connective tissue reaching into other parts of your brain. We know that this part, in particular, is thought to be involved in declarative and episodic memory. Deep inside the medial temporal lobe is the region of the brain we call the limbic system. These areas of the memory banks are still new to us and as for what they are capable of, well we are only scratching the surface really. I suppose what I'm saying is, we just don't know, yet."

I told them of things that no one had ever known, things lost in time and family stories. Details of Charles and his life that weren't previously known about and yet, I knew. It was a very personal thing, and everyone agreed it was a phenomenon that wasn't easily explained. Mr Marshall was intrigued and asked for me to stay in touch. This was as unique as case as he had treated but there was no derision or doubt. He completely believed everything I had tried to explain.

In time, all things returned to normal, my hair went a bit whiter and I had lost some weight whilst in hospital but, other than that, nothing had changed. After six months, no one would have known I had ever been ill.

I was told I had suffered a cardiac arrest on the table, and there were some slight complications during my procedure. They also said that they didn't have an explanation for my protracted unconsciousness.

Mr Marshall wrote a paper on my 'locked in syndrome' he presented it to his peers, they were none the wiser either; but at least now they all had a record of it.

The tumour was found to be malignant and yet it hadn't grown outside the areas Mr Marshall had explained to me. It was if it had almost been held in check.

I haven't had any more dreams of the war, nor Charles, as yet.

Epilogue

Thomas and Emily continued to live in Farnworth. Mae was joined by her sister, Doris and brother, Eric. He was my father.

Emily passed away in 1944 and Thomas finally joined his beloved wife, brother and sisters in 1971, he was 85 years old.

William Howard Atherton was discharged from the Army due to having Mastoiditis, the dizziness he suffered was incompatible with military service. He lived a full and long life, he died aged 73 in 1967.

Elizabeth never married and lived with her brother William and his family in Farnworth. She died aged 76 in 1964.

Mae married and became a music hall singer, quite a good one by all accounts, she died in 1996 aged 86 years.

Rebecca is a fictional character, but I would like to think she found love and married.

In all, the 20th Hussars lost nearly 250 Officers and Other ranks in the Great War, unfortunately it wasn't the war to end all wars. Their loss was mourned, and their deeds remembered as indeed they are all remembered by someone, somewhere. On the very same day that Major John McCrae wrote his now famous poem 'In Flanders Fields' Charles Atherton fell; a more fitting epitaph for this brave man and his friends couldn't have been written. Charles is commemorated along with his colleagues on panel 5 of the Menin Gate Memorial in the now, once again, beautiful city of Ypres. It is a magnificent monument and quite breathtaking when they play the Last Post there at 20:00 hrs every night. If you haven't been, you should go. If you do, say hello to Charlie I'm sure he's listening.

The End

In Flanders Fields

In Flanders fields the poppies blow
Between the crosses, row on row,
That mark our place; and in the sky
The larks, still bravely singing, fly
Scarce heard amid the guns below.
We are the Dead. Short days ago
We lived, felt dawn, saw sunset glow,
Loved and were loved, and now we lie
In Flanders fields.
Take up our quarrel with the foe:
To you from failing hands we throw
The torch; be yours to hold it high.
If ye break faith with us who die
We shall not sleep, though poppies grow
In Flanders fields.

Major John McCrae. 2nd May 1915